IN
DARKNESS
DWELLS

JAMES FOX
A K DUBOFF

www.cadicle.com

Published by Dawnrunner Press

ISBN-10: 195434421X
ISBN-13: 978-1954344211

0 9 8 7 6 5 4 3 2 1

Produced in the United States of America

TABLE OF CONTENTS

THE CADICLE UNIVERSE

The events in *In Darkness Dwells* are a self-contained story arc in the larger Cadicle Universe.

Tarans are the predominant race in the Cadicle Universe; humans are a Taran genetic offshoot. Most of the Taran sphere falls within the purview of the Taran Empire, governed from the planet Tararia by a council of High Dynasty families. Earth is one of several rogue colonies on the outskirts of the Empire, separated so long ago that they have forgotten their Taran ancestry.

The Tararian Guard is the primary military force for the Taran Empire. Its counterpart, the Tararian Selective Service, includes a specialty branch with Agents gifted in telekinetic and telepathic abilities. The TSS is headquartered at a base inside Earth's moon, and its iconic Agents are known in Earth lore as the mysterious 'men in black'.

Chronologically, *In Darkness Dwells* takes place immediately before the Taran Empire Saga. However, prior knowledge of that broader story universe is not required in order to read and enjoy this book.

CHAPTER 1

"EASY DOES IT," Captain Hailey Suro instructed her son, more out of habit rather than need, as he piloted the *Andvari* into position alongside its target.

For the first time in weeks, Hailey felt a glimmer of hope. The twisted starship wreckage was easily the best salvage target they'd seen in months. *We might actually be able to make our next lease payment.*

Darin smiled, his blue eyes shining under a lock of his highlighted brown hair. "Just want to get us a nice close look." He'd grown up flying ships, and at nineteen now was as capable a pilot as any old-timer.

The *Andvari*'s control board flickered with streams of data as Darin eased the freighter next to the once-mighty TSS warship, now reduced to little more than a lonely bit of scrap.

As the two vessels continued to edge closer together, additional details came into focus on the flight deck's front viewscreen. This wasn't just any warship; with its boxy munitions launchers—the kind designed to house and fire long-range torpedoes—and side thruster ports to compensate for the massive release of kinetic force, the remains of this warship had the potential to yield a massive score. From the looks of it, even the rear drive section appeared to be intact, which meant it might still have a functional power core. If so, they could be looking at a single payday to rival their earnings from the entire last year combined.

Oh stars, please be worth it!

Their salvage contract with Renfield was still months from being suspended, but their heroic efforts to locate lucrative wreckage had thus far yielded paltry payoffs. The last few scraps the *Andvari* located had been disappointments, and their small crew's resources were running dry. Renfield had already voiced some frustration about their 'mining in well-trod claims'. Even so, they were already skirting the very edges of the territory that their salvage permit allowed.

Worse, from all reports, this should be relatively virgin space. Sadly, it was rapidly becoming apparent that they were a few weeks behind another crew—at least one, and Hailey was beginning to think quite a few more. It seemed that their 'hot lead' on this part of space wasn't as significant a breakthrough as they had once thought.

Space was a big place; it was intensely aggravating to always be late to the party.

The door to the flight deck hissed open, and the waifish Dr. Mina Hurn ambled in. Her eyes were downcast on her tablet, the curls of her dark mahogany hair framing her face.

"Good morning, Captain," she greeted, glancing up and smiling amiably. "I've done a preliminary scan of this target."

Darin pivoted around in his seat to look at Hailey. "Do you need me for this?"

"You don't want to know what we've got?"

He shrugged. "If it's anything like the last few, I don't need to hear it again firsthand."

That stung. He didn't say it in a mean way, but the meaning behind the words cut deeply into Hailey. *This salvage business was supposed to be my legacy to hand him, and instead we might lose everything.*

A quick glance at Mina's expression indicated to Hailey that she wasn't about to get particularly good news. Darin was right; he didn't need to be here.

"Take a break," she told her son.

"Aye," he acknowledged and swapped over the flight controls to her captain's station. He left the flight deck, giving a friendly nod to Mina on his way out.

Hailey leaned forward in her seat and put her hands in the small of her back while pinching her shoulders together. That same spot spasmed if she sat for more than a few moments in her blasted chair. It was most certainly the chair's fault, not the years of abuse and injuries sustained while in the Tararian Guard; couldn't be that. "Well, what's the verdict?"

The petite doctor stared at her, a slight wrinkle of worry showing on her brow.

"Just tension from the flight, Doc, nothing to see here," she said casually.

An elegant eyebrow arched slowly in way of reply.

Summoning her command posture, Hailey rolled her shoulders back. "Well, are you going to give me the report, or are we going to play grab-ass all morning?"

Mina faked an overly dramatic sigh of exasperation but couldn't quite contain the mirth that danced across her features. The doctor was the newest member of the crew, though she had been with them for almost a year now, and she'd slipped into the ship's social dynamic beautifully.

Head down while she read from her tablet, Mina launched into her report on the target vessel's classification, service duty, reported loss date, haul records, and armament details. The TSS *Valiant* was one of the vessels that the Tararian Selective Service had commissioned for the war efforts three decades back. Dozens of destroyers like it had been rapidly churned out from the Prisaris shipyard, sparing no expense in their manufacturing materials. A great score, indeed.

Then, Mina brought up magnified images of the *Valiant*'s exterior, showing tether holes dotting the side of the warship.

Someone else had beaten them to it. The target had already been picked clean.

Hailey's hope evaporated. "Well, that's foking great."

Mina scrunched her face up in irritation. "Stars, I'm sorry, Hailey. I know we're on the right track for wreckage from a number of big encounters. There have been no reports of other salvage contractors out this far. So, either these were caught very early on and have drifted this far post-salvage. Or someone is working off the books."

That was always a possibility. Especially if the scores were as impressive as this destroyer should have been.

Space may be large, but the simple fact remained that the number of ships lost in the war was undetermined. Last known trajectories and headings were all rough estimates. So far, the data that Mina had gathered was sound; they were certainly finding wrecks along their designated path. It wasn't the doctor's fault that someone else had gotten there first.

Hailey bit back her frustration. "Where do we go from here?"

Mina leaned in closer, the pepper and mandarin scent of her perfume assaulting Hailey as she peered out the viewport at the warship. "I'll double check my research and put in a call to Renfield. Maybe there's another crew just ahead of us. We can try to swing beyond them for the next target. Play a bit of leapfrog, maybe?"

No, we're out of time. We can't keep retreading the same ground with wishful thinking. Hailey tried to keep her worry from showing on her face.

The lease payment on the *Andvari* had already been deferred once, and they wouldn't be getting any more favors. Hiring Mina and leasing the *Andvari* had been an all-in attempt to build a sustainable business that Hailey could pass on to Darin. The high upfront expense had seemed like a worthwhile venture, but it had yet to pay off. If they came up emptyhanded again, that would be the end of the dream.

"We can't afford another dead end," she said, barely above a whisper. "We need a score—a good one."

They had been pressing hard these last few weeks, hunting for pockets of wartime debris and wreckage that hadn't already been picked over by other salvage crews. The more remote they got, the higher the likelihood they could score. On the flipside, venturing further from civilization also meant far fewer opportunities to sell off cheap scrap for a quick mid-run resupply. As it stood, they were already reduced to half rations to stretch out their reserves.

The truth was, there wouldn't *be* a proper resupply if they didn't get paid. Hailey was under consistent pressure to make the sacrificed health, happiness, and resources worth it. She *needed* this run to work out.

"There is another option, Captain," Mina began upon seeing Hailey's sour expression she hadn't quite been able to mask.

"At this point, I'm open to anything." She crossed her arms.

"We could head toward the Kyron Nebula."

The suggestion caught Hailey by surprise; she'd considered

Mina to be by-the-book. "That's outside of the permitted salvage zone."

Given their dire situation, Hailey wasn't opposed to breaking the rules. If they didn't meet the terms of their contract, they'd be doomed anyway.

"I'm aware," Mina continued, "but there's a gravitational backwater there, and the models show it's a likely spot for wrecks to wind up."

Hailey was nodding now; those were exactly the types of places she'd been hoping Mina would find for them. She'd been resistant to unlawful activity up to this point, but if everyone else played that way, she needed to do what was necessary to stay in the game. "There are benefits to being out in restricted space. So long as we don't get caught."

"Risk and reward."

If they were caught, they'd lose the *Andvari* for sure. And yet, if they didn't go, they'd most likely lose the ship, too. At least the gamble provided the barest shred of opportunity.

"All right, get me the coordinates," Hailey agreed. *Stars, I hope this is the right move!*

—   —   —

A string of disappointments would get anyone down, and it had become especially difficult for Darin Suro to see his mom struggling.

She's doing all of this for me, but she never asked if it's what I want.

He hurried away from the flight deck with no clear destination in mind, only certain that he didn't want to be within earshot of another dismal report about their bleak prospects. After everything that had gone wrong since getting the *Andvari*, he was slowly becoming convinced that the new ship was cursed.

Roaming through the outer edges of the Taran Empire had made for an interesting childhood, but he couldn't imagine a lifelong career as a salvage hauler. He'd tried to tell his mom that on several occasions, but she had a way of hearing what she wanted to hear. Once she'd gotten it into her head that Darin enjoyed scrapping, she'd done every bomaxed thing she could to set him up for a future in that line of work. The unfortunate truth was that he'd rather join the Tararian Guard and never see a salvage rig again.

You need to come clean, he chastised himself. *The longer you wait, the harder it will be.*

Despite the sound advice to himself, he hadn't yet found the right moment to follow through. After this salvage run, maybe—once they had found a good score and were getting back on track with the lease payments. Before then, he didn't have it in him to break his mom's heart with the news that he wanted to leave.

Feeling antsy, Darin decided to run a few laps through the central corridors of the ship. On the main habitation level, the corridors formed one giant loop that made it great for such activity.

On his second lap, Darin almost bumped into Jamaal exiting his cabin.

"Whoa, watch it!" the older man shouted, raising his muscular arms.

"Sorry," Darin muttered, nimbly sidestepping him. He knew from past accidental collisions against the living wall of a man that he would be on the losing side of the encounter.

The ex-Guard soldier tilted his head questioningly. "Shouldn't you be on the flight deck?"

Darin slowed his jog and turned around. "Meeting with Mina. I didn't want to hear it."

"Less about the content and more about the view."

He had to admit, Mina was quite pretty—and the only woman on the ship he wasn't related to. Still, that wasn't enough to balance out being stuck in a confined space with his mother while she got more bad news. "Next time, maybe."

A chime sounded, indicating a ship-wide communication.

"We're headed to the Kyron Nebula," his mother announced, her voice echoing in the metal corridor. "Get to bed early. I want you rested and ready for a long day." The comm clicked off.

Darin looked at Jamaal questioningly. "Kyron? Where's that?"

"Restricted space," he replied with a frown. "A former warzone beyond the outermost colonies."

"Shite. We're getting really desperate, aren't we?"

Jamaal clapped him on the shoulder. "Your mom is a good captain. We wouldn't be headed that way if there weren't riches to be found." Without another word, he headed down the hall in the direction of the washroom and gym.

Darin shook his head and sighed. *So much for being model citizens.*

Everyone knew that most scrappers skirted the law. Sure, everything was handled via official contracts and corporate dealings, but the real money was made by scouting out restricted areas and grabbing the left-behind tech that wasn't easy to come by in more inhabited zones. His mom had sworn that they wouldn't be 'those people' when they got this new ship. An admirable aspiration, however unrealistic.

With the halls once again to himself, Darin resumed his jog. After completing another dozen laps, he'd worked up an appetite so he headed to the galley for an early dinner.

The dining and kitchen area of the ship was compact and efficient like most of the vessel's living spaces. It consisted of seating for six, storage areas, and the various appliances one would expect for cooking and reheating items, all finished in polished metal for easy maintenance.

As he was completing the preparation of the mostly tasteless gruel that would comprise his meals for the foreseeable future, Mina wandered in.

"Hey," she greeted him. "Anything good on the menu?"

Darin looked up from stirring the off-white paste. "You didn't hear?"

"Hear what?"

He let out a long breath between his teeth, recalling that the doctor hadn't been at breakfast. "We're getting reduced to half-rations to stretch reserves out long enough to complete this contract. The captain announced it this morning."

"Oh. I see." A slight flush rose on the bronze skin of the doctor's cheeks.

"Don't worry, Doc. The complete lack of taste means you can pretend it's anything you want!" he joked as he grabbed his bowl and took his usual seat at the table with the best visibility of the viewport on the back wall.

"You're lucky to be gifted with such a vivid imagination." She sauntered over to begin browsing through the mostly empty cupboards along the side wall of the galley.

"The supplement powder is about all that's left," Darin said to save her the effort of looking. The stuff was better characterized as 'nutrition' than 'food', but it filled the empty spot.

Mina shook her head. "If you find these meals passable, you'll do just fine in the Guard."

"Shh!" Darin whipped around in his seat to make sure his mom or Jamaal weren't nearby.

The doctor eyed him. "You still haven't told her?"

"I will… eventually."

She closed the cabinets, having come up emptyhanded, and sat down across from him. "All she wants is for you to be happy."

"That's the problem. She left that life behind, so she's convinced it will only lead to loss and heartbreak."

"There were some extenuating circumstances, as I understand it."

Darin again reflexively checked they were alone. "Yeah, well, working with the Guard is what got my dad killed, so there's no way she's going to willingly let me anywhere near the service."

Mina nodded slowly, looking him over with her dark, perceptive eyes. "We all need to make our own way."

"And this is where your path led you, huh?" He'd been trying to get the story out of Mina since her first day on the *Andvari*, but she hadn't given even the slightest clue about how she'd gone from being a fancy Central Worlds medical doctor to running analytics on a salvage ship.

"Sometimes you need a change of pace," she replied. "Once you've had your time out there in the universe, maybe you'll understand."

He thought he understood well enough. He'd been traveling with the same three people for his entire life, barely ever seeing other kids his own age. Mina was a welcome addition to their little family, though her arrival had underscored how little he'd seen of the galaxy. He'd already been leaning toward joining the Guard, but hearing her stories about the affluent Central Worlds had solidified his plans.

Scrapping would never get him to those planets; becoming a decorated soldier might.

Still, he didn't want to leave his mom in a bind. He wanted to know the *Andvari* and its crew would be okay without him.

"Hey… are we going to find anything in this new place?" he asked Mina.

She smiled. "I believe so. I hope you're ready for an adventure."

CHAPTER 2

HAILEY SNOOZED ON the flight deck overnight, wanting to keep an eye on the scan data as they ventured into forbidden territory.

The *Andvari* dropped out from subspace half a day's travel from Mina's target coordinates. One of the reasons the Kyron Nebula was off-limits was that it lay beyond the network of SiNavTech navigation beacons accessible for civilian use. While the military patrolled the area and could execute jumps in the zone, a salvage hauler like the *Andvari* would be restricted to movement via its antimatter pion drive until it was back in range of the beacon network.

By early-morning on ship's time, they were approaching the identified salvage grounds. The sensors pinged with a positive contact.

There's at least one ship out here!

She adjusted course toward the specific target and settled back into her seat to wait until they were in visual range.

Eventually, the long-range scan blip was replaced by a magnified image on the holodisplay, showing an old TSS warship drifting in the black. It was largely intact, which was a good sign.

On instinct, she checked her handheld. 05:10. Behind schedule, but not by much.

She started a mission timer. There was no real reason for the mission clock, but it was an old habit picked up during her years in the Tararian Guard. It made her feel good, like a favorite old blanket that was threadbare and no longer had much thermal value but was still the go-to.

It truly amazed her how much relief some of those little idiosyncrasies could offer. Most of the soldiers in her unit had some kind of comfort they relied on when times were particularly tough, ranging from a trinket, to alcohol, to carnal pleasures. Being the one in charge, she had noticed each of her soldier's coping tactics.

For Hailey, it was her mission clock; it kept her focused and grounded.

She opened the ship-wide comms. "Rise and shine! We're about to be in business."

Not a single person on her small crew could be considered a 'morning person', though time was rather subjective out in the void. She didn't mind taking the night shift; it offered a rare chance to get alone time and quiet. The five of them were a tight-knit family—which resulted in all the good-natured annoyances one would expect. At night, at least, she didn't need to play the role of taskmaster mom.

A slight hum over the outboard speaker on the flight deck comms preceded her son's strong voice. "How far out are we?"

Hailey smiled. "About fifteen minutes. You and Jamaal get suited up."

There was a slight pause, then, "On it. Now if only Jamaal would stop complaining about being old and sore, we could get ready a lot faster." A muffled *thud* and the beginnings of a laugh were cut off as the commlink ended.

Hailey made the ship ready for soft-docking with the floating hulk of junk. Once their velocities were synchronized—which wouldn't take much, in this case, as there was very little spin—it would be easy enough to deploy tethers and winch themselves close enough to minimize the EVA distance.

Entering a depressurized spacecraft was rife with inherent dangers, and it was the captain's duty to mitigate as many potential threats as possible. Those concerns were compounded by the fact that she was sending her only son and her closest friend into the void. It gave her every motivation to do the best job she could on her end—not that she would ever slack off. The Guard had trained any propensity for laziness or corner-cutting out of her long ago.

The starboard lines fired, and the grapples spiraled out with their silvery filament trailing behind them. The hooks embedded deep into the hull of the twisted starship.

Gently, she eased back on the controls and flipped the switch to engage the winches, drawing the two vessels even closer together.

As their target enlarged on the viewscreen, a knot formed in her gut. There were other visible tether holes—several sets, in fact—littering the side of the craft.

Bomax! Her heart sank as she realized that the ship had previously been boarded. *Who would come out this far?*

Most likely, the ship had already been picked clean and left afloat. She had prepared for it to be a bust; the lack of rotational velocity she'd noticed on the initial approach usually meant a salvage team had already stabilized it for safe entry. Exactly what she was doing to it now, as it happened.

She kept her disappointment in check. All might not be lost; the stabilization may have been from a crew rescue op during the war rather than salvagers years later. It was still worth a closer look.

—   —   —

Mina Hurn rubbed her eyes as she struggled to wake up her mind for the morning. She'd never get used to the odd hours kept on the salvage ship. Waking up to the rising sun on a planet was the way to live, not being out here in the void.

That life is over. The thought, her mantra for the last decade, was always a sad one. *Let the past remain in the past, and be grateful for every opportunity, big or small.*

It wasn't her finest pep talk, but it was enough to get her out of bed.

She pulled on her clothes and then grabbed her tablet to check the latest scan data now that they were in close range of the target. The preliminary results were a disappointment.

How could someone else have already come out here?

While it was possible the tether holes were from a rescue during the war, TSS ships were more likely to use gravity manipulation to aid their rescue efforts, not physical lines. This derelict warship had most likely been hit by salvagers, as much as she didn't want to admit it.

Mina needed more information, and trying to navigate that data on her tablet was too big an ask for her weary mind at the early hour. With a yawn, she headed toward the flight deck.

Hailey was in the pilot's chair completing the approach when Mina arrived. The captain's brows were drawn together with concentration and concern as she directed the ship using the manual flight controls, confirming her position on the holographic overlay on the front viewport stretching the width of the flight deck.

Not wanting to distract her during the sensitive maneuver, Mina got to work at the analytics station in the back of the room.

Data about the vessel began populating as the computer pulled identifying information from the hull markings. No energy signatures were coming off the ship, not even an identification signal, so it had been sitting dormant for a very long time.

Not a good sign. Complete blackout meant no reserve power, which didn't bode well for finding high-value components. However, that didn't mean the cargo hold couldn't be full. *Try to stay optimistic! You're out of a job if this is a bust, so you better pray to the stars there's something good here.*

She turned her attention to analyzing the likely cause of critical failure that had led the crew to abandon the ship. While she was looking for obvious battle scars, a glow lit up on the scan data, rendering like a spatial distortion as if the ship was preparing to jump.

The disturbance vanished as quickly as it appeared.

"What the…?"

Hailey glanced up from her station. "Hmm?"

"I saw…" Mina faded out. There were no signs the anomaly had ever been there. "That's odd."

"I'm going to need better descriptor words here, Doctor."

"Sorry." She gathered herself. "I thought I saw a spatial distortion forming around the ship for a moment, but it's gone now."

"Sensor glitch?"

"Could be. This nebula has all sorts of energy fields we don't typically encounter out in open space, which might be impacting the system."

"One of the many reasons this is a no-travel zone." Hailey checked the readings on the HUD. "Do you think it's worth having Alton take a look?"

Mina considered the offer. Alton Kress was an amazing kooky old fart. 'The Gnome Below,' is what the rest of the crew called him whenever they knew Alton wasn't around. Just a hair's breadth away from crippled, the hunched over and ancient appearing man was constantly wheezing and red-faced. He was also an absolute genius when it came to machinery and engineering, which often made Mina feel incredibly ill-equipped for her position as an analyst.

"It's probably nothing," Mina said. "I'll keep an eye on it while you see off the team."

"Okay." Hailey headed for the door. "And start scoping out new targets in case this one doesn't pan out."

Mina only nodded in response, a pit growing in her stomach. She didn't want to admit it, but they were running headlong into a dead end. *Where could we possibly go from here?*

— — —

Hailey took a brisk pace to the airlock on the lower deck to brief Darin and Jamaal. She savored the crisp metallic smell of fresh welds and cleaner still lingering in the halls of the new ship. It was one of Hailey's favorite scents, perfectly encapsulating the hope for a brighter future this vessel represented.

It had been almost a year since the crew had leased the ship to expand their salvage operations, but she still found herself marveling at the attention to detail in the ship's design. Crisscrossing metal structural webbing. Raised serrated steel floor grating. Hidden track lighting. The ideal intersection of form and function.

She smiled to herself. *What is a captain without a ship?*

The *Anvdari* was one of Dainetris Galactic Enterprise's newer models, an H4V-280 Medium Duty Cargo Hauler. The design had been modified several times, but many believed previous iterations had taken steps backward. Complaints ranged from sluggish control actuators to poor internal layouts and inefficient cargo space 'upgrades' that created challenges when trying to load or unload cargo. This particular DGE model was the answer to all those complaints. It was a near perfect design, peerless in its class of vessel, and Hailey loved it like a little sister.

Voices became audible up ahead. Jamaal's brash, booming voice echoed down the hallway like a blindfolded bull bouncing from wall to wall. In the gaps between, she could hear her son's spirited laughter.

That sound split Hailey's face into a wide smile. The waves of memories that singular sound brought were always bittersweet. He sounded just like his father.

"About time, Captain!" Jamaal teased as she rounded the corner.

Trying to act casually, Hailey smiled crookedly at him, moisture threatening her eyes from a combination of frustration, tiredness, and nostalgia.

Keenly observant, also like his father, Darin noticed. "You okay?" An intense look of concern crossed his face, disturbing the still-boyish face of the young man.

At nineteen, she couldn't really call him a boy anymore, though she wished nothing more than to bundle him up and keep him young forever. Yet, she acknowledged that she needed to let him grow up. There were important things her son was meant to do; she felt in her heart, even though she didn't know what those things might be. She supposed every mother felt that way about their children. Biology was a strange thing.

"The bomaxed halls still reek of factory cleaning fluids," she said, wiping at her eyes. "Makes my eyes water just walking down the hall!"

Jamaal slammed a gauntleted fist into the bulkhead of the airlock. "Stars, ain't she pretty, though?"

"Best heap I've ever flown," Hailey replied jovially, the hurt beginning to fade from unbidden memories of Darin's late father. It wasn't often she thought about Karej anymore, or the circumstances that surrounded his passing.

"All right, well," Darin said, slamming his hands together and working the fingers of the glove to loosen them up, "shall we?"

"Be careful over there," Hailey cautioned. "The doc hasn't had time to research this one, so I'm not sure what you're walking into over there."

Always ones for an adventure, both Jamaal and Darin exchanged excited looks.

When Hailey held up her hand to forestall their enthusiasm, she felt like she was robbing them of their childhood. "I suspect we weren't the first ones to this rig," she revealed.

Both men frowned sharply.

Hailey took a deep breath and continued, "The rotational velocity was minimal."

Darin's brow furrowed and he slumped dejectedly against the airlock's doorframe.

Jamaal grasped his suit with both hands at the collar and hung his head, frowning.

"We work with whatever hand we're dealt," Hailey said. Being the bearer of bad news got old.

Maybe it's time to retire. Whenever she started to feel discouraged, she imagined herself finding a nice beach planet where she could hold down a hammock for the rest of her days, a nice glass of chilled wine in-hand. *Pay off the ship and give it to Darin, then it's the beach for me. No doubt about that.*

Summoning all her previous years of campaigning and leading soldiers into terrible situations, she put her hands on her hips and barked, "Why the long faces? Get your asses out there and find me something to sell, or so help me, don't come back at all!"

Darin's eyes went wide, but Jamaal just raised his head and grinned wickedly. After decades of working together both in the Guard and after, he knew her style better than anyone.

"Yes, ma'am!" both men shouted.

Hailey watched them transfer into the airlock and then headed back to the flight deck. She needed to crack this puzzle and figure out how to get themselves onto some loot before their time ran out.

It's now or never. The last thing she wanted to do was die on this bomaxed boat.

CHAPTER 3

IF THERE WAS one thing Darin couldn't live without, it was the exhilaration of floating through space. From the moment that the airlock door opened, he was giddy with excitement.

Growing up on salvage haulers, he'd never had any one place to call home. Being the only son of a working mother, he was often on his own and had needed to find ways to amuse himself. As such, he had learned a great deal about spacefaring life by his eighteenth birthday and was always eager to get into a wreck to practice his zero-G maneuvering skills.

Nothing, to date, had fulfilled him like pushing off a bulkhead and drifting out into the void. Deep space was like a field of the purest black satin. He wanted to reach out and touch it.

"Hey," the orotund voice of Jamaal crackled across the comms in his helmet, "what are you doing over there?"

Darin took note of his surroundings. Lost as he was in his reverie about the wonders of space, he had totally miscalculated his trajectory and was veering away from their intended breach point.

"Ah, sorry!" He hated how young he sounded when he got

caught being stupid. "Thought I saw something up under that munitions container." It was a lie, but a harmless one.

"What's the first rule of scrappers?" The grizzled ex-Sergeant brokered no shite, even on a good day.

"Stay the course." Reflex more than anything answered the question. It was one that Darin was often reminded of, unfortunately.

"Now get your scrawny ass over here." Though aggressive in nature, Jamaal's tone made it more congenial.

Having grown up without his dad, Jamaal was the closest thing Darin had to gauge the experience. This exchange, like countless before, had the distinct qualities of a wayward son being called over by a father. There was no bitterness in Darin about it—stars, he was *lucky* to have Jamaal around. More than that, he knew his mother would be lost without Jamaal.

Although the captain presented a strong façade, Darin had found his mom's emotional resolve to be somewhat mercurial, contrary to her military background. Jamaal, however, was an unflappable beacon of support—offering a sympathetic ear or a firm talking-to, as the case may be. Jamaal's steadfast reasoning balanced out his mother's sometimes emotional decision-making; whether it was the loss of his father or something else, there were clearly unresolved issues there.

Jamaal and Hailey seemed to be stuck together, the shadows of their past linking them. While Hailey never spoke much about their history, Jamaal exclusively told whopping fish-tales of stories of bygone military days. They were enjoyable tales, always worthy of a laugh or ten, but Darin knew that the boisterous old vet was mostly full of shite.

With a few quick maneuvering-thruster pulses, Darin course-corrected and was back on a trajectory to meet with Jamaal at an aft airlock. The exterior markings identified the unknown ship as the TSS *Heron.*

As he approached, Darin marveled at the size and scope of the craft. A hulking brute of a warship, this particular destroyer class was a feared opponent. Boasting a monstrous arsenal of railguns, plasma beams, and various torpedo types, it could rain a shitestorm of destruction down on unsuspecting craft.

Being in the midst of a space battle sounded like a grand adventure to Darin. He was reminded of the incomplete Tararian Guard application saved on his tablet back on the *Andvari.* Sooner than later, he'd have to sit down with his mother and discuss that. Having already aced the exams and passed the physical with flying colors, all that remained was filing the official application before he could be sworn in.

Though the idea of leaving his little family behind was bittersweet, he couldn't help but feel like there was more for him than life on a salvage ship. Something called to him from space, and he owed it to himself to seek out whatever that *thing* was. Joining up with the Guard seemed like the best option to make that happen.

Plus, if it was good enough for Jamaal and his mom, it should be good enough for him too, right?

Then why have I put it off so long?

Shaking his head to clear it and get back to the task at hand, Darin clasped the rigging-hook on the side of the airlock. With practiced efficiency, he reached up under his abdominal pouch, grabbed his carabiner, and pulled enough cable length out to attach himself to the hook.

Jamaal did the same on the opposite side. "Let's crack this open and see what we've got, shall we?"

"If it were already salvaged by another crew, why'd they shut the doors?"

Jamaal cracked open the panel on the airlock control

system. He pulled a small tablet from an outer arm pocket and began hooking cables together to interface with the heavy pressure door. "Some people just have good manners, I suppose."

Darin laughed.

"Would you two stop mucking about and get this job done, please?" His mom was using her 'Captain's Voice' on them. Darin recalled a time when it had scared him. Now, he and Jamaal just rolled their eyes at each other.

"Yes, ma'am, just interfacing with the door now," Jamaal said, so severely and sarcastically that Darin had to bite his lip to stifle another laugh.

Their little crew had a certain culture Darin was thankful they'd been able to maintain over the years, even with the recent addition of Mina; the doctor brought a level of professionalism and poise to soften his mother's and Jamaal's rough military edges. The fifth crewmember, Alton Kres, kept mostly to himself in the lower decks doing whatever engineers did to keep a ship running. When they all got together for meals or social time, the ability to joke around was paramount. A person would go crazy out in the void without genuine camaraderie and the ability to decompress.

The airlock door suddenly released, its two halves jerking away slightly from each other as the solenoids relaxed. The power reserves on the ship must be depleted if the doors couldn't retract on their own.

Reaching over his shoulder, Darin produced a long pry-bar and wedged it into the small gap between the two doors. He reoriented himself to stand on the door, then heaved on the pry-bar. Vibrations from the metal sliding against metal ran all the way up to his arms and into his shoulders. Without sound to accompany the struggle, it felt somehow *emptier* than it should have.

After some initial resistance and a little cajoling, he was able to lever the doors wide enough to squeeze through.

"All right Captain, we're moving in," Jamaal said into his comms and motioned for Darin to move out of his way. With the practiced grace of a lifelong soldier, he unslung the pulse rifle that was almost always within arm's reach of him, readied it, and eased himself into the breach headfirst. "Away we go."

Having spent most of his life out in the outer fringes of the galaxy doing runs like this, Darin knew the drill. He was supposed to wait outside until Jamaal had cleared the initial couple rooms, and then he'd be called in.

It chafed a bit. *Always the kid with this crew, I just need to remember that.*

In all fairness, had the roles been reversed, he would have run it the same way.

"Okay, big-guy, come on in and let's have a look." Jamaal's transmission was barely audible through an intense wave of interference.

Darin jerked his head to one side in sudden pain. The amplified sound through his helmet comms felt like a physical assault, as if a swarm of hornets had just shot through his ear and into his brain. The pain of it made him suddenly dizzy, and an intense wave of nausea overcame him.

"Ah, bomax!"

"Darin, are you all right?" The concerned sound of his mother's voice chimed in across the comms.

"Yeah, fine," he replied. "Just got hit with some interference. About blew my ears out of my helmet."

"Weird. Wasn't on my end," Jamaal said.

As best he could, Darin shook off the pain and gently pulled himself through the narrow opening.

The airlock was only slightly larger than those on the *Andvari*, able to accommodate four people if they were quite comfortable with each other.

Once beyond the airlock, the halls opened up into a four-way intersection. To the left and right, the corridors stretched off into the darkened distance. Straight ahead was a small alcove and a pressure door, which had been sealed. Blast marks scorched the walls, offering evidence of the chaos from the ship's final moments in service.

Jamaal floated upside down relative to the interior layout, using his shoulder-mounted light to inspect some of the damage around the door seam. "It looks like someone attempted to get in here." He indicated some abrasions. "See how the scrapes are over the blast damage? It happened after."

Darin could see what he was talking about, but he marveled at how keen one would have to be to notice the tiny marks amidst the other devastation.

It was then that Darin saw Jamaal was scrutinizing him.

"What?" He hated it when he sounded defensive, but he couldn't help it.

Jamaal grabbed Darin's helmet in both hands and looked into his eyes intently. "Did you hit your head out there?"

"What?" The intense light from the shoulder lamp was enough to bring on another wave of dizziness. "Of course not. I would have said so. Get that light out of my face, would you?"

Jamaal hesitated the briefest of moments before he moved away.

The comms crackled to life as Jamaal spoke, "Captain, I'm going to send Darin back. He—"

"No way in the stars you are!" Darin protested on a private channel.

"Talk to me, Hyko. What's going on?" his mom said, her

voice a sharp and precise staccato. It was always a bad sign when they started reverting back to their old military comm protocols. Last names came first, and as the stress or threat levels increased, they'd move on to their old ranks.

"Captain, he's looking a bit piqued and eyes are dilated." Jamaal evaluated him.

Darin raised his hands in an exasperated 'what the fok?' gesture. "This is a two-person job. If you send me back now, we're all screwed," he protested on the private line.

It was stretching the truth, but it was enough to make the former soldier hesitate. "You *sure* you're okay?" he asked Darin.

"I repeat, Hyko, what's going on?" Hailey asked, unaware of their private exchange.

Darin nodded. "I'm good."

"Disregard, Captain. I'll keep an eye on him out here, and I'll keep you apprised of any issues," Jamaal reported over the common channel.

"Your prerogative, Hyko." The captain didn't sound altogether happy with the decision, but the trust was there after their long history together.

"You let me know the second you feel queasy or light-headed, you got me?" Jamaal said on the private line.

Darin hesitated.

The truth was, he was already feeling all those things, and considerably more. Some facial numbness was beginning to crawl up his neck and into his jaw and cheeks. His head was spinning, and his vision was blurring somewhat. Even so, there was no chance in the universe he was going to tuck his tail and run back to *mommy*.

"I got you," he said as confidently as he could. "Now, let's crack this egg and see what she's got for us."

Jamaal was still watching him.

Exasperated, Darin said, "Burning air here, Sarge!"

Jamaal just grunted over the comms before returning to his inspection of the door. "All right, smart ass, how should we go about this?"

Darin considered the question. They had entered through an obvious personnel airlock and now faced what they presumed to be the pressurized door to the main cargo hold. On this type of vessel, there would be two other personnel airlocks, and a total of four additional cargo hold doors—one personnel door, and three others for loading and unloading of cargo, aft, starboard, and port side.

Pressure doors were thick polynanocarb that would take ages to cut through. There was also not enough power in their jump packs to hotwire the doors open. With sufficient power, they could bypass the security measures and get the door open without so much as lighting a plasma torch.

"I think we should jump the ship from the *Andvari*, power up the door systems, and put it into recovery mode. That should disengage all the pressure locks throughout the ship, make it easy to access. Once the doors are open, we can disconnect the power tether and the *Andvari* can rotate aft for each loading."

Darin was proud of his solution, and as he continued, he let a little of that pride into his voice, "But first, I'd recommend that one of us do a circuit and make sure this baby is still sealed up before we go to all that work. One man readies the tether, while the other does a lap?"

Jamaal cocked his head, thinking through the plan. "All right, who's on what?"

Darin definitely wanted to explore the ship, but he knew how Jamaal thought. Reverse psychology was the best strategy here. "I'll go pull the high-voltage lines and get them hooked up. I've never done it before, but I'm sure Alton can walk me through it."

The psychological strategy that Darin had deployed was a risky maneuver. On the one hand, Jamaal would be reluctant to send Darin off exploring a potentially dangerous derelict vessel on his own. On the other, Darin had pointed out two very important facts about running the cables.

First, they involved incredibly lethal high-voltage power lines. A single 'whoops!' would more than likely equal sudden death.

Second, it would undoubtedly get Alton involved in one of Jamaal's operations, and the grandfatherly man was agonizingly slow and methodical. This smash and grab would immediately become an all-day affair.

By pointing out, in a very subtle way, those two bits of information Darin had exponentially increased his odds of being sent out to trailblaze.

"Fine, go explore," Jamaal said, "but don't think for a moment I didn't see what you were doing there."

Darin just grinned broadly and turned to launch himself down the corridor by pushing off the wall.

The ship-wide comms tone sounded, followed by Jamaal. "All right, Alton, ready the hot line. We're going to jump this baby."

The slow, gravelly voice of Alton came over the comms, "Roger that, Jamaal. Readying the hot lines in External Access Six."

"ExAc Six, copy."

Ignoring the pounding in his head, Darin pushed off the wall and began rocketing through the corridors. Ice crystals floated lazily by like little stars as he zoomed through them.

The walls were covered in the patterned diamond-plate metal that had become quite common during the war efforts. At the time, ships had been pumped out at back-breaking speeds, and every effort had been made to conserve materials and time. Many of their salvage targets were from that vintage, so Darin took it as a good sign that they were on the right track.

He assessed the damage as he made the circuit around the ship, looking for any signs of depressurization. Whatever had happened to this ship hadn't been good.

Several sections of the halls had buckled where supports had been blown out or given way from trusses being compromised in other parts of the ship. A fire had burned through the corridor down at the rear of the ship, the direction he was heading. It gave the area an otherworldly aspect like he was traveling down a tunnel toward oblivion. Thick char clung to the walls wherever something combustible had been. Soot and ice commingled in the air with other unidentifiable bits of burned-up debris.

The aft deck of the ship was likewise damaged, with the entire rear sections pancaked on top of one another. While he couldn't access the aft cargo hold doors like he had hoped, he could see through the tangle of debris that it was unopened. A good sign, since it was the most likely route for a scrapper to haul out the goods. The likelihood that no one had accessed the main hold just increased ever so slightly. It was enough to get his pulse racing.

Tucking into a tight ball, Darin rotated in midair while letting his forward momentum carry him toward the mangled steel trusses blocking the aft halls. He planted his feet and bent his knees up to his chest, then shoved off with all his leg strength.

Like a bolt, he shot back through the sparkling detritus still swirling from his previous passage just moments ago. It had a kaleidoscope-like effect and tricked his eyes into believing he was moving faster than he really was. Jamaal called it the 'hyperspace effect'. Since there was no air to disturb the motes beyond physical contact, his passage left a near-perfect tube to delineate where he'd sped by.

Growing up out in space with his mother, this had been one of his favorite things. While Hailey and Jamaal had explored cargo holds looking for treasures, Darin had spent countless hours playing in his own wake of twirling space dust.

Looking back, it had been amazing zero-G training. He had been little more than twelve years old when he had first looked up the Tararian Guard Basic Training requirements. Only fourteen when he was able to complete the grueling course. Fifteen when he could hit the performance mark for 'exemplary' in several categories. It wasn't just his dream to be a soldier *in* the Guard, he wanted to be the *best* of them.

"Coming back with the hot line now," Jamaal's voice interrupted Darin's serene voyage through the corridors. "Have you got the other decks scoped out yet, kid?"

Always with that 'kid' shite!

"Not yet, Sarge." Darin grabbed the ceiling rafters and then pushed off to propel him faster down the hall. He flew past their entry point, rocketing toward the forward decks. "Two minutes."

"You're telling me," Jamaal sounded incredulous, "that I went all the way back to the *Andvari*, had to talk that old geezer Kress out of some juice-line to hotwire this derelict windbag up, and you're not even done checking it out yet?"

"It's a big ship!"

Flipping in the air, so his feet were pointing toward the approaching wall, he touched down ever-so-gently, his muscular legs easily absorbing the minimal impact.

Darin grinned to himself. *They may as well skip me past Basic Training and make me the zero-G instructor.*

He checked the forward cargo door. It stood ajar, the pry marks from flat bars easily visible even from the fifty-meter distance.

"Bad news, Sarge," Darin said.

"Fok!" Jamaal spat into the comms, inferring the meaning of Darin's report. "I thought for sure she was sealed tight."

Darin pushed off the wall and floated slowly over to the cargo hold. With a quick adjustment of his shoulder lamp, he peered through the cracked-open door.

The inside was a dizzyingly massive void. Overhead struts loomed like talons from a grasping monster, with cables, chains, and filaments glittering from the various implements used for loading and unloading cargo. The hold was so colossal it could have easily held a half squad of fighters.

Unfortunately, it was utterly, despairingly empty. Darin didn't even notice any of the usual tiny debris floating about.

"Total bust in here. Not a drop left for us," Darin announced over the general comm channel.

It would be a crushing blow to the crew. His mom, in particular, was starting to buckle from the anxiety.

Survive a war, just to be defeated by bills.

There was nothing he could do. Even if he left for the Guard at their next port stop and she had one less mouth to feed, it'd be too late. The lenders would only delay for so long before they called the port authority to lock down the ship, and that would be the end.

"What about wiring, mechanical bits, scrap metal?" She didn't sound desperate, but Darin knew she was at the end of her line. "Grab anything you can, Hyko."

"Roger that, Captain." Jamaal would cut into the ship and rip out anything worth a shite. It wouldn't even come close to what they needed.

It was imperative they score something big, and fast.

"All right, I'm making my egress," Darin said.

"You good on your own?" Jamaal asked.

"Please, Sarge," Darin chided. "C'mon, it's me we're talking about here!"

The open comms filled with laughter from everyone active on the line.

He smiled. It was good to cut the tension and apprehension.

Suddenly, a new wave of pain shot through Darin's forehead. He grunted and exhaled with the force of it. White-hot, searing agony lanced up and down his spine in electrical pulses.

"Jam—" he managed to gasp out into an open comm before another jolt hit his forehead like a hammer blow.

"Darin? Darin, what's wrong?" Jamaal was cool under pressure, but his voice was tight, clipped, and authoritative.

Darin wanted to respond, wanted to tell him to hurry. He couldn't.

The pain was so intense that his jaw was clamped down like a vise. He could feel his teeth creaking under the pressure. His cheeks were beginning to tingle, and his neck had gone ice cold. No part of his body was responding the way it should.

"Darin, I'm coming, *stay there!*"

The world began to darken around the edges. Silvery white star-like spots flickered into existence everywhere. Another wave shot through his head and down his spine.

The fuzzy black edges of his vision collapsed in on themselves until all he could see was a rapidly growing white light at the center. Then, even that too faded.

All went black.

CHAPTER 4

SHITE!

JAMAAL HAD only taken his eyes off the kid for a couple minutes—mere heartbeats—and something like this had to happen?

The big worry was an ambush. It was unlikely, as the scanners along the *Andvari*'s hull would have alerted them to heat-signatures.

That left the possibility of an environmental hazard. Any number of things could be on the ship that might harm a person. Jamaal had heard about some nasty weapons employed during the war, so it was possible Darin had been exposed to residue during his run through the ship. Darin knew those risks and he was usually extremely cautious.

"Talk to me, Jamaal." Hailey's voice was tense, clipped, and rigidly in-control. Those were all bad signs. It meant she was struggling to hang on.

"I'm making my way to Darin now." He thrust himself headfirst down the dark hallway toward Darin's last known location.

Jamaal engaged the floodlights on his suit, which

immediately illuminated the corridor at least ten meters ahead of him. The light sparkled off the ice crystals and dust. After a little searching, he spotted a distant shadow floating near the ceiling up ahead.

If anything happened to that kid on my watch, I'll never forgive myself, Jamaal thought as he closed the distance to Darin's limp form.

There was no blood around. That was a good sign.

Neither were there any signs of a breach in his suit. Also good.

There was, however, no movement from the kid. That wasn't at all good.

Flipping over, Jamaal squared his legs toward the wall just beyond Darin and began to slap the bulkheads streaking by overhead to slow himself. He struck the far wall and rebounded toward Darin. The maneuver was as natural as breathing.

Reaching out, he grasped Darin by the shoulder and rolled him over so he could peer inside his visor. No blood, no sign of seizures or stroke. For what it was worth, the kid looked asleep.

"Okay, Captain, I've got him. He appears to be unconscious. No visible damage." Using a carabiner on his suit and a hook on the upper part of Darin's back, he tethered the two of them. "Coming back, ready the medbay."

"Already on it, Mr. Hyko." Doctor Hurn's velvety voice gave him a little chill.

There was no denying a mutual level of interest between the two of them. Jamaal knew it was purely physical for him but wasn't exactly sure on her motives. Their recent banter had been a little on the arousing side. And, well, he liked it. He liked *her*.

The weight of Darin tugging against the carabiner felt

suddenly heavier than it should've.

He had a responsibility now. The Suros relied on him. He didn't need the distraction of 'what if?' fantasies about the lovely doctor right now.

Focus, Jamaal!

This kind of mind-wandering shite was what had gotten him into so much trouble in the Guard.

"There have been no anomalies in the vitals readout from his suit, Captain," said Dr. Hurn. "I'll do a thorough workup once he's on board."

"ETA, Hyko?" Hailey had lost a bit of the barely restrained panic to her voice. It was subtle, but he could tell.

"Three minutes, Captain." The words left his mouth as he and Darin exited the derelict TSS *Heron*.

Thanks for nothing, you floating piece of shite!

He and Darin launched out of the open airlock door. Using the side thrusters, he fired short little bursts to align with the *Andvari* and his target airlock.

"Coming in alpha-two, copy?" Alpha, for airlock, two for the side he was aiming at.

"Alpha-two, copy. Will meet you at the door."

Of that, I have no doubt.

Whether it was good news or bad, Captain Suro was *always* impatiently waiting at whatever threshold there was. Jamaal often thought she'd die first, just so she could be waiting in the afterlife with the same toe-tapping impatience she had in life. Whatever it took, he planned to make sure that didn't happen. That was one race he fully intended to win.

Jamaal's mind churned through what he knew of the incident so he'd be ready to debrief Hailey.

He and Darin had both entered the ship, and neither had detected any kind of known biohazard or high levels of radiation. Sensors also would have alerted them to the presence of other people. The placed had been sealed up tight and there were no signs of disturbance, so it seemed unlikely that someone had been lying in wait in a stealth suit for the opportunity to knock a teenager unconscious.

Given all that, the most likely cause of Darin's current state was an inadvertent impact. Jamaal knew full well that Darin liked to show off in zero-G. Stars, he'd taught the kid everything he knew!

Darin had probably clipped a bulkhead or support beam with his head and was going fast enough to knock himself out. He'd wake up with a killer headache, but otherwise be no worse for wear. Maybe a little dumber, but the smart-ass could likely afford that, too.

There was that half-spoken message, though. It didn't seem like an accidental clip to the head. You wouldn't *drift* unconscious if that had happened. With a hit like that, it was lights out.

Something just wasn't sitting right.

Facing Hailey without having all the details was going to be like sticking his manly bits into a cheese grater.

Actually, the cheese grater might be more comfortable.

Sighing heavily into his suit, he steeled himself for what was to come. At the end of the day, he just hoped to the stars that Darin was okay.

CHAPTER 5

MINA SCRAMBLED TO remove everything from the examination table in the tiny ship infirmary. *What in the stars happened over there?*

Aside from the flash of spatial distortion she'd observed—which she still figured was a sensor glitch—there was nothing anomalous about the derelict TSS ship. However, young, healthy people didn't pass out for no reason. She tried to prepare the room for a response to the most likely medical scenarios.

The compact infirmary was illuminated with diffused light and had drains in both the examination table and floor. Its autodoc was a low-end model that had come with the ship, but it would serve in a pinch for moderate injuries. Thankfully, they were fully stocked on the rest of their medical supplies, having had no previous occasion to use them. The downside was that Mina had been mid-inventory—hence the clutter she was removing.

What began as a delicate and purposeful extraction of the supplies quickly devolved into raking items off onto the floor with her forearms. It was her job to clean and organize all of it, anyway, so there was little harm in the disarray to anyone other than herself.

The comms crackled with an open, ship-wide, line.

"What the fok, Jamaal? Talk to me!" There was no panic in the good captain's voice, but there was a cold and calculating tone of command. It gave Mina the shivers.

"I am not sure, Captain." Jamaal was clearly upset and confused; his tone wavered close to hysteric. "I saw him fly down the hall, you know doing that thing he likes to do. He had some really good speed built up."

"Maybe he struck something?" Hailey didn't sound convinced with her own theory.

There were some sounds of movement, grunts of exertion. "His suit is sealed; all the pressure readings are normal. I see no visible signs of impacts or punctures."

Flinging cabinets and locker doors open wide, Mina rooted around in a desperate rush to find the field-trauma kit. *Where in the stars did I put it?*

When she finally located the case, in a location where she knew for certain she hadn't placed it, she emptied it out on the stainless steel table and started to organize the various implements.

From the rapid dialogue taking place over the comms, she gathered that Darin's condition could be anything from some kind of radiation exposure to head trauma. Either would be fairly easy to diagnose but would ultimately require a true hospital. Unfortunately, the nearest facility was a solid two days away.

Mina would reserve judgment on the recommended course of treatment until after she'd examined her patient. Depending on the severity, managing Hailey's reaction—and Jamaal's, based on the sound of it—might prove to be a challenge.

Now that her makeshift triage table had been arrayed to the best of her resources and abilities, Mina made her way to the sink to wash her hands.

Her mind raced. This incident undoubtedly meant their mission would come to an end. There wasn't enough time left on their salvage contract to go to the nearest station with an adequately equipped hospital and surgical center, treat Darin, and then head back out to strip a vessel. Not even if they knew where to go.

Scrubbing furiously enough to hurt in the scalding hot water, Mina suddenly felt a wave of intense remorse. Her heart ached in her chest. The crew had been so welcoming of her, so grateful for the expertise she had to offer. Yet, she had failed miserably at every task she had undertaken while on the *Andvari*. They'd leased the new ship because of her—with the promise of being able to go after more ambitious salvage targets off the beaten path. So far, she'd done nothing but lead them toward disappointment after disappointment. It was her fault they were now behind on the payments and on the brink of losing everything.

"Dr. Hurn?" Hailey's voice thundered over the speakers in the little infirmary.

"Yes, Captain?" Mina was more than a little aware of the squeak in her voice. It happened when she got nervous, and she hated it.

"Are you ready for your patient?"

"Yes, all set," she confirmed, trying to sound more confident this time.

It had taken her years, but she had transformed her predisposition toward anxiety into a strength. It made her sharper, cleverer, and hyper-focused. Failure had made a bitter enemy of her.

Not this task. I will not fail Darin.

"We're at the airlock," Jamaal announced. "Beginning re-pressurization."

With squinted eyes, Mina scrutinized the table in the way only a trained doctor was able. She was as prepared as she could be. On a whim, she sprayed a second coat of an aerosolized disinfectant on the table and surrounding area; you could never be too careful when it came to infections.

"Pressurization complete," Hailey said breathlessly; she was obviously on the move. "Take him to the infirmary. I'll meet you there."

"When you arrive, Mr. Hyko," Mina began, "please help me get him onto the table as quickly as you can. Touch as little in the area as possible and leave promptly. We must maintain a sterile environment, and if it was a radioactive or biological exposure event, you could make that exposure worse."

Or even expose me, or the rest of the ship, which could kill us all. It was a sobering thought.

There were so many risks to space travel, even for an advanced civilization such as they were. Thousands of years of existence traveling throughout space, and yet the right biological organism could overcome all of that experience, all of that technology, with ruinous results.

"Copy that, doc," Jamaal said in short breathy grunts. "In and out. No problem."

The airlock wasn't far from the medical room. With only a few tense moments of waiting, the door opened to reveal the bulky Jamaal with Darin slung over one of his broad shoulders. Both were still in their full pressure suits, which was good. Not only did they not waste any precious time removing them, but if Darin's condition *was* exposure-related, the suit could very well be keeping them somewhat quarantined from the rest of the crew.

As instructed, Jamaal marched right up to the table and carefully lowered Darin down.

Mina watched from the side, ready to jump in if necessary.

As he righted himself, Jamaal stared right into her eyes with an intensity that spoke volumes. The hollow look of a soldier winding his way down the path of survivors' guilt and treading on familiar territory.

On reflex, she started to reach out to comfort him before catching herself.

He stepped beyond her reach with the grace of a large cat. "Appreciate the thought, Doc. I'm fine. You fix him up."

The door hissed shut behind him.

As soon as the seal clicked, Mina activated a hard lock protocol to isolate the room's air and water drainage. It would protect the rest of the ship from potential contamination as much as possible.

All right. Let's find out what we're dealing with.

She removed Darin's helmet. Though a tricky maneuver, it was something that she had repeatedly practiced in medical school. Any EVA brought with it an insanely high risk of a medical emergency and accounted for almost a full half of spaceborne fatalities.

With the helmet off, she saw no external signs of head trauma. *So much for an easy diagnosis.*

As quickly as she could, she used medical shears to begin cutting away the pressure suit from the young man she had grown so fond of.

She saw no sign of the suit being penetrated or abraded as the pieces fell off the table and onto the floor. Good news.

The bad news was that she had limited means on board the salvage ship to diagnose and treat more complex issues. While it was never ideal to suffer some kind of exposure incident, it was far better than some of the other possibilities.

As the last bits of pressure suit fell to the floor, it revealed the shipsuit normally worn as a base layer to provide extra protection in case of rapid decompression. The formfitting charcoal-colored fabric highlighted every muscle and curve. Doctors lost all modesty in medical school, and in a few short moments, Mina had stripped Darin down to his undergarments.

She began her full analysis of Darin. No visible cuts, abrasions, or bruising that she could immediately see on his front.

"Is he going to be okay, Dr. Hurn?" Hailey asked from the intercom at the door.

"I need to finish my examination," Mina replied while wiping sweat off her brow with her forearm, "but all the easy stuff is coming up negative. Everything from here on out is a bit more…"

"Complicated?" Hailey provided.

"Yeah. Let's go with complicated."

"Just like a Suro to keep things interesting." Hailey chuckled humorlessly.

It was a painful sound.

Mina had initiated enough banter back and forth amongst the crew to know that Hailey had lost her husband in a violent way. It sounded like her experience was a type of loss that most people would not face over a long lifetime. That was tough. It no doubt made any threat to her son's wellbeing that much more difficult to bear.

Knowing that, Mina would need to choose her words carefully. There was a lot to consider when discussing a patient with a loved one. Sometimes a distraught relative could make a bad situation much, much worse.

Mina considered trying to soothe Hailey, but ultimately decided the captain was a seasoned military veteran who wouldn't respond well to platitudes. Focusing on Darin was what was important right now.

The next diagnostic step was to perform a full-body scan to identify any internal issues. She ran a handheld scanner up and down the breadth and length of the young man's body. There was nothing abnormal.

Mina secured the portable unit in a clamp over Darin's head. The real-time readings streamed to her handheld. His vitals looked good. Really good, in fact. It was almost as if he were sleeping, or in a trance.

With an extreme sense of foreboding, she fingered open an eye and shone a bright penlight over it.

Bomax!

She checked the other eye, then repeated the cycle. Depressed brainstem reflexes. That and his vitals suggested he was in a coma.

But why?

Her mind running through potential scenarios as to why an athletic young man coming into his prime would suddenly drop into a coma, she grabbed an electromagnetic radiation scanner. The unit flared to life, the initial reading was off the charts so far that it caused the unit to reboot. Frustrated, Mina smacked the side of the device.

Once it finished its boot-up cycle, she passed it back over Darin. This time, however, the unit stayed dormant. Totally normal readings.

That's not ominous or anything...

As delicately as she could, Mina rotated her well-muscled crewmate onto his stomach. His limbs were hot, but not overly so, and completely lifeless. The examination of his backside yielded no new revelations.

"Okay, Hailey, I think it's safe for you to come in," Mina said as she disengaged the lockdown protocol.

Her last words were still hanging in the air when the door and Hailey ran in, leaving a hand-wringing Jamaal in the hallway. He had evidently stepped outside and immediately stripped to his shipsuit, piling his pressure suit against the bulkhead.

"I don't like guessing games, so just hit me with it," Hailey said as soon as the door shut behind her. The overly gruff tone was meant to be a strong front, but Mina had been around enough wounded soldiers to know she was quaking inside.

"He is stable," she began gently. "His vitals are quite good, actually. However, for some reason that I have yet to determine, it appears he's in a coma."

"A coma?!" Hailey exclaimed.

Mina raised both of her hands in a placating gesture. "There's no cause for immediate alarm. He's stable, he's strong, and we're adequately equipped to treat most of the circumstances that would result in such a condition."

A sudden look of fear stole its way across Hailey's face. "Radiation poisoning?"

Mina considered for a moment.

"No, I don't think so. There were no unusual readings." She brought her finger up to tap thoughtfully against her lips.

"Should *I* get checked for radiation?" The sudden booming voice of Jamaal over the intercom made Mina jump.

"Yes!" Hailey snapped.

"Not necessary…" Mina started to comment but trailed off at a stern look from Hailey.

The door opened and Jamaal peered inside, hesitant.

"Come on in, Hyko," Hailey said. "Might as well get this over with."

Jamaal stepped inside gingerly as if his mere presence could worsen the situation. Mina grasped the scanner and met him halfway to the table. With practiced gestures, she scanned him from head to toe, front to back.

"Nothing but your magnetic personality, Mr. Hyko," Mina said with a wink.

She was rewarded with an intense wave of blushing on the grizzled soldier's cheeks.

"Okay, well, should we head for the nearest trauma center? Where would that be?" Hailey asked forcefully, having missed the entire exchange while staring worriedly at her son stretched out mostly naked on the exam table.

"At this stage, I don't think traveling to a medical facility is necessary," Mina replied, skirting the truth.

Under typical circumstances, she would suggest they immediately head to the nearest hospital to have a specialist take a look. An *unexplained* coma was in reality quite a bit worse than one with an obvious cause. However, Mina couldn't ignore the larger context of their situation. If they left the Kyron Nebula now, that would be the end of their livelihood.

Ultimately, she was confident that her patient was stable and his condition was unlikely to worsen if they delayed medical treatment until after completing their salvage mission. They'd already risked too much coming here. So, forging ahead was the smartest move.

"I don't see how—" Hailey started to protest, as Mina expected.

She was ready with her reply. "For now, I'll start him on fluids and a catheter to keep him from developing any kind of infection or dehydration. The autodoc can handle the rest. It's entirely possible he'll wake up perfectly fine, so let's wait and see."

What she didn't mention was that if something changed and his condition suddenly worsened, being in a hospital would be the far superior option. Mina knew what was at risk, however, and wanted to enable Hailey to make the difficult decision to remain on course as a captain with a responsibility to her crew. Not just a decision from a distraught mother worried about the health of her child.

Having never been a parent herself—though she hadn't ruled out the possibility—Mina didn't know what that must feel like to put another so thoroughly before oneself. However, that lack of parental perspective didn't change the fact that she was right about the decision to move forward with fulfilling their salvage contract.

"I think we should turn around and head directly to the nearest hospital." Hailey planted her hands on her hips and raised her chin slightly. It was more than a simple declaration; it was far closer to a direct challenge.

With as much patience and grace as she could muster, Mina met Hailey's gaze and gave her a regretful shrug. "We certainly can, if that's what you order. It'd be a shame to lose our contract only to discover that Darin is perfectly fine."

For all her bluster and commanding presence, the captain suddenly looked dubious. Mina watched her patiently and let the silence of the moment do her talking for her. Hailey wasn't stupid; she would realize that her emotions were clouding her judgment. It wouldn't take long for her to come to the same conclusion that Mina had already communicated.

With a frustrated sigh, Hailey made a motion like swatting a large insect out of the air between them. "Fine."

That was that.

Restraining a smile, Mina watched as the captain glanced

once more at her comatose son and then stalked out of the room, her back rigid as a steel strut.

"He's going to be okay, right?"

Mina jumped slightly; she had forgotten Jamaal was there. For such a big man, he sure could be stealthy when he wanted to.

"I believe so, Mr. Hyko," she said thoughtfully.

She had an urge to be more reassuring, to remove the weasel in the statement; causing undue worry was not ever her intention. Yet, it was a certain point of pride for her to never diminish the risks present in the situation. She didn't want to give hope where there was none, or allow her ego to influence her prognosis. With Darin, she simply did not know yet what to expect for his recovery.

In these matters, she trusted her training and experience. She'd once been a shining star in the biomedical facility, before the event that led to her unfortunate exile. Even then, her diagnostic aptitude was never the issue. Since her instincts now told her Darin would be okay, she stood by her recommendations.

Jaw set, with his teeth grinding together, Jamaal scrutinized the young man on the table.

It was no secret to anyone that saw the two together that Jamaal cared a great deal about Darin, and vice-versa. As hard as this was for Hailey, she could tell that Jamaal felt ultimately responsible for anything that happened to Darin outside the ship.

Without another word, Jamaal turned and plodded out. Everything about his posture screamed defeat and despair.

Mina let out a heavy sigh. She'd left behind her medical career to become a data analyst. Now she couldn't even locate a decent salvage site to save her life, plus she held a literal life in her hands. The day couldn't have gone much more sideways.

Nonetheless, she had a job to do. *I brought us here. Now I need to get us out of this mess.*

CHAPTER 6

THERE HAD BEEN too much hardship in Hailey's life. It seemed like today would garner more.

Slumped in the pilot's seat, she held her face in her hands and sobbed silently. Her shoulders twitched and air hissed periodically over her teeth, but otherwise, she endeavored to not make any sound.

Years of being in challenging leadership roles had trained her to be fairly cloaked with her emotions, maintaining an unwavering front of level-headed leadership. But here, alone, she allowed herself to let the emotion pour out—a necessary purge.

Seeing Darin on the exam table had brought back a flood of memories of his father. She missed him every day, but in moments like this, the most.

Karej Suro had been one of the most good-hearted people she had ever encountered. She had met him during a raid on the glacial moon Hiovis. Her unit had been ordered to eliminate a threat with 'extreme prejudice', but when Hailey realized there were civilians trapped within the building, she had defied orders and sent her team into the collapsing inferno.

As usual, Jamaal had entered the building right behind her with his typical unflappable dependability.

The building had been a mess of raging fire, blood, and death. The macabre scene still disrupted her dreams most nights. Hailey had found Karej with a group of small children, administering triage care as much as he was able. As a research scientist not trained in first-aid or medicine, he had found a first-responders bag and done what he could to 'figure it out' on his own. Of the thirty or so wounded children he had personally pulled from the wreckage, he had managed to save seven lives. A heroic effort for one person without adequate medical training.

When Hailey and her team had tried to extract him and the surviving children from the wreckage, he had fought her with a passion. Screaming, kicking, and even biting her in an effort to continue administering care to corpses. It had broken a part of Hailey, witnessing that depth of despair. Ultimately, she had had to knock him unconscious and carry him over a shoulder to safety.

It was a week later that she had found herself compelled to visit the stranger in the hospital where he was receiving physical therapy for injuries he had sustained while rescuing the children.

Back then, Karej had a haunted look. He spoke little, and his vacant stare was gut wrenching. Without any words exchanged, it was obvious that he blamed himself for those twenty-three body bags. His eyes seemed to say, "Seven. Just Seven? That's all you could do, was seven?" Any time someone said the word 'seven' around him, he'd flinch as if struck.

Hailey had made it a habit to visit him whenever she could find the time.

Slowly, painfully, Karej had come out of his darkness. She

wasn't sure if she had been of any help, but she liked to think so. As he opened up to her, and began to talk about his experience, his history, and what futile hopes he had for the future, she finally got to know the man beneath the pain. Like a child clutching a beautiful butterfly and peering through interlocked fingers to catch glimpses of the splendor, her heart had warmed to him. And reluctantly, so had his toward her.

It took a full three years after the incident for them to admit it to each other. Jamaal had known from the start, because the idiot seemed to know *everything* when it came to potentially disastrous personal matters. Other than him, everyone just assumed theirs had been a friendship born of strife and pain. What they didn't see was the mutual respect and admiration they shared for each other. It had been the foundation of their marriage, and they'd had it until the very end.

The comms clicked to life, and the hoarse voice of Alton Kress filled the space, "Captain?"

Despite being the oldest among the crew, Alton was polite and deferential, often showing a level of awareness Hailey wouldn't expect. From the soft inflection of his question, it was almost like he knew he was interrupting a tender moment.

Hailey wiped furiously at her wet cheeks. *This isn't the time to reminisce.*

She cleared her throat and returned her thoughts to the present. "Go ahead, Alton," she said with her crisp, *make-it-quick* tone.

"Well, I guess I'm just wondering what to do now." There was an awkward pause, then he continued, "Jamaal is wanting to suit back up and go scrap what he can from that hunk outside."

"No!" she cut him off, and while not overly loud it carried

with it the weight of her rank.

"Okay, should we figure out where we're headed, then?" Alton was trying to distract her from her worry. Hailey recognized this, but she didn't care. He had a kind heart, and she appreciated him immensely.

"Yes." She sniffed loudly to clear the streams of snot threatening to drown her. "Has Dr. Hurn made her calculations?"

"She has, but... she thinks our best chances of making a trip worth it is to go deeper into the nebula," he grumbled softly, which over the comms reminded Hailey of the multitude of reverberations in a shipyard she'd visited in her youth.

No surprise there.

They didn't have a choice, really, so there was no point in Hailey pressing the issue. The decision to head toward the Kyron Nebula had already taken them outside the designated salvage grounds and outside of jump range, and they needed to stay the course if they were going to have any chance of making their next lease payment.

"Have Dr. Hurn get me the coordinates. But if we get the feeling it's a bust, I'm turning us right around and making for the nearest trauma center."

"I think it's better than our other options, Captain, that's for sure." The comms clicked off with a faint *snap-buzz.*

Within moments, the coordinates to a point inside the massive Kyron Nebula were transmitted from Mina, and Hailey began plotting the course.

She could tell that this was as close to a 'sure thing' for a good score as was possible. A ship on the outside of the nebula was one thing, but they should have a veritable ship graveyard to peruse inside. By all accounts, wrecks from several major battles spanning hundreds of years should have drifted toward the enormous planetary nebulae and become mired in its gravitational tide.

Unfortunately, their new course put them much further away from the nearest medical facilities.

Hailey had to put her faith in her doctor. As opposed to other analyst they'd interviewed with a narrow skillset, Mina's medical background made her an asset in situations exactly like this. The last thing Hailey wanted to do was jeopardize the sustainability of their operation by overreacting to an injury. If she had abandoned everything and taken Darin to a hospital just to be told he had bumped his head on a strut and would be fine in a few days, she would never forgive herself. The opportunity to have their own ship and carve out their destiny, ruined by overactive maternal instincts.

She had made up her mind, they were pressing on. If Dr. Hurn told her she could keep her son stable, then that was that. Hopefully, they'd get what they needed to fulfill the contract quickly and get to a hospital.

The doorway hissed open and Mina entered. For once, her face wasn't buried in her tablet. There was no trace of her usual smile, either.

Hailey felt a sudden stab of anxiety. It had only been an hour or less since she had left the infirmary. Surely that wasn't enough time for something bad to happen, right? Her military training told her otherwise.

"Darin is still stable, Hailey," the doctor reassured her.

"Thank you, Dr. Hurn." It came out a breathy whisper as Hailey pushed down her worry.

"Okay, we're going to fix something right now that should have been addressed a long time ago. Please, Captain, stop calling me 'Dr. Hurn', 'Doctor', or whatever. Call me Mina."

Hailey started to protest but Doctor... *Mina*... held up a hand to silence her.

"Okay, I think I can do that." Hailey had spent too much time in the military; titles were important to her.

"I mean, I don't feel bad calling you Hailey," Mina said dryly. "Do you resent that I don't call you 'Captain' all the time?"

Hailey did, in fact. But she wasn't about to throw back the offer of deepening friendship with Mina. "No, of course not."

"Oh my, you're a terrible liar!" Mina laughed.

Despite herself, Hailey smiled.

"What can I help you with, Mina?" Hailey faked a gruff 'Disapproving Captain' tone but found herself becoming increasingly annoyed with the delays. She wanted nothing more than to get into the nebula, find anything worth salvaging, and then get her son to safety.

"I've looked up the last known flight data for several large craft that have yet to be registered as salvaged." Mina finally brought her tablet up to her face, scrutinizing the displayed data. "I think we're in for a treat. There are dozens, possibly hundreds of potential targets that could be stuck in the gravitational backwater. My models show potentially twenty lost carriers—power cores and all!"

Finally, something going our way! Despite the fantastic news, the thought was bittersweet for Hailey; her son was below decks in a coma, so she wasn't in a mood to celebrate. Instead, she just nodded.

Finding a stash of power cores would be the answer to all their financial troubles. The perpetual energy modules—or PEMs—powered everything on a ship from the jump drive to subspace communications. Though PEMs were commonplace throughout the Taran Empire, the components required to construct them were extremely rare, so they fetched top dollar in salvage. In particular, voydite crystals were the base component of the nanocrystal chambers that were essential for the function of the PEM, so even a depleted power core held significant value if the voydite chamber was intact. That made the power cores the prime objective of every other salvage crew out there.

For once, being far from the well-trodden salvage path, the *Andvari*'s crew might actually get to claim that top prize. If their speculations about their destination turned out to be accurate, they'd be alone in a sea of premium salvage targets.

That was why Hailey loved having science types on her crew. Without them, they'd just be flying around hoping to stumble across something. Traveling into the nebula was a calculated risk, sure, but they had the potential to get the payday of their lives.

Nothing is guaranteed yet, she reminded herself.

Their lack of success to date meant they'd need at least basic scrap from several carriers just to make their quota. Hauls from twenty ships would fulfill the remainder of their current salvage agreement. On the flip side, harvesting only PEMs would meet their financial needs but wouldn't satisfy the materials minimums in their contract. The power cores were small enough that they could fit them and the other scrap on the *Andvari*, but it was a time-consuming process to strip down a vessel. They were already down a man, which would slow the process considerably. And their mission clock had almost run out.

If we do come across a treasure trove, how long should we commit to harvesting? Did we just take what we need and get out? Or do we make the most of it? For the first time in her career as a scavenger, Hailey hoped there were just enough targets to keep the debt collectors out of their hair for a few more months. That way, she wouldn't have to make that difficult decision about what to take and what to leave behind.

The comms crackled to life as Alton spoke, "We're all ready here, Captain."

"Let's make tracks." Hailey did everything she could to project confidence she didn't feel into her voice.

Without further communication, she felt the subtle vibration of the sub-light drive spinning up. Hailey cross-referenced the coordinates she had been given with what she had entered, just to make sure everything was set properly. Then, she engaged the drive.

The *Andvari* lurched violently.

Both Mina and Hailey staggered but managed to remain standing.

The systems all went haywire, alarms flashed, panels spontaneously rebooted.

Shite! What could cause that? Hailey reached over and flipped the comms on, "Alton, what the fok's going on? Did we blow our drive?"

Silence.

Mina and Hailey shared a concerned glance.

"Alton?" Hailey transmitted, this time ship-wide.

A click. "Did you guys feel that?" The elderly man was coughing and wheezing the words out.

Mina hid an amused smile behind her delicate hand, while Hailey just gnashed her teeth in frustration.

"Of course, we felt that, Alton! What was it?" Her tone was clipped and angry. The fact that she had to confirm that she had felt something so substantial was exasperating. Alton was old but he wasn't senile—yet.

"Electromagnetic surge, I think," Alton said, totally

oblivious to her ire. "A mother of one, too, by the looks of it. Whole systems on the fritz down here!" He chuckled. The man *actually* found this a good place for mirth.

Hailey had half a mind to stomp down to the engineering level and yell to the old fart's face. With a start, she realized the ship was still vibrating subtly beneath her feet.

"Alton, I had just engaged the pion drive when that wave hit us…" She trailed off, unsure of how to ask the question. *Did I just doom us all?*

"No problem there," Alton said reassuringly. "However, the PEM is unresponsive." For the first time today, Alton sounded genuinely worried.

"Unresponsive? Was it damaged?" If Alton was sounding concerned, she felt like she should be screaming in terror.

"There is no visible damage, but it's completely powered down," Alton said.

"Powered down? Is that even possible?" Hailey felt her brows draw down together in confusion.

"Before today I wouldn't have said so, no." Alton sounded more curious now, "I have never heard of a PEM losing power, aside from shorting out. That's kind of the point of the system—infinite power supply, you know?"

"Should we reverse our course and head back to a station while we still have full use of the sub-light drive? We can drop Darin off and get the ship repaired at the same time." It just felt like no matter what she did, Hailey was being forced back to port.

We're going to lose the ship. It was beginning to feel inevitable.

"Captain, at this point, we're closer to the salvage site than we are the nearest port. If we can find the right scrap, I could potentially swap out our PEM so we could jump to port as soon as we get back into beacon range. Might be faster to press on and cobble together a fix on our own than to limp back the whole way at sub-light."

Hailey confirmed the distances, and Alton was correct. It'd take them almost four times longer to get back to port on the sub-light engines than it would if they were to continue on their present course to the salvage site, make repairs, and then jump back the rest of the way. The risk, of course, was that once they reached the wreckage, if they failed to procure the proper materials, they'd likely not make it back at all.

Mina had leaned over the sensor control panel and was tapping her lips thoughtfully. It was just distracting enough to break Hailey out of her spiraling fears.

"Do what you need to do and keep me apprised of any trouble," Hailey said.

"Will do, Cap!" Alton acknowledged, and she could almost hear the rustle of clothing from a physical salute over the comms.

Alton had served in some fashion or other, but unlike Jamaal or herself, he never spoke of it. All of his mannerisms were that of someone who had been in the Tararian Guard. That special bond of servicemembers, even from different eras, was part of the reason they had grown so close as a crew.

"Hmm," Mina said.

A pit of cold suddenly opened in Hailey's stomach. "I don't like that sound at all." *The punches just keep falling!*

Mina looked up, confused at the comment. She glanced back down at the controls and then nodded. "Ah, right. Sorry, I was just going over the diagnostics reports from the ship. There's something quite odd here."

Hailey came over to peer at the readouts herself.

Mina indicated a few lines. "It seems like we were scanned

during that EM pulse."

"Scanned? Like by another ship?" Hailey immediately switched into combat-mode.

After a moment of hesitation, Mina frowned and narrowed her eyes. "No, not another ship, I don't think. It was too big, too fast. I think we would have noticed a battlecruiser right on top of us."

Sudden concern overtook Hailey, and she again reached over to access the comms. "Jamaal."

After a brief pause, he replied. "Go for Jamaal. What's up, Captain?"

"Go check on Darin," she requested.

"Already with him, Cap. He's fine. Well, not *fine*. You know, the same."

Hailey sighed. "Thanks." She sat down heavily in the pilot's seat. "Well, it looks like the only way is forward now." Not having options was the worst—by far her biggest pet peeve.

"When the Universe is telling you the way, sometimes you can't fight it." Mina patted her on the shoulder and strode out.

Screw that. I'm Tararian Guard. I can fight anything. Hopefully, even years after retirement, that still held true.

CHAPTER 7

BLOOD DRIPPED FROM Jamaal Hyko's abraded knuckles onto the metal floor tiling. He always worked out hard; it was a point of pride for him. This, however, was something else. This was punishment.

Red impact splatter glistened on the woven punching bag, where his bloody fists had left their marks. It had likely been an hour since he had worn through the tape wound around his hands to protect them from the coarse bag. The pain didn't bothered him; he found peace in it.

A nagging in the back of his mind accused him of all the faults that had landed him in this situation. Arrogance. Lack of focus. Stubbornness. *I let Darin down. I let Hailey down. I should have been able to keep him safe.*

Closer than most married couples, Jamaal and Hailey had been connected by fate or function since their late-teen years. While in the Tararian Guard, they had killed, and watched die, hundreds of friends and foe alike. It was not uncommon for them to stitch each other back together in the field after significant injuries.

It was no secret that they loved each other, deeply. Just not *that* kind of love. That place in his captain's heart had been reserved for her dead husband. Jamaal respected him, and though it pained him greatly, honored his memory. It still hurt, every bomaxed day!

Before Karej came along, Jamaal and Hailey had briefly entertained the idea of fooling around. Unfortunately, she had been one of those soldiers that got promoted rapidly—while he was one that was more likely to get reprimanded. It didn't take long before fraternization rules in the Guard made the possibility of an intimate relationship between them a major infraction.

Not wanting to put either of their careers in jeopardy, Jamaal had drifted off to the sidelines—never *too* far, but watching from a safe distance. However, once Hailey met Karej and decided to get married, well… things changed.

He couldn't begrudge her the choice. A bucket-head grunt like him, with a bad reputation and a penchant for mischief, wasn't exactly marriage material.

They had remained close friends over the years—more, he'd wager. Though, his standing was never quite on the level he had hoped for. It made their interactions difficult. When Hailey had left the Guard, Jamaal had blindly followed. That had been a difficult time. Comforting someone over a significant loss in their life, all while fighting the urge to dance over maybe, *finally*, having a chance, was a delicate balance.

All the while, he'd been there for Darin, watching him grow. He was the closest thing to a son he'd ever have, so knowing he was in peril now gutted him.

Pounding a bag until he was bloody was a good way to recenter. Jamaal's crew—his adopted family—needed him. He couldn't run from the problems or beat them out of existence. Facing the circumstances head-on was the only viable move.

The humbling thought returned him to the reality of the moment.

Now his hands hurt. Quite badly, in fact.

As he stared down at the sprinkling of blood across the floor and running freely down his clenched fingers, all he could think about was Darin.

What happened to him over there?

Darin had looked a bit off, and he'd complained about phantom 'interference' on the comm line, but he'd though the kid was just tired from the early morning. His decline had been so sudden. Why wasn't anything unusual showing up on the scans?

An exasperated breath rushed from his lungs, and he reached out to steady the still tumbling bag with his scarlet-stained hands. He'd been over the events two dozen times and was no closer to understanding what had gone wrong.

While Jamaal walked toward the hydrosonic shower room, he stripped off the tattered remnants of protective tape and dropped them in one of the disposal bins. Not for the first time, he made a mental note to improve his taping protocol. At least his medical nanites would heal the surface abrasions in short order.

The vanity room, which served as a bit of a foyer for the communal shower, was dimly lit. Though not overly large, it offered sufficient facilities to allow for several crew members at a time to practice their hygiene routines.

He grimaced at his reflection in the mirror, speckled with his own blood and with dark circles under his eyes. *Shite, you're better than this.*

Jamaal had been a soldier of some renown within the Tararian Guard. Nothing too overwhelmingly noteworthy, but his boxing skills had been peerless. Now, in his mid-forties, he found himself getting winded more easily. The soreness between visits to the gym often made him long to stay in bed. The body that reflected back to him in the mirror was still cut from a warrior's cloth, though a little less lean than he had once been, still strong and sturdy. He was letting himself get wrapped up in emotion, and that wasn't the way to accomplish the mission.

Yet, seeing Darin stretched out on the doctor's table was a living nightmare. Never had his heart raced faster than it had on that short trip back with the boy's limp body in his arms.

And it was all his fault.

Jamaal had lectured Hailey about Darin pulling his weight on the ship. He had all but forced her to let him take Darin on the EVA salvage runs. That had never been the deal, nor had it ever been the plan. The only son of his best friend had been intended to take over as captain of the *Andvari* when she retired—which would be sometime soon, he imagined, based on Hailey's disposition of late.

Even before, Jamaal had had no idea where Hailey's retirement would leave him. Now, if anything happened to Darin...

No, he'll be okay. Stop dwelling on the worst case scenario.

With just a few practiced motions, Jamaal stripped his pants down to the floor and stepped out of them. He made a quick gesture to the hydrosonic control, and a scalding hot mist flooded the cylindrical chamber. The fine particles gathered on his body and streamed down into the bowels of the ship where it would be filtered and reused.

As the heat eased his fatigued muscles, he leaned his head against the ceramic wall, eyes closed. It felt good but did little to calm his frantic thoughts.

Aside from Darin, everything about the excursion had

been routine. He couldn't help wonder if there was any underlying medical condition that could have triggered Darin's coma.

Don't try to rationalize it. It was my fault, nothing else!

Jamaal didn't flinch when the door to the shower chamber opened. He cracked open one eye and peered through the illuminated fog. A shadowy figure strode through the open door, then it vanished as the door shut.

"I'll be done in a minute," Jamaal growled into the dark mist-filled room. "Oh, and I'll clean up the mess outside, too, so don't bother giving me any shite over it." *I'm not in the mood.*

There was no immediate reply. Through process of elimination, he determined it to likely be Dr. Hurn. She was an enigma. Never before had Jamaal encountered a bashful doctor, yet he couldn't walk shirtless down the corridor without Mina blushing furiously. It was quite fetching really; he liked a little color in those sable cheeks.

A smile tickled at the corners of his lips. If she smiled at him shirtless, she must be near to blabbering with him in the shower.

Jamaal shut off the shower and used his hands to scrub the moisture out of his hair, down his face, and across his chest. He stepped from the shower chamber back into the vanity room.

"All yours, Doc…"

He stood alone in the room.

"Huh," he chuckled softly. "Wishful thinking, maybe?"

Shaking his head, he wrapped a towel around himself and gathered up his sweat-sodden clothes.

"Jamaal…"

He spun around, and the clothes and his towel dropped to the deck with the sudden movement.

Still, the room was empty.

That voice had sounded like... Darin.

"Darin?" The confusion in his voice was entangled with a burgeoning sense of hope aching in his chest.

There was no response.

The door opened behind him, and the room burst with light, forcing him to shield his eyes as he spun around.

"Why are you standing in the middle of the room naked?" Alton strode past him, a sonic toothbrush sticking haphazardly out of his crooked mouth.

Feeling even more confused, Jamaal regained his meager composure, and subsequently his coverings, from the floor. That was definitely not the voice he had heard previously. Maybe he had worked out harder than he had thought.

Or maybe it was radiation.

Well, that was a sobering thought. It would take significant exposure to outpace the constant healing of his medical nanites.

"Alton, you didn't come in previously, did you?"

The older man's bushy eyebrows drew together as he replied around the stem of the device buzzing in his mouth, "Can't say I did."

Dr. Hurn suddenly came back to mind, only following a much different train of thought. Thinking now that he might have been exposed to whatever had affected Darin simultaneously made Jamal feel better and just a touch scared. Nobody wanted to go into a coma, especially not a control-freak ex-soldier who organized his sock drawer based on length of service, color, and comfort.

Alton gargled and spat water out into the sink, with his beard catching what dribbled out. "You look sick, Jamaal. You all right?"

As the other man gently patted his face and beard dry with a hand towel, Jamaal just stood there, his anxiety spiking.

"Jamaal?" Alton asked softly.

"What?" he coughed out. "Yeah, yeah I'm fine. Just worked the bag a bit too rough, I guess. Tired. Stressed about... you know."

Alton nodded and thumped him on the shoulder as he walked by. "He'll be fine. Doc has it under control."

The door opened and then closed silently behind him.

Jamaal's soldier conditioning forced him to take a walk around the small chamber. Empty again.

Once he was assured he was alone, he strode up to the sink to finish his routine. There was something sinister in his expression that made him feel queasy. The short hairs on his neck stood up. Every instinct told him something was wrong.

Anxiety was raising his blood pressure; his neck was stiff and cold. With shaking hands, he splashed cool water on his face several times as he leaned over the wash basin. With several deep breaths, he regained some of his composure. He reached for a nearby towel and pressed it over his face. Eyes closed, he breathed in the gentle, clean smell of the linen.

The anxious moment passed in the shrouded darkness of the towel.

With a sigh, he lowered the cloth. He was wadding it up to toss down the laundry chute when movement in the mirror caught his eye.

Darin stood behind him, blood pouring from his eyes and mouth, reaching out toward him with trembling hands.

With a surprised shout Jamaal spun. "Darin!"

The room behind him was empty.

Jamaal turned to examine the mirror's reflection, but it too only showed an empty room beside his own bewildered expression.

No, it wasn't confusion. It was outright terror that his reflection revealed.

As quickly as he was able, Jamaal gathered his belongings and fled the room.

He stumbled out into the main corridor that connected the various parts of the ship. The walls rocked back and forth, and his vision was going double. A dull headache pounded in his temples, and his jaw felt ice cold. He walked hastily down the corridor as if drunk, a familiar feeling devoid of all the fun that usually accompanied it.

As he rounded a corner, he half fell, half barreled into a surprised Dr. Hurn.

"Doc," he said weakly, his own heart slamming in his ears like too-quick thunderclaps.

"Jamaal, are you…?"

The cold floor met his face in a silver blur. Flickering blue-white lights danced across his vision. There was a vague thought about how he'd feel *that* in the morning.

The edges of his vision darkened, closing in toward the center.

Jamaal tried to talk, but the words just spilled out as inaudible groans mumbled wetly into the cold floor.

Then, all went black.

CHAPTER 8

"WALK ME THROUGH it again." Hailey was still sitting on the chair in Jamaal's cabin with her eyes fixed on her sleeping friend's body sprawled across his bed. Mina stood to her side, glancing between the two. She wasn't sure Hailey had blinked since entering the room.

Mina couldn't blame Hailey for being overwhelmed. Within twenty-five hours, two of her crew members had been incapacitated—one her son—while their final resources and options dwindled. Talk about a rough turn of events.

Getting the heavily muscled soldier here all by herself had been a feat of strength and determination for Mina. Jamaal outweighed her by, what, *double*? The fact that she had managed to stop his face-first swan dive into the floor of the corridor had impressed her. Dragging him all the way to his quarters should be catalogued right alongside the great mythic feats of lore.

"I came around the corner," Mina answered the captain, trying desperately to keep the annoyance out of her tone and only half succeeding. "Then he says, 'Doc' and started to drop headfirst at my feet." She shrugged. That was it.

"Okay, then you carried him here?" Hailey sounded skeptical.

"Well, no. I had to drag him." Hopefully that information stayed between the girls. Regrettably, it was not a short distance, and she was almost positive he'd have abrasions in unfortunate places.

The captain arched a delicate eyebrow. "And how'd he get undressed and in bed?"

A flush crept up Mina's cheeks at the memory. It wasn't that she was a prude, and she had been to medical school. In fact, she'd consider herself rather *healthy* regarding her sexual appetites. The simple reality of the situation had demanded she do a preliminary diagnosis on Jamaal, and that had required checking for injuries. The way he had collapsed could have been anything from cardiac arrest, food or alcohol poisoning, radiation exposure, or infection. Any number of things! Never in a million years would she admit to admiring, however briefly, the chiseled perfection of the career soldier's body. Nope. Wouldn't happen.

No need to talk about how I had to wrestle him up there, either. Thank you very much!

"Please, Captain," her thoughts had turned the slight flush into a raging inferno, and her pulse was pounding in her neck, "I'm a medical professional, and my attempts to triage and stabilize Mr. Hyko were necessary."

"Well, that's too bad," Jamaal mumbled and he let out a faint groan from the bed.

Hailey chuckled. That ribald camaraderie soldiers shared could be so annoying at times.

Mina did her best to just smile through it. Instead of scolding him, she simply asked, "How are you feeling, Mr. Hyko?"

He cracked open an eye and peered at her. "Back to using 'mister', are we? Here I thought this was going somewhere."

She sighed. "All right, I think we're out of the woods with this one. I'll leave you two alone so he can debrief you on the situation."

As she stood to leave, quick as a lightning strike, his hand reached out to grasp her by the forearm. It hurt slightly, and she glared at him, ready to voice her disapproval. His gaze halted her tirade. The single most sincere look of gratitude she had ever received was etched into the unused portions of his face; it looked uncomfortable for him.

"Seriously, Doctor Hurn," his voice was soft—gentle, even. "Thank you."

There was nothing to do but stand there, stupidly, and bob her head.

Before she knew what she was doing, the door was open and Mina was out in the corridor, breathing heavily. There was really no reason for her to be so discomfited by him. If anything, the two of them had been overly professional to date. Certainly, a bit of flirting here and there, but no more than she could be accused of with Darin, and she was twice the boy's age! But unlike the captain's son, there was no compelling hands-off policy when it came to Jamaal. A person could only spend so much time in close quarters on a ship before—

Nope, don't start down that path.

That did it. There was nothing for her to do except to get out of the bomaxed area as quickly as her feet would allow.

Frankly, Mina's cabin just wasn't far enough away from the quarters of her *patient*—she needed to remember that distinction—so she decided she should go check on her other charge in the infirmary.

She sighed. All this nonsense was for the young and

foolhardy. Jamaal and she were grownups and should act like it. *No more silliness allowed*, she decided solemnly.

The corridors of the *Andvari* created a giant closed circuit around the craft, with each section designated by a junction of another, smaller connected track. It made it wonderful for jogging but disastrous when trying to flee a particular site in any kind of expedient manner. This was especially true when one was on the complete opposite side of the ship from the intended destination.

The walk to the infirmary was long enough that when the doors opened, she felt much clearer minded. Familiar smells of ozone and disinfectant made her nose itch slightly. Were she ever asked to declare a place where she felt most comfortable, she'd say the infirmary or medical ward of whatever ship or building she was in. More than half of her life had been spent tending to the sick and infirm in the sterile environments, so it's where she felt the greatest sense of familiarity and authority.

One important thing about infirmaries was the abundance of tasks required for proper upkeep. It was a never-ending list, which made it a perfect place to distract oneself from certain infuriating notions.

Mina busied herself at one of the cabinets, using her handheld to begin her reorganization of various medications after the disastrous mess she made for herself upon Darin's unexpected situation. Now more than ever, it was worth being ready for anything.

She couldn't help her mind wandering to thoughts of her other patient while she worked. Mina suspected that Jamaal may have gone off on a bender, drowning his overwhelming guilt over the incident with Darin. Mina knew that sometimes things happened, and she certainly didn't doubt the man's devotion to his young friend. Holding the grumpy soldier accountable for something as yet unexplained made no sense. If only he would allow himself to accept that.

A sudden wave of dread washed over her. It was almost a palpable thing, like a dark cloud passing over the sun. A chill ran down her spine, and goosebumps rippled up her legs.

Behind her, the monitors tracking Darin's vitals began to chime, and various alarms sounded. The autodoc immediately sprang into action, administering life-saving intravenous drugs.

Mina took a steadying breath and walked purposefully over to the table, reading the incoming data on the overhead tablet. Her knowledge and surgical talents were her strengths, not bedside manner. Had she been more adept at the latter, she may have still been serving in the Terminus Grace Hospital, where she'd been one of the primary residents for a number of years after medical school.

The tablet was piecing together a narrative of a cardiac event. Not an ideal situation.

But the question was, *why*?

As far as comas went, Darin had been stable up until that moment. There was absolutely no reason she could think of that would cause this kind of spontaneous heart failure. Again, things happened. In her line of work, not usually good things, much to her consternation.

With the kind of efficiency that only artificial intelligence could produce, the autodoc stabilized the young man and averted further catastrophe. Now, she had to get to the bottom of the burning question: what was causing all of this?

A sound, like small bells tinkling in a breeze, echoed behind her. Mina started to turn.

Without warning the medication vials she had previously been inventorying exploded like shrapnel from a fragmentation grenade. A million searing spots of pain erupted across that side of her face and body.

On pure reflex alone she doubled over, shielding her face, and fell to the floor in a heap.

A shriek like some dying animal reverberated shrilly through the small room. It wasn't until Mina drew a shuddering breath that she realized the scream had come from her.

She lay in the fetal position on the deck for some time, scared even to open her eyes more than a crack. With a whimper, she finally allowed herself to look around at the mess.

Most of the glass polymer materials in the room—vials, testing equipment, and screens—had been reduced to little more than a fine powder of razor-sharp splinters. The engineered material was all but indestructible under most circumstances, designed specifically to withstand everything from rough handling to high temperatures. A spontaneous explosion was inexplicable.

Mina slowly pushed herself up. Small droplets of her blood fell into splattering puddles amid the glittering debris. Liquid from the smashed vials and containers leaked out of the cupboard.

"What did this?"

Darin had no answers to her question, not that she expected him to respond.

It looked as if the young man had fortunately dodged most of the carnage; between Mina's own body and the bulk of the autodoc, he had been reasonably protected from the blast. At least luck had been on her side there. All Mina needed was a nicked artery or embedded glass shards to deal with, on top of whatever else was going on with him.

Standing, she surveyed the destruction. At least half of the glass objects in the room were now in ruins. Otherwise, the walls were intact, and there was no obvious gas leak or compromised structural integrity.

As if coming out of a daze, she walked over to the doorway and reluctantly flipped the master alarm, which immediately doused the room in a slowly pulsating amber light and sounded a ship-wide alert.

Mina felt bad doing so—Hailey would immediately think something was happening to her son—but it was the responsible thing to do. The ship could be damaged in a way that endangered everyone.

Blood ran down her forehead into her eye, which burned terribly. It was also beginning to dapple the floor at her feet, enough that it spurred her to begin addressing some of the larger lacerations.

After rummaging through the shattered contents of a cupboard, she managed to find a laser cauterizer. She set about tending to her wounds.

While she was sealing one of the larger cuts across the length of her forearm, the door opened, and the entire crew complement rushed in carrying various emergency supplies. Toolboxes, mobile welders, and laser cutters, even a pressure suit in the hands of a *still* half-naked Jamaal.

Hailey was pale with worry, but her gaze was filled with focused determination. Mina had to marvel at the woman's composure. Had the roles been reversed, she'd likely had been a gurgling puddle of tears and despair.

"Darin is fine," Mina opened her hand in a calming gesture, "but..."

The thought trailed off as the crew skidded, some slipping on the glass fragments, to a stunned stop.

Alton, being the engineer, immediately assessed the supporting structures of the room, peering in corners and seams. "Any signs of decompression?"

Mina shook her head. Not that she knew, precisely, what to look for.

With bushy brows furrowed until they almost touched above his nose, Alton grunted and then rested his toolkit on a countertop. Obviously, he was about to dig into the problem, so Mina set that aside for the moment.

"Hailey, Darin suffered a cardiac event of unspecified origin." There was her lack of bedside manner again. She quickly added, "He's stable now, but it's worrisome that it's inexplicable. It happened just before, well, *this*. I have no idea what happened, things just started exploding."

Hailey stood stoically, processing all the data.

Jamaal was looking at Mina wide-eyed. "Do you need help, Doc?" He indicated the crimson streaks down her arm.

"Yes, Mr. Hyko," she said smoothly, if just a touch on the cold side, "I'd appreciate some help with my primary hand." Usually, she'd let the autodoc address her wounds; it did amazing suture work. However, it was currently busy monitoring Darin. Hopefully, hand-wrapping would be enough to sufficiently close the cuts so her medical nanites could take over and heal her injuries without leaving a scar.

Jamaal got straight to work. Mina approved of his steady hands, and as she watched him work, she realized he likely had done quite a lot of these on the battlefield. The quick, efficient, and precise movements spoke of a muscle memory that would impress any of her distinguished mentors.

When not watching the procedure, she observed Hailey as subtly as she could manage in the small space. The creases on the other woman's brow were deepening by the moment. Mina could read her thoughts like a book, the conversation playing out in her mind. Her worries were valid, but the argument operated from a place of emotion, not logic. Ultimately flawed, the idea of turning around and limping to a station brought with it much more inherent risk than proceeding as they had planned.

"No," Mina told her firmly when their eyes met. The fact remained that going deeper into the nebula would actually get them back to populated space *faster*, assuming they could locate a replacement PEM.

"I didn't say anything." Indignation added a little bite to the words.

"You were just about to proclaim we should turn around and head to the nearest medical facility." Mina stopped to take a breath as the heat from the laser burned just a little deeper than it should have.

Hailey inhaled and opened her mouth to speak, but Mina held up a hand.

"We can't. The ship is too damaged. Turning around now would put us weeks away from the nearest hospital now that we're restricted to sub-light. I've looked." That was mostly true, Mina had done a cursory search of nearby medical facilities that were adequately equipped to handle their needs. While there were others that were closer, they wouldn't offer anything beyond their capabilities on the *Andvari*. "If we reach the backwater and can find what we need to make the repairs, we'll cut the travel to a quarter of the time," she reminded Hailey.

With a scowl that would have sent a Guard cadet scampering off into the dark corner of a barracks, Hailey glanced at the members of her crew. Alton exhaled through his unruly beard and nodded reluctantly. Jamaal wouldn't meet her gaze, instead leaning forward to tend more fervently to

Mina's lacerations.

Mina waited patiently. Hailey was intelligent. She'd come around to this once she assessed the situation with a leader's eyes instead of a mother's.

"Alton, I want a prioritized list—with backups and piecemeal options—for every hunk of scrap we need to find to get us back home. I am not talking about flagship parts here; whatever gets the job done the quickest. You hear me?"

"Yes, Captain." Alton continued his structural assessment of the room.

Hailey paused only the barest of moments. "And I want to know exactly what the fok happened here. Within the hour."

The last bit made Alton glance up, but Hailey had already spun and was leaving, her back straight as a board and all rugged military discipline.

After a few half-heard grumbles about how *unappreciated* he was, Alton followed after the captain. Mina once again thought, as she often had since joining the crew, that it must be quite hard to have been a soldier and to then find oneself in the civilian world, confined by legal and resource limitations.

"There we go, Doc." Jamaal sighed, standing. "Not my best work, but it's been a rough day." He started to smiled, but it twisted into a pained wince from the bruising that was just beginning to appear on his face after his recent encounter with the deck.

She tilted her head with sympathy. "I'd offer you some sedatives to help you sleep, but I've suddenly found myself without my stockpile."

Getting the infirmary back in order was going to be a nightmare. The room was thick with an orchestra of offensive odors mingled into one pungent calamity of burnt metal, bleach, and cloves. A headache threatened to manifest behind

Mina's eyes from the irritation it was causing her sinuses.

Being the observant warrior that he was, Jamaal recognized her discomfort. "Do you need some help cleaning this mess up?"

Mina smiled as warmly as she could through the hundreds of tiny cuts decorating the left side of her body. "No, please, go rest. As you said, it's been a rough day."

With a reluctant glance at Darin and the destroyed room, Jamaal nodded and turned to go.

When he reached the door, Mina suddenly said, "Let me know if you need anything."

After a brief moment of silence, he turned with a small smile, "You too."

As the door closed behind him, Mina realized for the first time since she was a child, she was scared to be alone in a room. It was something that most people grew out of, and she was no exception. When she had been a youth she had been absolutely terrified of bathrooms. Something about them made her feel vulnerable, and even as a kid she had hated that feeling. However, as she grew older, the fear was rapidly replaced with the peace that solitude would bring—especially once she had moved away to medical school and lived in a dorm.

Standing here now, though, with Darin unconscious and the supplies in shambles, the room felt hostile. Like an enemy that had struck the first surprise blow and was readying itself for the next onslaught.

She left the door open, not wanting to be sealed inside alone, and got to work cleaning up. It was difficult, tedious work sorting out the broken materials from the salvageable, but Mina needed to get the infirmary back in order. It was the once area where she felt like she had any control left in her life.

The sound of soft footfalls called her attention to the

corridor. She looked up to see Jamaal return and lean casually against the open frame.

"I do need something." There was a nonchalance in his voice that was uncharacteristic of the seasoned soldier.

"I'm afraid I haven't located my sedatives yet." She surveyed the remaining mess in the room.

"Not meds." He moved closer to her, deliberate and intent.

Mina felt the heat of him as he approached, his attention fixated on her. He reached out and stroked her cheekbone above one of the minor lacerations her medical nanites had already started to close.

"You should be in bed," she said softly.

"I'd like you there with me."

She couldn't help letting out a little laugh. "Seriously?" She waved her hand. "Look at this place! Look at us. We're—"

Jamaal tenderly caught her hand in his. "I need to escape for a while. I think you do, too."

He was right about that. Everything had gone so terribly wrong *so fast* that the distraction was an intoxicating proposition. It wasn't like she hadn't thought about it before...

Mina glanced to her side, all too aware of Darin's unconscious form barely more than an arm's reach away.

"Are you sure about this?" she asked Jamaal, gazing into his eyes to look for any signs of uncertainty.

In response, he slid his hand behind her neck and pulled her gently toward him. As her lips found his, she forgot where they were for a moment.

She pulled back. "Not here." Taking his hand, she led him toward her cabin. Cleaning up the rest of the infirmary could wait.

CHAPTER 9

THE ALARM CHIMED again.

For the sixth time, the system reboot had failed. Hailey was about to rip her hair out.

A loud *clang* from underneath the control board preceded a pained grunt from Alton. He was laying on his back, with just shins and feet stuck out from the bottom access panel to the labyrinth of circuitry and crystal control matrices found below.

The access hatch was small, and Alton was not. It made it somewhat awkward for Hailey to stick her face down somewhere south of his crotch to peer through the small opening into the ship's innards. Unfortunately, it was the only way they could communicate at present.

"Failed," she reported.

An absolute litany of curses and banging followed, and Hailey had to suppress laughter. Alton was slow and steady, not one for bursts of excitement or fits of frustration. Situations like this where he lost his calm disposition were somewhat rare and always ended up being entertaining. If only their current situation wasn't so dire.

As quickly as the smile had stolen its way across her face,

it was replaced with a razor-sharp scowl. It seemed as though everything was going to shite.

With grunts, groans, and kicking legs, Alton scraped himself out from under the control station. "...And complete waste of fokin' space!"

The first part of the sentence was lost to her, but she felt similarly. By all measure, this ship was still brand new. It should still have that *newness* that was so thrilling after a purchase. There should be no scenario where they were having to limp across the bomaxed sector of space. Not to mention, in the span of two days, her son had inexplicably fallen into a coma, thousands of credits' worth of medical supplies had spontaneously exploded, and a large portion of the data on her ship had been lost in a bizarre system failure.

"It's the strangest thing I've ever seen, Captain," Alton scrubbed a hand through his coarse hair. "The best way I can describe it is we were subjected to a deep system scan that corrupted files as it went. Some kind of *aggressive* scan."

Hailey sighed. *Why does it always have to be bad news?* Just once she'd like to be surprised with a good report. Was that too much to ask?

"Will it stop us from getting to the salvage grounds in the nebula?" At this point, she wasn't even concerned with keeping the contract, saving her ship, nor her legacy. *Just fix the ship and race to a hospital.*

Ever since they had docked with the *Heron*, things had been going wrong. They had been exposed to something, and now there was a looming sense of dread that had settled on her shoulders. The clock was ticking. She didn't want to find out what happened when it ran out.

"I see nothing that should prevent us from reaching the target area," Alton replied slowly, thinking out loud. "As near as I can tell, this invasive scan happened after we had already locked in our course. So long as we don't divert, we should arrive as scheduled. It has, however, completely wiped out our travel logs."

"So, all the data we've collected on the various salvage targets is gone?"

Alton just nodded slightly in response.

Months of data collection. Vanished. For an inexplicable reason.

The process of tracking down wreckage was not something to leave to pure luck. Sure, opportunistic encounters were a part of it, but space was *quite large*. By using data collected from conflict-loss reports, tracking down known wreckage, and obtaining the direction, velocity and distance travelled, they were able to narrow down data related to still-missing vessels.

That's where Dr. Hurn had become invaluable. By applying the right science, and a bit of ingenuity, she had been able to reliably identify several wreckage sites that were still reported as lost. Unfortunately for them, for one reason or another those targets had already been picked clean and their discovery undocumented. Hailey made a point of dutifully reporting every salvage mission, to save other crews the trouble they currently found themselves in.

Losing all that data they had collected was a major blow to their continued operations.

"All the more reason we need a major windfall. Mina's gotta be right about this one." Hailey sure wished she sounded more confident than she felt.

"It's the best shot we've got," he grunted back sourly.

Suddenly, the room filled with the sounds of alarms. The screens began flashing, and systems launched and failed in rapid succession.

The sounds were so chaotic and loud that both Hailey and Alton had to cover their ears.

"What's happening?" Hailey's shout was lost in the cacophony.

Unable to hear her, Alton just shook his head, his eyes pinched together from the pain.

As quickly as it had begun, the sounds suddenly ceased.

The ensuing silence was dizzying.

They stood there, looking back and forth from each other to the ship's controls. Both of them were breathing heavily.

After a minute, Alton finally broke the silence, "Hailey, I think we need to get off this ship. Sooner rather than later."

"Find out what that was, Alton," Hailey commanded. "Right now."

Alton sat down in the pilot's chair and started several diagnostic tests. He had yet to offer any explanation about what had happened in the infirmary, and Hailey held little hope that this analysis would be any more conclusive.

Off to the side, she braced against an overhead control panel to steady herself. Too much was going wrong too quickly. This didn't seem coincidental to her. It felt malicious. Intentional—like an attack. She was all too familiar with that feeling.

Hailey hated surprises, especially the kind where she was being sneaked up on. *What the fok is happening to my ship?*

"It was another deep system scan, more aggressive than before." Alton was more comfortable with a torque wrench in hand or waist-deep in cables, but he was no slouch when it came to the more sensitive ship systems.

"What did they scan?" she asked.

He was already navigating through the log files to find the

access entries. The better question, she realized a moment later, was *who*?

When he triggered the search, information began scrolling on the screen.

Almost in unison, the two gasped audibly as the list ran, and ran, and ran more.

"Alton," Hailey whispered, "tell me what I'm looking at here?"

Slack-jawed, he watched the screen, the reflection of the seemingly infinite list dancing in his wide eyes. His mouth worked but no sounds came out. When no answer was forthcoming, she turned her attention back to the scrolling data.

It suddenly felt very cramped in the compartment and on this ship. Hailey turned on her heel and palmed the door open, leaving Alton staring at the screen.

With no intended destination, she started down the port side of the vessel. This was the operational side; consisting of access to the cargo holds, engineering, the mess, and vital systems access. On a whim, she strode directly to the galley. Eating something would take her mind momentarily off what was happening.

Everything was falling apart. It was too much. *Why has everything gone wrong so suddenly? What could cause…?*

The thought trailed off.

All the trouble started after they interfaced with the *Heron* wreckage. She needed to find out more about that ship.

As she went about the mundane task of preparing a small bit of flavorless mush that subsisted them during lean financial times, she let her analytical mind run free. They had docked with the *Heron*, and everything had been fine until Jamaal had left Darin alone to check the cargo doors for entry points. She had listened in as the check had happened; first one side, and then the incident happened before he could get to the second set of cargo doors. Between those two locations, something had attacked her son.

Now it was attacking them.

Which meant that whatever it had been on the *Heron* was almost certainly now aboard their ship.

The bowl of mush slipped through her fingers and fell to the floor.

Hailey raced toward the flight deck.

When the door snapped open, she was just about to doll out orders, but she instead skidded to a stop.

Alton lay crumpled on his side in an earth-tone heap on the floor. A bulbous bruise had already formed on the crown of his head with rivulets of blackened garnet streaking his silvery hair.

For the briefest of moments, Hailey couldn't move. Even if she had spontaneously combusted, she would have been locked to the spot. So long as she didn't check his pulse, he couldn't be dead.

Every soldier instinct in her screamed to intervene, to administer first aid as rapidly as possible. And yet, it was if her heart had stopped—perhaps even time itself.

Focus. Her mind cleared. She had a mission to fulfill.

Hailey became a flurry of action, practically leaping upon the older man in her haste to loosen the clothing around his throat and check for signs of life. She found a strong pulse thumping rhythmically on his neck.

"Alton," she said softly and stern, like that of a mother rousing a child from an overlong nap. When no reply was forthcoming, she repeated the call with a bit more volume, and a gentle shake of his raised shoulder.

Thankfully, her efforts were rewarded with a grunt and muted groan.

Moments passed, until finally an eyelid fluttered open.

"Hailey…"

"Shhh," she soothed. "Lay still. You've had quite the afternoon. I'll fetch the Doc."

The pupils on Alton's eyes were dilating in pulses, and from the way he looked at her slightly cross-eyed, his vision was potentially doubled. She had often gotten that look before from Alton, were she being honest, though not from being struck by anything but rather as a result of his lust for spirits.

Another groan, this one a bit more forceful, and he closed his eyes and raised a hand to his wounded dome. When his fingers came back sticky with blood, he winced and rested his head back down on the cool floor.

"I won't move a muscle, Cap," he muttered.

Hailey ran, hardly waiting for doors to open.

Someone, *something*, was on her ship.

And her people were under attack.

— — —

Jamaal glanced at the door to Mina's cabin for possibly the hundredth time since he'd arrived. Sweat stung his eyes, and he panted as he flopped onto his side in Mina's bed.

She slipped out from the bed next to him and stood gracefully, flipping the bedsheet casually aside. Sweat made her dark skin glisten like dewdrops in the first amber beams of the morning sun. Something about the abrupt departure from the bed and, well, the lack of cuddling afterward their little encounter, told Jamaal she was upset about something.

The real issue was, so was *he*! Not that he could share it

with her. There wasn't a woman he had met that would want to talk about his unrequited love, just after a stress-induced quickie. Bringing it up was a bad idea. Probably the worst. He definitely shouldn't do it.

Resisting the urge to try to explain or excuse his constant glancing at the door, he reached out and grasped Mina's hand.

She glanced over her shoulder at him, eyes sparkling dangerously.

There was something else there. Hurt? Confusion? It shot a pang of regret through his chest like an unexpected knife wound.

"We should get cleaned up," she mumbled, turning back toward her small closet.

There'd been plenty of flirting between them over the past year, but this was the first time they'd acted on those feelings. It had been intense, and not in the way he'd been expecting—less about making a connection and more about a desperate attempt to escape.

Jamaal was fuzzy about what any of it meant. Sure, it was a fun release, but hook-ups at ports—albeit most of them disappointments—were certainly a lot less complicated. What were the expectations now that they'd finally crossed the line they'd been dancing around?

While the stoic captain had little need of intimacy, Jamaal was a vastly different animal. There were needs that were not being met, and while he was rather proud of the effort he poured into subduing those passions, desire inevitably won the war. Every time.

Jamaal had come to care about Mina. Maybe he wasn't *in love* with her the way he was with Hailey; there was too much history between them. That did not mean what he had with Mina was *less*, or not *worth it*, though. Right?

"Not just yet," he said softly. When she didn't immediately turn back, he tugged gently on her hand. "Let's not rush back to reality quite yet. Okay?"

An uncomfortable silence stretched on, but finally she relented and flopped back into the small bed. Mina was petite enough that the small bedframe barely protested when she moved around on it.

She didn't turn to face him. Instead she nestled her back into his chest and curled her legs up in front of herself. He wrapped her up and pulled her close. Her skin was wet and colder than his, and she smelled of warm honey and dried flowers.

"What is this?" Mina asked abruptly.

Ah, fok!

When he hesitated a moment too long, she spun to face him, ripping the bedsheets in a tight grip to her chest.

"Does it need to be defined to be nice?" Hoping to deploy a little charisma to disarm her, he smiled and waggled his eyebrows at her.

She wasn't having it.

"Yes," she said in a dangerously low tone, "it absolutely does."

Well, here we go.

The worry for Jamaal was two-fold. First, and foremost, if he pissed her off enough, would she immediately run to Hailey and confront her about what they had been doing, just as a spiteful way to hurt him for whatever perceived slight she had suffered? He thought it unlikely, but it wouldn't be the first time that a woman had surprised him.

Second, and by a longshot he was ashamed to admit, he actually had developed feelings for the woman. Despite his intentions to keep this encounter purely a convenient physical release, there was no denying this was more than one of his port hookups. They'd resisted for a long time. All the anticipation gave meaning to this consummation, regardless of the other factors.

In many ways, it would have been easier if they'd given in when they'd first acknowledged there was interest there. Jamaal had chanced upon her in the shower room and been instantly attracted to her. Being a life-long military man, he had seen his share of coworkers in the shower, including Hailey. Mina was different. Where Hailey and most career military women were all sharp angles, with lithe bodies built for strength and dexterity, Mina was all enticing curves and sumptuous grace. There was a *warmth* and *welcome* insinuated by her glowing body.

Nothing had come of that encounter, and obviously Jamaal had played it as cool as he could.

But he couldn't help but notice she had lingered overly long, allowing him to strip and enter the shower. Being on a small ship meant knowing everyone's routines; it was just part of being a tight crew. So, as she lingered on her hair for the entire duration of his shower and cast furtive glances at his reflection in the mirror, he knew the appreciation was mutual.

That had happened on a few more occasions, until, well... here they were.

A sigh of irritation snapped him out of his thoughts as Mina made to stand up again.

"Sorry! I was just thinking about how we," he stumbled a bit, looking for the right words, "you know, how this all got started.'

Words! Bomaxed words were his worst enemy. *Just give me a rifle and let me shoot something!*

She raised an eyebrow at him, everything in her body

language practically screaming 'plan on answering my question?'

Unfortunately, Jamaal was an honest man. Well, mostly honest.

Heaving a deep sigh of his own, he decided to just shoot straight. "I'm not going to lie and say I don't have feelings for Hailey. We have a history. A long, *long*, history. We have seen and done things together that nobody else could ever understand."

Both of Mina's eyebrows shot up her forehead.

"Not like that." Jamaal coughed, his throat suddenly tightening uncomfortably. "Hailey and I have never... I am not sure we *would* ever. Anyway, never mind about that."

Mina physically tensed every time he said the captain's name; he could feel her muscles twitch.

"It's just that," he fumbled again, not knowing how to say what he felt. Stars, he didn't even really know *what* he felt! "Look, I like you. I like *this.*" He gestured to the space between them.

She watched his gesture, which just so happened to point directly at her breasts. Her eyes widened a bit accusatorily.

"Not that," he said quickly.

"Excuse me?"

"What?" What was she upset by *now*?

"Are you saying you don't like my tits?" She pushed away from him, staring him full in the face.

"No!" he blurted out, and her reaction spurred him to continue, quickly, and quite apologetically. "I mean yes! I... You have amazing tits! I love them! The no was that I wasn't saying that."

This was going terribly.

Could their ship just be attacked by pirates or something

else equally critical, so that he could be saved from further foot-shoving-in-mouth?

"I don't make commitments, okay? That's not who I am. But I will say that I enjoy your company."

She relaxed somewhat, so he continued.

"And I certainly enjoy your body."

Finally, the tension left her and she giggled. The sound made his skin tingle slightly.

"In that, the feeling is very mutual." The words were a seductive purr. She leaned in and nipped at his lips.

He pulled back, the serious look on his face never leaving. "I mean it, Mina. I do like you."

She studied him for a moment. "I hear a 'but' coming."

Why am I such an asshole? The thought made him grind his teeth in frustration. "I am not sure I can ever let it be more than it is now."

There. He had said it. Now, she could throw her fit and toss him out. He'd miss the opportunity for a convenient hookup while out in the void, obviously. But he certainly wouldn't miss the sneaking around and guilt that would accompany it.

Mina regarded him, expressionless, for quite a long moment.

"Well," the words were quiet, subdued, "I'm okay with that. So long as you're honest with me. And who knows what the future holds?"

That... went better than expected.

She hopped up, taking the bedsheet with her. The cold air hit his wet, now totally bare body, like a slap. After inspecting him top-to-bottom-and-back, she said, "Besides, I'm just in this for the sex."

Then, she swayed straight out of the cabin with the diaphanous, sweat-streaked sheet clinging suggestively to her.

Animalistic instinct itched at him to pursue. In fact, he almost hopped out of the bed and gave chase. However, the thought of Hailey catching them stopped that thinking dead in its tracks.

Instead, he lay there, imagining Mina washing up in the shower, and considered the mess he was in.

Will Hailey even care?

The worst part of all of this was that he honestly had no idea how she'd react. Would she be relieved to finally be rid of his undying advances? Would it hurt her to lose him? Why wasn't he good enough for her? He had poured his entire life into her and Darin. Stars, the kid felt like *his* son!

Dark thoughts swirled in his mind, until he heard voices outside. Two women talking in hushed tones just outside the door.

Shite! Jamaal judged the time, trying to determine if Hailey had encountered Mina on her way back from the shower or way there. It had to be the way back by now... not while her hair was mussed and her cheeks were still flushed. He found himself looking around for somewhere to hide if Hailey suddenly barged in demanding an explanation.

Jamaal held his breath, straining to hear what was being said.

"Attacked? Alton?!" Mina exclaimed.

Jamaal snapped to attention. *Another attack?*

"He seems okay," Hailey said. "He's still on the flight deck."

"I'll have a look at him."

The two women rushed off. His protective instincts told Jamaal to go investigate the potential attack, but he couldn't stomach the idea of emerging from Mina's cabin and trying to explain that to Hailey straight away.

Instead, he waited until the voices had vanished to make his hasty retreat to the showers. Cursing Mina quietly for how the little episode had ended, he pulled on his clothes and slinked into the empty corridor.

CHAPTER 10

A SOMBER MOOD hung in the galley as Mina sat with Jamaal and Hailey around the dining table for a meager meal. Metal dishes clanked together ever-so-slightly on the storage rack from the low vibration of the sub-light engines. It wasn't loud enough to bother most people, but for Mina it was one of the most annoying sounds she had ever heard.

For having just gotten laid, I shouldn't be this irritable! It was the unrelenting stress of the past week catching up with her. From the emotionally charged situations to the bizarre glass-exploding incident in the infirmary, her nerves were fraying. Even having completed her cleaning, that sanctuary would never be the same.

She'd expected her romp with Jamaal to make her feel better. However, Jamaal's detached affect now that they were in Hailey's presence underscored his admission about his feelings, and it irked Mina that he could go from passionate lover to indifferent toward her so quickly.

He sat slumped haphazardly in a chair across from Mina, picking at his gruel; the man hadn't so much as made eye contact with her since they got to the galley. Of course not.

Around Hailey, no one and nothing else mattered.

Mina tried to swallow her frustration. It wasn't like she was looking for a marriage proposal from the guy, but she didn't want to be someone's dirty little secret. They were all adults. Hailey could accept that her friends had their own needs. What was the big deal?

Adding to her deteriorating mood, the length and breadth of Mina's body had begun to itch. As time progressed and the myriad of tiny lacerations healed, she knew it would get far worse. Between that and the constant clinking of the dishes, she felt like she was about to scream. Or lose her mind. Maybe both?

Everyone now sat in silence. No one was willing to give voice to the concern, but Mina would bet her last credit that every single one of them was thinking the same thing: they had picked up an uninvited passenger during the salvage operation on the *Heron*.

That had to be who'd harmed Darin and Jamaal, and now Alton, too. Similarly, it logically tracked that this someone had somehow deployed a sonic weapon in the infirmary. The only remaining question now was *how* had this person done all this without being detected?

Captain Hailey sat with eyes downcast, jaw muscles working furiously. Occasionally, the squawk of her teeth grinding together was audible, even from several meters away.

Jamaal, meanwhile, had a somewhat haunted look to his face, no doubt still brooding about what had happened to Darin. Mina would never understand the guilt people heaped upon themselves for things that were outside of their control. Whoever, or whatever, was harming them was cunning and had the element of surprise. One couldn't plan for every eventuality. Trying to live one's life with that kind of paranoid anxiety was far from healthy.

Much like she would read a patient record sheet, the creases in Jamaal's forehead spelled out his thoughts. *He's wishing it had been him that had been injured instead of Darin.*

Noble, but ultimately stupid and selfish. They needed Jamaal's help to hunt down this hidden threat.

Not for the first time that evening, Mina felt her stomach complain, most uncomfortably, about the lack of nourishment. With supplies dwindling, and the PEM non-functional, there was scant hope of anything outside the reduced ration of protein-dense engineered slop. Mina struggled with which was worse: eating it or starving. The verdict was still out.

She finally took a spoonful of the lukewarm mush. It slid into her mouth with a subtle savory flavor that kept it just outside the realm of completely tasteless. Unfortunately, it was not a particularly pleasing sensation. Most people would call her upbringing somewhat entitled, she'd have to admit. With everything she had lost in her life, and all the requisite transformations, food remained an area where she struggled to conform. She didn't really miss the comfortable job, lavish parties, or fortune; but the lack of food variety was a difficult adjustment.

Mina jerked to attention as the door whisked open.

Alton, his head bandaged tightly, hobbled through the threshold carrying a tablet. His complexion was ashen, with dark wrinkled circles shadowing the sockets of his eyes. He gripped the side of the doorway to keep himself from falling over.

He should be in bed! Mina's patients aboard this ship were among the most obstinate she'd encountered in her career. Tell them to rest, and that was almost a guarantee they'd keep going about their duties like nothing had happened.

Hailey was first on her feet. "Alton, what are you doing up?"

Mina nodded her agreement, casting Alton her perfected glare of disapproval at his flagrant disregard of her medical advice.

The elderly engineer winced as he stumbled from the doorway, angling to take an empty seat at the table, with obviously pained intensity. "I scanned the ship…"

The words trailed off as Hailey threw her arms up in the air, an exasperated bark of laughter escaping her clenched teeth. "Because of course you did," she muttered. "Far be it to have a member of my crew actually listen to me for once when I tell them to take a break!"

Suddenly, the silence around the table grew uncomfortably awkward. Alton, despite clearly being in the wrong in Mina's opinion, glared defiantly at his captain and longtime friend. His mouth worked wordlessly.

Likely chewing on some astoundingly colorful curses. For some reason, the thought made him seem more charming than surly.

"I think you'll be glad I did," he finally grumbled out.

Hailey rolled her eyes and redirected her angry stare away from the table and the group.

"Did you find anything?" Mina couldn't help herself. Curiosity flowed through her veins.

The twist of Hailey's lips punctuated her displeasure. Yet, the captain perked up with interest when Alton grimaced and bobbed his head.

Mina watched with fascination as the old engineer got to work on the tablet, recalling scans that he had previously performed. Despite his age, he had nimble fingers and a quick mind, displaying true mastery as he compiled a multitude of scans of the ship's interior.

"These readings were taken shortly after my unfortunate

encounter." His hand subconsciously wandered toward his bandaged forehead. The scans resolved into a rainbow-hued rendering of the ship, with bright spots accounting for the various people aboard.

Mina felt her mouth turn down in a sudden frown. "Wait." She chewed her lip and edged closer to the screen. With a delicate finger she counted each of the bright points on the image; five in total. "What are we looking at here, Alton?"

"Ourselves." He let out a defeated sigh.

"That's impossible!" Hailey blurted out, irritation heating her tone. "There has to be someone else here!"

Alton nodded his bandaged head again. "I thought that, too. So, I ran it a dozen more times, in the entire EM spectrum. Captain," he breathed out heavily, "we are the only living things aboard this ship."

Mina didn't like the way he emphasized the word 'living' at all. Goosebumps suddenly sprang up her arms and down her thighs.

Jamaal inhaled sharply. "Ghosts?"

Hailey scoffed. "Of course not."

Alton merely shrugged.

Mina felt somewhat nauseated. Obviously, as a medical professional, she had no real *fear* of 'ghosts' or the afterlife. However, enough weirdness had occurred over the years to her and others that it made her at least somewhat openminded. Maybe 'ghost' was the wrong word, but there were certainly *things* beyond conventional understanding out in the darkness of space.

The entire situation would have been less disconcerting if the scan had revealed a stowaway. Physical violence she could handle, being no stranger to it. The supernatural, not so much.

Jamaal abruptly stood, knocking his chair to the deck

behind him. There was a wild look in his eyes, like that of prey smelling blood in the air.

"Easy, Sergeant." Hailey wasn't exactly soothing, but it was that gentle insistence a strong leader could utilize to great effect on their subordinates.

As she sat and watched Jamaal, Mina noticed his heart thudding hard enough to see his pulse raced up and down his jugular. Sweat had begun to bead on his forehead, glistening prismatically in the cabin light.

"What's wrong, Mr. Hyko?" she asked. The formal address seemed strange after the intimate moment they'd shared, but she felt it important to draw a clear line when it came to her medical responsibilities.

With his eyes pinched together, Jamaal scrubbed at his head with both hands. His breath came in ragged gasps between words. "When I was showering earlier, I saw…"

The words trailed off into a whisper.

"What?" Hailey asked at the same time Mina said, "Go on."

Never before had she seen Jamaal scared. To her trained eyes, he looked on the verge of a panic attack.

"I saw—" The words choked off strangely, like a tight fist had suddenly clenched around his throat.

Without warning, his eyes bulged like a spooked animal. Then, he stood and promptly fled the room without so much as a glance over his shoulder.

They all stared at the door in disbelief.

"What was that about?" Hailey asked no one in particular.

Stress was a weird beast. That was especially true when it came to soldiers suffering from any kind of post-traumatic stress. Sure, Mina couldn't be sure about Jamaal or his mental condition, but she certainly recognized an anxiety-induced panic attack when she saw one.

Hailey set her clenched fists at her sides and started to walk toward the door after Jamaal.

On a sudden instinct, Mina stepped in her way.

Cold fury thundered across Hailey's features. For the briefest moment, Mina thought that the captain was going to hit her or shove her out of the way.

"Let me talk to him," Mina requested. She did her best to sound assertive, but it came out little better than a squeak. "The injury and... well, the guilt he feels for what happened to Darin, I'm sure. It's had an ill effect on him. I can talk him down." She strategically left out the part about what else was going on between the two of them.

"Doctor, he and I carried mutilated bodies together and dropped them in holes. Women, children, pets. They all went into the same holes." The captain's voice was ice and fire. "I've talked him down more times than I can count. And he's done the same for me."

With otherworldly grace, the captain neatly sidestepped her, pivoted sharply, and was out the door in four quick strides.

Mina had barely taken a breath to utter her, albeit flimsy, rebuttal. *The dexterity of a soldier is a really unfair advantage in confrontations.*

"Well," Alton said with a husky grunt, "that could've gone better, eh?"

A half-chuckle, half-sob, bubbled out of Mina's throat. *Well, one thing at a time, I guess.*

"Alton, would you walk me through what you've done with these scans, please?" The quaver in her voice made her furious, but she pressed on regardless. "I'd like to know what exactly is happening here, and I think you're on the right track."

CHAPTER 11

AFTER TWO DECADES of friendship, Hailey was certain she knew Jamaal better than anyone else in the universe. It wasn't the first time he'd rushed out of a room on the verge of a breakdown, and she'd helped him through many of those times. They were always there for each other. It was the one consistent element amid so many other uncertainties in their lives.

She found Jamaal in his cabin, as she expected. He sat on the edge of his bed, hunched over with his head down and forearms on his thighs.

He looked up when she entered the room after a light knock on the doorframe. "It's my fault," he murmured. "Darin. I saw him the other day—my mind playing tricks on me. I should never have let him come—"

Hailey sighed. "I'm only going to say this once, so try to get it through that thick skull of yours. Darin is a grown man and knows the risks of an EVA. Whatever happened to him isn't on you. What you *did* do is get him back to the ship alive so he could be treated. You did everything you were expected to. Shite happens."

"You know it's not that simple."

Hailey grabbed the metal chair near the door and flipped it around to sit in it backward. She folded her arms on its back, resting her chin on her hands. "Accidents can happen anywhere. If anyone's to blame, it's me for leading us into this mess."

"I shouldn't have left him alone. He—"

Oh, for fok's sake! Hailey let her narrow-eyed glare do the talking.

Jamaal stopped cold, swallowing whatever else he was about to say.

"I could beat myself up all day about 'if's' and 'could have's' about this foking *disaster* of a situation, but where would that get us? The best thing all of us can do right now is keep level heads and do everything we can to find a replacement PEM. I need you for that, Jamaal. Don't quit on me now."

He bristled at the suggestion he might be giving up, just like she knew he would. "I'll do whatever is needed."

"Foking right you will, Sergeant. Don't make me report you to Command." She cracked a playful smile.

"Aye, ma'am." He gave her an intentionally sloppy salute, returning her smile.

Their days in the Guard were long past, but habits died hard. She'd never stop feeling like his superior officer, no matter where life had taken them in the years since retirement from the service.

That perspective had always kept an invisible barrier between them. No matter how close she felt or how attractive she knew him to be, it was a line she'd sworn to never cross.

They'd come close a few times—usually with Jamaal pushing the boundaries. Those feelings had never gone away; she could sometimes see it in the way he looked at her. The way he was looking at her now.

"Hailey—"

Shite, it's never a good sign when he uses my first name.

"—I really don't know what I would do without you."

There was more to the statement than the meaning of the words themselves. The complicated history of their years together hung on the air in the space between them. The yearning for more than she was willing to give.

"We'll always have each other's backs," she deflected.

She hated it when he got emotional like this. Few things were more awkward than shooting down an advance, especially when she did care so deeply for him. But they just didn't have *that* kind of relationship. It wasn't going to happen, no matter how long he waited around for her.

"We're bound to each other. Family," he said slowly. "It kills me to see anyone in danger—especially Darin. It seems like yesterday when I was holding him or when he was climbing up my arms. No one wants to see their kid hurting."

The phrasing ignited an unexpected burn of annoyance in Hailey. Jamaal had been a father-figure to Darin for most of his life, but it wasn't the same. He couldn't possibly understand what she was feeling as Darin's mother.

"He's strong. He'll be okay," she said to keep herself from saying something she'd regret.

"Yeah. He's got his family looking out for him."

There it was again. Jamaal's protectiveness of Darin wasn't the same as the two of them being a couple caring for their shared child. She needed to set that straight once and for all. "I appreciate everything you've done for us, from the bottom of my heart, but you and I… we're always only going to be friends. This isn't a love story. Don't keep waiting around for me to feel differently."

"I haven't."

The statement caught Hailey by surprise. He'd been pining after her for so long that it had become a *given*. It wasn't like there was anyone else around who…

The realization struck her like a physical blow. *Mina.*

Hailey had noticed the flirtation between them, but it hadn't seemed like anything serious. If anything *had* transpired, it must be a recent development. The ship was too small and the crew too close for it to have gone unnoticed for long.

Irritation seared the back of her neck. Anything *recent* meant that two of her crew had been fooling around while her son was unconscious in the infirmary. That her best friend was off screwing Darin's *doctor*, who should have been tending to him.

The betrayal stung—magnified by her already high emotions from the chaotic string of events since the *Heron*.

Hailey's eyes narrowed. "How could you be so irresponsible at a time like this?"

He gaped at her. "Oh, *now* you're jealous?"

How is it possible for someone to be that clueless? She scoffed. "Unbelievable."

"No, please explain to me how finding a shred of relief in this foking shiteshow we're living right now is such a big deal."

Hailey stood. "You never could overcome your arrogance." *So much for coming in here to talk him off a ledge. I should have let Mina follow him.* An unwanted mental image of the doctor and her friend together made her queasy. She couldn't take any more of the conversation.

"Maybe it's *you* who needs to get over your deep-seated fear of being loved."

Her heart wrenched. *I already had my one great love. And*

he died. Whatever he has with Mina isn't anything like that.

Hailey slammed the chair back to its proper place by the wall. "Get some sleep. I expect you to be well-rested and ready for a long shift when we reach the salvage target." She stormed out.

—   —   —

Jamaal swore under his breath as the door to his cabin slid closed. No doubt, Hailey would have slammed the door in his face if that had been physically possible.

They'd had the same argument many times before, but this one felt different. Before, there'd always been a little opening left—a 'not now, but maybe *someday*' feeling that he'd latched onto. It'd been enough to keep him closed off from pursuing other possibilities for years.

Recently, he'd felt Hailey pulling further away. It was why he'd finally given in to the flirtation with Mina and sought out her bed. He didn't regret the tryst, but it was unfortunate that it was driving a wedge into the most important relationship in his life.

That was the problem, though: he always put Hailey first.

Curse the stars, he *still* wanted to put her feelings above all others even after she swore him out. He didn't know what it was about the bomaxed woman, but he'd dive into a black hole for her. One person shouldn't have that much sway over another. He knew that, logically, yet he always found himself blindly following her lead no matter what.

Jamaal shook his head and sighed. *Stars, Hailey, why did it have to be like this?*

He understood why she'd been drawn to Karej. The man was as close to a saint as a mortal person could be—giving and generous even to his own detriment. Ultimately, his generosity had killed him.

He recalled that final day; he had memorized every detail of it.

Pirates had taken a port-of-call by force. Karej's civilian aid group was accompanying Jamaal's unit, as they often did. Jamaal hated that the man was always so willing to run headlong into danger, with Hailey and a new baby at home. Starting that family had meant Hailey giving up her career on the frontlines, having been forced into an ops support role— the Guard was firm like that—so it seemed reckless for Karej to disregard the reasons behind the regulations surrounding combat careers and parenthood.

The Guard had field medics, so there was no reason for Karej's team to be alongside the first boots on the ground; let the pros clear the way first. Ego certainly played a part.

What they had found upon their arrival on the planet's surface shocked even the hardened veterans. Jamaal could still taste the bile from being sick. Men, women, children, charred to crisps hanging from doorways and streetlights. This wasn't just a pillaging, it was a razing. Later, they'd learn that the local government had had backroom dealings with the leader of this particularly brutal band of pirates. When he had been caught skimming from their take, well, an example needed to be made.

While the soldiers rooted out the pirates, Karej and his medical team had dutifully attempted to triage anyone with a pulse. The effort was commendable; Jamaal would've just called it a total loss and been done with it. Not the noble Karej, though! The easy way out was never good enough for him.

Somehow—the details were never shared with Jamaal— Karej had become separated from the rest of the unit. Far too deep into enemy controlled sections of the city, while trying to evacuate a terrified group of survivors, he had wandered into an ambush that had been set for the Guard.

Jamaal had been the one to find the aftermath. They had nailed Karej to the wall in the main room of a family dwelling, the occupants already deceased. Then they had used his own cauterizing tool to seal his mouth closed. Or that had come later, Jamaal wasn't entirely sure. Then, they had tortured, beheaded, and burned those he had been trying to save at his feet, like green timbers.

Karej had died of smoke inhalation. The process had not been a quick one.

That scene still invaded his sleep with disturbing regularity.

The pirates had not taken kindly to the Tararian Guard's involvement in their carefully crafted production. What they had done to Karej was as much a warning to the Guard as it had been to the local government.

Jamaal had wanted to shield Hailey from the specifics. Sadly, another company had stumbled upon the scene while he was trying to cut Karej down. It didn't take much longer than the ride home for word to get back to Hailey, in agonizing detail.

Much of the next few months were a blur for Jamaal, as he had watched Hailey dip into crippling despair. If he were to be totally honest with himself, which he didn't make a habit of doing often, he'd admit that Darin was the only thing that kept Hailey from following Karej into the afterlife. Nothing Jamaal could say, or do, could penetrate her depression.

Eventually, she began to talk again. He would never forget the first words she spoke to him after that day. "Jamaal, I'm leaving. I'd like you to go with me."

Naturally, he had said 'yes'. The where, or how, or why—

none of it mattered.

What he didn't expect was that that decision would forever cement him in her mind as a supportive friend, closing off the possibility of more between them.

Jamaal had stepped in to help his best friend as a part-time father. It had brought them even closer, and he admired Hailey even more for her ability to compartmentalize, if not fully get over the tragedy. Had it not been for her, Jamaal would have done at least a decade more in the Guard. But he recognized that she needed him, and they could build a new life together as civilians.

The scrapping gig had fallen into their laps eventually, after taking too many random jobs to count. Jamaal liked to think that they'd managed to give Darin a good childhood. It might not have been what Hailey and Karej had envisioned for their son, but there were certainly worse ways for a boy to grow up. He was loved. What was more important than that?

As a result, without meaning to, Jamaal had spent the past twenty years serving as Hailey's emotional crutch at his own expense. Getting with Mina had been his latest attempt to snap out of the cycle. Not that such tactics had worked with other women in the past.

Everything is going great now, he thought with thick sarcasm. *Couldn't be better!*

He tried to suppress the disgust with himself. How he'd pathetically hung to the hope of Hailey coming around. How he'd shamelessly jumped into bed with Mina while they both should have been keeping watch over Darin. Jamaal knew better, but he'd gone along with all of it like a lovesick puppy.

"Jamaal…"

The voice snapped him to immediate attention. It sounded like Darin. Just like what he had heard in the shower a couple days before.

Jamaal was about to shrug it off when the door suddenly opened. Darin stumbled forward through the doorway, wearing only his underwear and clutching his midsection.

"Stars, boy, you're awake! What are you doing out of bed?" He rushed forward to help him to a sit on the bunk, overcome with relief to see the young man conscious and on his feet.

"I needed to talk with you. I have to understand," Darin said. Something in his face was wrong—like the spark was missing behind his eyes.

"Talk about what?"

"Why do you put up with it? You'll never replace my dad in this family."

"What...?" Jamaal's heart pounded in his chest. It was unlikely the boy had awoken from a coma and immediately hacked into the ship's security system to observe the conversation he'd just had with Hailey. "I care about your mom. And you. I was never trying to 'replace' anyone."

"Your sense of loyalty is so strange. Why do you follow one person and not another?"

Jamaal felt Darin's forehead with the back of his hand. He seemed a bit feverish. "Let's get you back to the doc. We can have a nice heart-to-heart about the complexities of life after you're back in top form."

"Typical. You refuse to take responsibility for your own actions. Always following orders, never leading. You let others take the blame even when it's your fault."

"What are you talking about?"

"It's your fault I got hurt. You left me alone."

Jamaal's gut clenched. Darin had never been judgmental like this before, but he didn't blame him for being angry. *I did leave him alone. I should have been there to keep him safe.*

"Now you're just sitting in here moping while the ship is under attack. What kind of protector are you?"

Jamaal frowned. "There's nothing on the ship."

"You sure about that?" He raised an eyebrow. "I'll show you."

"Show me *what*?"

"There isn't any time. Hurry!" With a sudden surge of energy, Darin jumped up from the bed and ran out of the room.

Shite, what has the kid so worked up? Still, it was better to be prepared for an encounter than not. Jamaal grabbed his handgun and followed Darin into the corridor.

A flash of movement caught Jamaal's eye as Darin disappeared around the corner, heading toward the infirmary. Jamaal was about to follow him when another voice sounded behind him.

"It should have been you."

Jamaal tensed. *That voice...* He whirled around.

Standing in the center of the hall, in the opposite direction Darin had ran, was Karej, appearing no older than the last day Jamaal had seen him. The day he had died.

Jamaal closed his eyes and massaged them with his thumb and forefinger. "This isn't real. You aren't here," he murmured.

Karej walked toward him. The metal decking vibrated with his footfalls. "How do you define reality? You see me, hear me, feel my presence. But none of that matters now. It doesn't change that you let me die."

"You ran off, Karej! I told you to always stay with the team."

"You could have stopped me if you'd really wanted to."

The guilt welled in Jamaal's chest. Most of the time, he could keep the feeling at bay, but it was always there right beneath the surface. He had failed that day to protect the husband of his best friend.

"Why did you do it?" Karej pressed.

"Do what?"

"Let me go off alone. Was that your plan? Did you hope something would happen to me so you'd have her to yourself?"

Jamaal's breath caught in his throat. "No!" he choked out.

"Be honest. You don't need to lie to yourself anymore. You can tell me the truth. Who am I going to tell? I'm dead."

"I never wanted you to get hurt."

"Just scared enough that I would quit, right? Enough that Hailey would think I was a coward and she'd leave me for a brave soldier who'd never back down."

Jamaal took a step back. "It wasn't like that."

"You can't deceive me." Karej advanced toward him. "She lost her future dreams when I died. She'll never forgive you for that."

Jamaal took in the words, knowing the truth of them. He'd been clinging so tightly to Hailey that he'd never stopped to think about what was best for her. They'd leaned on each other for so long that they were inexorably linked—too close to allow anyone else in, yet they couldn't offer each other the intimacy that they individually needed to be truly happy.

He didn't want to believe it. *I was there for her. She wanted it like this.*

Jamaal forced out a defense, the rationale sounding flimsy even to himself now that he was forced to look critically at the situation. "Hailey has made a good life for herself."

"Has she?" Karej tilted his head with quizzical skepticism. "She's in debt, stressed, and lonely. Face it, you're holding her back. You always have been. She can't move on so long as you're in her life."

Tears stung Jamaal's eyes. "We need each other."

"*You* need *her*. What else do you have? You're dragging her down, slowly suffocating her. She'll never be happy so long as you're here—not really. You remind her of what she lost."

"Go away. You're not real!" Jamaal pressed his temple with the heel of his hand.

"There's nothing imaginary about these thoughts." Karej took another step forward. "Don't you want her to be happy? To be free? You know what you have to do."

— — —

Mina listened intently while Alton applied his craft. The old engineer, she decided, was a humble and reluctant genius.

Sitting at the galley table with their heads bowed together over Alton's tablet, they reviewed the scan results and looked for further clues about what might be causing the strange goings on. Mina nodded along as Alton explained his methodologies and reasoning, only occasionally asking a question or clarifying a point.

She became absorbed in the work, fascinated by this new type of data analysis. Already, she could think of several applications of the techniques to her own work in salvage target evaluation.

An alarm sounded, flooding the galley in amber light.

Mina jumped in her seat at the sudden blare filling the confined space. "What's that for?"

Alton sprang from his seat and shuffled as quickly as he could toward the door. "Someone activated an airlock!"

"Why would…?" She faded out, unable to think of a reasonable explanation. Aside from docking, cargo transfer, or an EVA to effect repairs, there was no reason to open those doors—and certainly not without alerting anyone. That increased the likelihood that it was either their invisible guest or some other catastrophic event.

Either way it's not going to be good news...

A blood-curdling wail echoed down the metal corridor.

All injuries forgotten, Mina and Alton ran toward the scream as fast as their feet would carry them.

CHAPTER 12

THE COLD METAL bulkhead pressed painfully into the side of Hailey's head. A cold, constricted feeling spread across her chest like ink dropped into water. Her jaw was clenched so tightly it creaked inside her skull from the agonizing pressure. Tears burned her eyes and slipped down her cheeks to splatter bitterly onto the floor beneath her, glimmering like rubies in the flashing red indicator lights.

Someone was shaking her, their voice sounding distant and muffled—vaguely reminiscent of wearing a helmet with the external pickups turned off.

Although it shamed her to be crying in front of subordinates, she couldn't help it. Emotionally she was completely numb.

First Darin, now… Jamaal. Fresh tears formed in her eyes. *What the fok is going on?*

In short order, her life had been completely upended. None of this was fair. The *Andvari* was supposed to be her fresh start; something she could leave her only child. Within what seemed a heartbeat, that had all fallen apart. Evaporated. More than anything else, now all she wanted was to get off this cursed ship without losing another integral piece of her life. There weren't many left to lose.

Jamaal Hyko had been with her for nearly half her life. They had been friends, *real* friends for two decades, sharing an incalculable number of pivotal life events. Though their years in the Guard had been tough on them both, Jamaal had suffered most of the emotional trauma. She hadn't been fully clued in on everything he had endured. The thought that now she never would know somehow stung even more.

Reluctantly, reality returned. Voices above her spoke worriedly.

"...very common with shock, Alton," Doctor Hurn was saying.

"Shouldn't we turn the ship around and," the sounds of ruffling clothes filled a frustrated silence, "I don't know, go *look* for him?"

Hailey raised her head and wiped at her damp face. "No," she said quietly. "He couldn't have survived, and we have to get Darin to a hospital as quickly as possible." The next part choked its way out in a desperate gasp. "I can't lose them both."

They both bent down to her, consoling whispers escaping their lips in the practiced way that people did when they weren't sure how to help but cared too much to stand idle. Under the circumstances, Hailey couldn't bring herself to push Mina away even though the revelation about her and Jamaal still burned. Her energy was sapped, and she needed all the support she could get.

The soothing words just washed over her while that coldness continued to spread like ice racing through her veins.

After soaking up their strength for just a moment, Hailey gently pushed them aside and stood. There was no memory of collapsing against the bulkhead, it didn't feel like something that she would have done under normal circumstances.

Alton silenced the alarm and closed the airlock's exterior hatch from the panel on the outside of the pressure door. "What happened, Captain?"

Doctor Hurn just watched her with that hawk-like stare that all medical professionals seemed to acquire during their careers. The most troubling part for Hailey, she found, was that already her soldier's conditioning was cloistering her feeling of loss—locking it down in some deep vault inside her mind, where her other hurts huddled together. One day that box would open, and it would crush her.

Not today.

"You already know what happened," Hailey spat back. The venom in her voice wasn't meant for him but for the situation. She couldn't help it. *Did Jamaal do it because of me? Did I push him over the edge?*

Mina swallowed hard. "Were you with him when…?" she began tentatively. A sheen of tears formed in her eyes. "We were reviewing scan data, then the alarm—"

Hailey took a steadying breath, her emotional vault threatening to crack open. "We talked. I told him to soldier up and left him on his own. Then I heard him talking in the hall, and by the time I got out there, he'd already sealed the door, and…" She couldn't complete the statement. *I can't tell them we fought. If they think I pushed him to do it, I'll lose all control of this ship.*

Mina and Alton exchanged concerned glances.

Before they could ask for answers Hailey didn't have, she changed the subject. "How far from the target coordinates in the nebula are we?" Standing straight-backed, her voice projected more command than it had in all her post-duty years combined. It carried considerably more confidence than she felt; that much was at least true.

Alton side-eyed her skeptically.

Doctor Hurn checked her handheld, a slight quaver to her hand. "Approximately fourteen hours out." She glanced at Alton then back to Hailey. "Captain, if you want to talk about what just happened…"

Hailey wasn't about to let this woman diagnose her mental health. Not after watching her best friend airlock himself into the void only minutes before. Absolutely not.

"Noted, Doctor." With nothing else to say, and no further patience, Hailey marched down the corridor away from what remained of her crew.

There was nothing left for her to do at this point except complete the salvage mission. After so much loss, she couldn't leave emptyhanded.

Before anything else, she intended to find out why her best friend and faithful companion over the decades had just flung himself from the ship they'd worked so hard to acquire. *It couldn't have been because of what I said, right? Something else must have driven him to do it.*

The self-assurances were meaningless. She needed evidence. Thankfully, every centimeter of the *Andvari* was monitored with cameras, oftentimes multiple cameras covering the same areas.

The corridors were eerily silent. No laughter floating from the residential cabins or sounds of chatter from the galley. It all felt wrong. Somehow, they had stepped into a warped reality. There was no way this could be happening. Could it?

Hailey stopped by the infirmary to look in on her son as she passed by. He still slept, seemingly peacefully, on the exam table. The room, unfortunately, wasn't equipped to house a live-in patient, and she regretted their lack of a proper medical bed. While the table wasn't a great long-term solution, it would do for now. He was stable, and that's what mattered.

"I'll get you out of this infernal place," she whispered to him. "By the stars, I won't let you die here." She kissed his forehead and then continued to the flight deck.

Hailey had always taken great pride in her ability to process the here-and-now. She felt it was the hallmark of a good leader. No one liked hard times or difficult decisions; that went without saying. But the hard facts of reality couldn't be ignored. Being able to face those difficult truths and spin a negative into a positive made a leader someone worthy of following.

There was no spinning this.

Her son lay clinging to life by a thread.

Her best friend had thrown himself out of an airlock like worthless scrap.

Their ship was limping its way toward very slim chances of salvation.

Those were the facts as they currently stood. Nothing would polish this turd of a situation.

As the doorway to the flight deck opened, Hailey immediately noticed the now dried pool of blood mere centimeters from the threshold. Taking care not to disturb it, for what reason she couldn't say, she stepped over it and bellied up to the ship's sensor systems console.

The piloting and sensor controls were two separate stations. On any other day, it'd not give Hailey a moment's pause. Today, however, straddling the two sets of controls felt as overwhelming a challenge as boarding a hostile ship with little more than her underwear and a pocket wrench.

Shaking off the lurking darkness that threatened to reduce her to a blubbering pool of depression, she steeled her resolve.

This needed doing. The loss hurt, but she was unwilling to sacrifice everything she had left to wallow in the misery.

The sensor array fired up without any fuss—not that she expected any, just with how the last few days had gone, her defenses were on a hair-trigger. The security camera footage was automatically logged and flagged with anything that the ship's artificial intelligence control system—CACI—deemed necessary for human oversight. Obviously, a lifeform launching itself out into space without any form of protection would be caught by the reason-based AI and subsequently flagged.

When the footage appeared on-screen, Hailey felt a stab of remorse as penetrating as a cold length of twisted steel. There was her friend in his final moments of life.

On the video, Jamaal came into the foredeck of the airlock, and immediately Hailey knew something wasn't right. He had his hands to his head and was shaking it violently as if to clear his vision. She watched the screen, scrutinizing the situation. Jamaal was agitated, that much was clear. It seemed like he was talking to himself.

Hailey flipped a switch to bring up the audio feed.

"...Leave me alone!" Jamaal wheezed out in a pained whisper.

Nothing and no one responded in the silence.

Jamaal drew his firearm and pointed it at the door, as if tracking a target, it moved along the wall.

"No!" he shouted into the quiet room.

Still his gun tracked whatever invisible target was threatening him.

Terror gripped Hailey's heart at what was coming. The end of this story was known to her, but her search for *why* was unfortunately spawning more questions than providing answers.

With her heart pounding, she watched as Jamaal backed into the airlock, looking desperately for some other means of escape. Finding nothing, he locked the door from the inside and began the procedure for opening the outer hull door. There were no audio recording pickups in the airlock proper, but she could see his mouth moving. He was yelling now, screaming, holding his head between his hands as he pressed the firearm into his temple.

Then he was just… gone.

Alarm sirens sounded; lights flashed. The rest she was familiar with. It wouldn't be long, and she would arrive.

Hailey couldn't watch any more.

She rewound the video back to when Jamaal entered the room. Whatever apparition was hounding him had chased him there, so she switched to the hall camera. Sure enough, Jamaal was backing up, gun pointed at something and speaking to whatever it was. Studiously, she checked every camera and every angle. There was no one even remotely around him. Ever.

There were more issues in play than him being upset over an unrequited romance. He had been talking to someone unseen, and that entity had driven him to his final act.

Hailey had suffered loss; it was the most consistent thing in her life. This was different. A part of her had died today.

If she let it, despair would consume her. She knew herself well enough. She needed to spend her energy in *doing* rather than thinking if they were going to make it out of this alive.

Who were you talking to, Jamaal? What did they say?

It occurred to her that there might be more clues on the video logs from the past few days. Something was on her ship causing trouble, and she wouldn't let anyone else get hurt.

—

"Captain."

Alton's voice was gentle but insistent. It reminded Hailey briefly of her father's.

For some reason, her mind resisted waking. Usually, it would snap to alertness so fast that her body would be left reeling to catch up. This time, her brain was sluggish—a survival instinct telling her she should stay draped in slumber for as long as possible.

Like being plunged into cold water, the pain washed back over her.

Hailey cracked open her eyes, crusted eyelashes pulling uncomfortably at her lids. Someone had draped a blanket over her, and there was a sweaty smear on the control console where she had been resting her head. As awareness swelled to full height, so too did the realization of loss. Her subconscious had been right; she wasn't ready to come out of her emotional hibernation just yet.

Alton sat in the nearby chair, poking at some of the controls and peering intently at the resulting readouts.

It was too late; Hailey was fully awake now and there'd be no sleeping for a while. She wasn't even sure how long she had been out.

"What is it, Alton?" It was a bit ruder of a delivery than she would've liked, but there it was. Her fortitude was worn to a breaking point. The fact that she was able to communicate at all was impressive.

Alton regarded her with that brand of compassion he was so good at. Not quite judgmental, but only just. Hailey had noticed he looked at misbehaving machinery with the same expression. The fact was, she didn't deserve someone of his skill level or emotional resilience. Neither did she deserve his friendship.

"We're here." Alton glanced back at the screen he had been scrutinizing. "I'm afraid you're not going to like this very much, Hailey."

The use of her familiar name—not Captain, not Suro, but her *first name*—set her shoulder blades to twitching furiously. There wasn't a time in recent memory she could recall where he'd addressed her that way. Whatever information he was about to share, it was most certainly ominous.

"Just once," Hailey mumbled, while wiping at her crusty eyes, "I'd like to wake up to good news."

"I'm sorry to say that must wait for another day." Alton passed her the handheld.

The device displayed information from a deep scan of the Kyron Nebula. Immediately, something looked strange. There was some kind of grid pattern, evenly spaced, across an entire section of the nebula.

"Is this noise?" Hailey made some attempts to run clearing filters, only to realize that they had already been applied.

"No."

Oh. The thought echoed dully through her mind.

Doing her best to not just completely lose her shite, she sighed. "Alton, could you just tell me what I'm looking at? If you haven't noticed, I've had a pretty bad few days, and I'm not in the mood."

Alton took it placidly. It rankled somewhat that she got the feeling that he was expecting an outburst from her.

He shrugged and heaved a sigh of his own through his gray beard. "I don't know, I'm afraid." The words sounded foreign on his tongue. He made a face like it tasted bad in his mouth.

"Is it some kind of interference from the nebula?" Hailey

zoomed in, trying to figure out what exactly it was she was looking at.

"As near as I can tell with the deep scanners…" He trailed off, looking out the main viewport into space.

"Alton? What is it?"

Another sigh, then he stood, stretching his back with both hands pressed into the area above his hips. "I'm old, Hailey, but those are spacecraft. A *foking lot* of them. They are spaced *exactly* one point six eight kilometers apart. In all directions."

Well, that *was* weird!

"It gets worse." Alton knuckled the spot just below his right ribcage.

"Oh good, I was just wondering how we could make this worse." The sarcasm was lost, and the joke wasn't funny. Of course, she wasn't sure she had been aiming for humor.

"All the ships are transmitting our identification number."

CHAPTER 13

EVERYONE STARED AT the perfectly aligned grid of ships.

It was one of the oddest things Mina had ever seen. And, having spent her career as a physician and scientist, she had seen some exceedingly strange stuff.

No one spoke. Not even an acknowledgement when she had entered the flight deck.

It was all too much to take in. Her analytical mind took over to keep her emotions in check. She could process her feelings about Jamaal's death later. Right now, she needed to focus on what in the stars was going on in the Kyron Nebula.

Alton stood with his arms crossed over his chest, gazing out into the prismatic nebula and the dimly illuminated targeting reticles of the scanner which overlaid each ship. It made the control system appear to be in some kind of strange diagnostic mode, with all the little boxes so neatly arrayed across it.

Hailey ground her teeth audibly, the grip on the back of the pilot's chair white-knuckled and unrelenting. It seemed like she was physically resisting losing her mind. The frustration was a reasonable reaction to the cacophony of dreadful events she'd suffered lately. Most people would have already cracked or given up.

"Okay, people," Hailey growled out between clenched teeth, "let's start discussing options here. Alton?"

Alton shook himself, as if coming out of a daze, and glanced rapidly between Hailey and the ship's main viewscreen. His mouth worked, like he was going to start saying something, but then closed it again. This repeated for several seconds until Hailey sighed loudly.

"Sorry, Captain, this is a bit beyond my comprehension," he managed at last. There was shame with a heavy helping of awe in his voice—almost like as much as he wanted to be frustrated or angry, he couldn't get beyond the wonder of what they were witnessing.

"Fine. Doctor?"

Back to formal titles, I see.

Mina considered the situation as she might evaluate a severe wound. It certainly *looked* bad. However, they still had an objective to fulfill. "It's super strange, but it doesn't change what we came here to do."

Alton's eyes widened ever so slightly in surprise while Hailey nodded slowly.

"You recommend we continue on?" the captain asked.

Mina detected a bit of hope in Hailey's voice. This is what she wanted; she was just worried the decision would endanger her dwindling crew further.

Best tackle the heart of the issue, then. Mina clasped her hands in front of her, as she would when delivering a difficult medical diagnosis. "I do. Nonetheless, I think it's important to address the elevated risks in play here. *Something* strange is going on; that is beyond question. Stars know what! And, frankly, I'm not interested in finding out. I say we scan the nearby wreckage to check for the parts we need, smash, grab, and go. All of that as quickly and efficiently as possible."

Alton backed away from the front console, eyes still riveted to the viewscreen. "I'll get you the list." The door whisked shut behind him.

Mina and Hailey continued to stare at the disconcerting view.

"What the fok is happening, Doctor?"

Mina valiantly attempted to restrain her shock, with mixed results. The whispered question from Hailey was so faint, so delicate and vulnerable, that Mina thought for a fraction of a moment that someone else was in the room with them. Never in her wildest dreams had she expected someone as stalwart as Hailey to open up to her.

Reluctantly, Mina became aware that the thought terrified her. If Hailey Suro was *vulnerable,* the rest of them were most likely well and truly doomed.

"I wish I had the answers for you, Captain." It sounded so hollow, so politically correct and tasteless, but it was the only answer Mina was capable of giving to such an enormous question. What *was* happening?

Hailey smirked and glanced at her before she said, "I wish you did, too."

With that, Hailey spun smartly on her heel and stalked out of the room. With her confident strides, squared-off shoulders, and martially efficient movements, she looked like a large predator stalking prey. The moment of quiet reflection had passed; she was once again the formidable leader Mina had come to rely on.

Left alone, Mina crumpled into the pilot's seat. The air rushed out of her in an enormous sigh.

She liked her shipmates, genuinely, but the circumstances

they found themselves in were increasingly stressful. Nobody was handling it well, and she found herself just wanting to be alone *all the time*. Which was very unlike her. Usually the life of the party, a self-proclaimed social butterfly, the fact that she was admitting to herself she *wanted to be alone* was alarming.

Then again, the last person I started to get close to just jumped out an airlock! A painful pang struck her heart. Jamaal had been a sensitive soul, despite his gruff exterior. She wished she'd had the chance to know him better.

He didn't seem like the kind of person to vent himself. Weird shite was going on. Her own experience in the infirmary proved that much.

But, now they had a new problem to face. Ships did not perfectly arrange themselves within nebulae. She was the scientist on board, so it was on her to get answers.

With a few keyed commands on the main console, she began a ship-to-ship scan of the arrayed vessels. The *Andvari* was close enough to the first rows of the grid that they'd yield relatively precise data from the scans, but the deeper into the grid they dug, the more superficial the information would become. Maybe they'd get lucky and strike gold in these closest ships so they could scoot in and scoot out without having to enter into the strange anomaly.

As the sensors started their sweep, information on each ship in the grid was displayed on the monitor. Immediately, something was off.

The manufacturer, service dates, action-loss-reports, and models of craft were all a hodgepodge of data. Nothing lined up. Well, very few things; here and there, a part number would match another part number, or craft make, or service date. For the most part, however, each ship was like a strange sort of salvage chimera. Bits and pieces of ship parts spanning decades, if not centuries, all put together to look like the *Andvari*.

Perfect replicas of their ship, arranged in a perfect grid.

Mina wasn't particularly religious and had never really considered there might be a higher god-like being out there. That was, until this very moment.

It was completely outside the boundaries of logic that someone could arrange this sea of ships, precisely spaced and synchronized in their drift so as to appear motionless. Not to mention how the ships were assembled from various bits of smashed vessels to form an astonishingly close approximation of their current ship. Let alone in the time allotted!

They had only decided to *come here* a few days ago. It wasn't just improbable, it was impossible!

Yet, here it was. Almost like they were meant to come here somehow.

Almost like it was... destiny.

As that thought sank in, an alert chirped. Something unknown had triggered an alarm.

"What...?"

A bright flash of light filled the compartment. Painfully bright, like an arc from a welder the size of the screen, or the heart of a nuclear explosion. Mina couldn't see anything, but she heard herself scream and felt her knees and side slam onto the cold deck.

A presence pressed like a weight against her mind. She screamed again, or rather, she thought she did.

The cry filled her mind with an intense desire to be released into the world, but she couldn't be completely sure her mouth was moving. Her senses ripped away like a sheet caught in a hurricane's wind. The pain consumed her.

Then she was engulfed in blackness.

— — —

Alton tried the comms again.

"Captain? Doc? Are either of you there? I have the parts list ready for you."

When no response was forthcoming, he sighed and released the comms button.

Alton didn't know Mina very well, but she seemed responsible enough. She was a doctor, for stars' sake! But he had known Hailey since she was a pudgy and carefree squirt of a girl, and he knew her to be the most responsible person he had ever met. All of this was adding up to some terrible unknown that prickled the hairs on his neck.

With a growl of frustration, he leaned back in his seat. The chair was old, coming apart at the seams, and let out a squeal reminiscent of a dying animal with even the tiniest fraction of movement. He found the sounds immensely comforting, like the familiar chatter of family members in the neighboring room.

We need answers. That thought tumbled over and over again in his mind.

Something was happening aboard the *Andvari*. That was a fact.

They had come under attack at the previous wreck. Also an undisputable fact.

Someone was attacking them.

The thought hung in his mind as he examined it from every possible angle. It seemed the only logical conclusion. Ever since they had stopped at the wreckage of the *Heron*, they had seen an increasing level of disturbances.

So, assuming that someone had managed to sneak aboard

their vessel without them knowing and was launching some kind of coordinated attack against them, that begged the question of motivation, didn't it? What was their goal?

When attacking an enemy, the goal was to capture territory and claim resources. Destroying everything was a last resort, not an initial strategy; that was a fundamental of space-based warfare. Therefore, the motivation must be the conquest of the *Andvari* itself.

The problem was it didn't *feel* like that was the goal of these attacks. Not to mention, the scans of the vessel hadn't revealed any signs of an additional presence. Sure, stealth tech would be capable of masking those organic signatures, but it added a level of complexity to an already bizarre set of conditions.

Sweat dribbled into Alton's eyes and he scrubbed at his face. He was used to the feeling of having a bomaxed blanket on his face, having worn the beard for decades, but the ferocious itching drove him mad sometimes.

Alton leaned back so far in his seat he was nearly parallel to the deck of the compartment, pensively stroking his beard in a futile effort to scratch the itch. He couldn't think of anything to bridge the established certainties of the situation and the unanswered question of *why*.

An unusual sound echoed down the open metal corridor behind him, which led to the heart of the ship. The pleasant hum and whirring of the various systems were interrupted by the discordant noise. It wasn't loud, but something was definitely out of place.

On any normal day, Alton would have run a system diagnostic, and barring any errors, just ignored the sound. With everything the way it was the last few days, though, there was no way he could dismiss the oddity.

He stood as silently as his big frame would allow and

reached under the console for the pistol he kept stashed for emergency defense. It released from its magnetic holding plate with a quick tug. The weapon was old, almost as old as Alton was himself, and the weight of it in his hand brought back a flood of memories. Some were good, enough that it invoked a longing-like nostalgia; most, however, were full of blood and pain.

The hallway toward the main engineering deck was really more of an enclosed catwalk, less than half the width of the other corridors found throughout the ship. The expanded metal floor provided glimpses of the mechanisms and systems in the main engineering compartment below. The ionized air had a tingling, metallic quality that made his nose tickle in a pleasantly familiar way. Having spent most of his life in engine rooms, it was as close to 'home' as he had ever had.

The fact that there was something foreign making noises in this place meant more to Alton than it would anyone else. This was *his* space. Aggressors be warned.

He rounded the corner to the overlook, a bit of the walkway that curved back around the perimeter of the main PEM enclosure before it extended down a short staircase to the lower engineering deck. Nothing appeared out of order. The room hummed as it always had, the discordant sound no longer audible.

Suddenly, motion in his peripheral vision caused him to jerk his head to peer down one of the electrical ducts, which supplied power to various parts of the craft. A shadow had moved toward the end of it.

How did someone get in there?

While not impossible, he supposed, it would be incredibly uncomfortable. Not only was there very little clearance between the groupings of conduit, but the heavily insulated area was continuously supercooled to reduce power degradation. Whenever he had to go into those ducts, he wore the equivalent of an EVA suit.

It suddenly made sense why they had been unable to locate whoever had stowed away from the *Heron*. No one had considered they'd be hiding in such a dangerous area.

Cursing his oversight, he walked down the stairs to the lower landing. A locker housed the two sets of engineering thermal suits, which were much bulkier than the garments they used for going out into space. While there was very little fear of decompression while crawling around in the frigid guts of the ship, the thickly insulated suit was constructed to provide protection from freezing while in direct contact with supercooled surfaces.

The garment went over his clothes with some effort and sealed in the front. It was heavy, unwieldly, and the helmet provided terrible range of vision.

As the suit sealed, he immediately began to sweat. Swearing to himself that he'd work on losing a few pounds, he blew the sweat off his nose which splattered against the visor.

Before turning toward the duct access, he peered into the locker to make sure he hadn't forgotten anything important. It would be just like him to wander off without the gloves, or boots, or something else equally critical. He'd lose his own head if it wasn't attached.

It seemed he had all the critical portions of the suit, but a flashlight also hung in the locker, which Alton took reluctantly. Wielding both the handgun and the flashlight in such a small space would present a considerable challenge; he'd have to crawl in headfirst and push the flashlight ahead of him. Though not an ideal situation, there was no way he was going to let this intruder escape now that he knew where he was.

Grunting with the effort, Alton leveraged himself into the duct headfirst. Kicking his legs frantically to try to wiggle his bulk up into the channel made him somewhat self-conscious. His insulated gloves stuck to the frost-covered metal ducting. The sudden change in temperature caused the visor to steam up, and the sweat streaked down in rivulets. As the suit automatically adjusted, the fog began to clear.

He clicked the flashlight on, illuminating the darkness stretched out before him. It was a tight fit, much tighter than he remembered from his last trip into these ducts during the initial inspection of the ship upon lease signing. Alton began wiggling his way deeper into the horizontal shaft with an increasing level of trepidation.

There was no way he would be able to turn around, and wiggling out backward was totally out of the question. Consequently, he was committed to moving forward until the first junction at a minimum. The junctions were spaced every ten meters so it was not terribly far to travel in theory, but in practice it was almost an unbearable distance.

Slowly and exhaustingly, Alton used his knees and elbows to wiggle forward bit by agonizing bit. Pushing the flashlight ahead of him, and holding the pistol out, he felt significantly exposed. The intruder had already been confirmed as dangerous, and his current position wasn't exactly optimum for self-defense.

The light ahead of him began to fill a void, where the conduit branched off into various directions. The junction was rectangular and steaming slightly. Small flashing indicators didn't provide much in the way of illumination, as they were just a way to quickly reference power systems. For Alton, at that moment, they were like marking the entry gates to his salvation.

He had already decided if there was nothing visible at the first junction, he was going to turn around and get help from someone smaller. The thought of watching Doctor Hurn wiggle into the conduit made him flush slightly.

Stay focused, Alton. Time and place, you old fart!

The conduit he had been following suddenly dropped down at a ninety-degree angle, disappearing into the floor of the chamber. Alton pushed the flashlight out ahead of him, which clattered to the floor.

Sighing, he wiggled out into the void and slipped gracelessly out of the tunnel and into the small room—landing right on top of the flashlight. The bomaxed thing likely bruised a rib, even with the protection of the padded suit.

He groaned and rubbed the sore spot, swearing under his breath.

The room, if it could be called that, was only tall enough for him to crouch and barely wide enough for him to turn around without colliding with the intersecting conduits.

Biting back more curses for the pain radiating out from his bruised side, he collected the confounded flashlight off the floor and peered down each intersecting tunnel.

Each one was slightly different, with the number of conduits and the overall size of the access varying widely. None were what he would consider easy to traverse, but some would be decidedly impossible for him to navigate. Frustratingly, none showed any signs of the intruder.

After shining his light down each a number of times at random, hoping to catch a glimpse of something worth pursuing, Alton began to feel a bit silly. He would have sworn that the shadow he had seen was real. That was the problem with getting old; the mind was still sharp, but the body's senses were slowly becoming less and less reliable.

Breathing in shallow gasps from the physically challenging feat of getting through the tight space, he tried to catch his wind for the return trip. Obviously, he was going to report this to Hailey, but he couldn't help but feel like the doddering old fool of the crew. Maybe it was time to retire.

A loud *CLANG* echoed down one of the tighter-looking tunnels.

Quick as he had been in his youth, he sprang into action, launching himself headfirst toward the still echoing sound.

This particular access was so tight Alton couldn't even use his elbows and knees to propel himself, resorting to wiggling his shoulders and digging his toes in behind him to push ever so slightly. As much as he was able, he kept from thinking about getting stuck as he inched deeper and deeper into the buzzing innards of the ship.

Nobody would be safe until this threat was handled. Up until this moment, they hadn't the foggiest idea where the intruder had been hiding. If Alton could get one clean shot, he could rid everyone of this menace and things could get back to normal. Or, at least as normal as they could be, what with Jamaal dead and Darin still in a coma.

One problem at a time.

The thought swirled amid the anxiety of what he was attempting without alerting anyone to his intentions, compounded by the significant pang of loss he felt whenever he allowed himself to think of Jamaal. Neither of them would have proclaimed they had been particularly close, but they had been friendly enough. Alton treated Hailey like a daughter, which made Jamaal the close friend that always showed up uninvited to family dinner.

Focus, man!

Alton knew full well that his situation was precarious. As

the conduit tightened perceptively around him, and each shove-off with his toes brought with it a grunt of exertion, just *how* much danger he was in began to override every other thought.

The conduit pressed into his back and sides, making it hard to expand his diaphragm enough to fill his lungs. As his body began to lack for oxygen, his breathing increased rapidly. The inability to draw in a full breath gave rise to panic.

If only he had brought a handheld, maybe he would've been able to call for help. Not that he'd be able to reach it in his present circumstances.

Bright flashes of silvery-blue pinpricks of light began to dance in his vision as the edges blurred and darkened. He was slowly suffocating.

As the panic really took hold, a fierce clenching pain suddenly spasmed in his chest. A cold sensation began crawling up his neck.

Alton had seen enough. He tried to back out of the tunnel…

And failed.

CHAPTER 14

AFTER HOURS OF tossing and turning, Hailey decided to get up.

Exhausted and frankly just plain fed up with everything, she flipped the sheet off herself and sat on the edge of her bed.

For being the Captain's Quarters, they sure were spartan. A bunk, slightly larger than standard, was built into an alcove of the wall furthest from the door, flanked by a small sitting desk similarly built into the wall. A simple chair sat in front of it. Displays and readouts on ship system performance hovered on viewscreens above the desk, casting the frosted glass top with dim multi-colored illumination in pleasant patterns. The only other furnishing was a floor-to-ceiling closet space near the edge of the bed, which held enough clothes to allow for a decently hygienic rotation. No awards, no pictures or decorations; just functional sterility. It was more than she'd had during her years in the Guard but not quite what she'd aspired to in her dreams as a youth.

Sitting there on her bed, she mussed up her hair and gave her scalp a thorough, vigorous scratching. Then she hopped up and swung her arms around, the room just barely large enough to allow for the exercise. If she couldn't sleep, she may as well get the blood moving.

Once she'd completed her stretches, she grabbed her coat off the back of the chair and exited her modest dwelling with a sigh.

Out in the hallway, she realized she had nowhere to go.

After the briefest hesitation, she turned to walk to the infirmary. She'd check on Darin while she sorted out what to do next.

If there was one thing that really grated on Hailey, it was feeling out of control. Too many years serving in leadership positions for the Tararian Guard had instilled in her an overwhelming need to have a plan of action. Nothing she was doing seemed to be working. Regret had begun to creep up in the back of her mind. If she had turned the ship around immediately after the accident with Darin, perhaps Jamaal would still be with them.

There were too many questions. What had happened with Jamaal? Sure, he hadn't really seemed himself since the accident with her son, but not suicidal. Certainly, she would have noticed that. Right?

The corridor to the infirmary was quiet, save for the subtle vibrations of the sub-light drive propelling them closer to the strange formation of ships arrayed in the nebula. Hailey had seen a lot of weird shite in her day, but she was having real issues reconciling this one. There was an odd sense of deliberateness to the arrangement of ships, like they were put on display and meant to be browsed. The whole thing made her think of an elaborate buffet. The comparison was alarmingly accurate, given their need to find suitable replacement parts for their ship.

When the door hissed open, she heard movement and her heart caught. *Is he finally awake?* The last few strides she took at a jog and entered the room, only to find Darin suffering a seizure under restraints on the exam table.

Fear and disappointment warred within her as she approached her writhing son.

Saliva had bubbled and foamed out of his mouth, and his eyes were rolled back in his head, but it was near the end of the episode, it seemed. After a few violent thrashes, he once again calmed and then eventually stilled.

Tears welled in her eyes at the sight. Parents weren't supposed to watch their children suffer.

No!

Hailey shook herself. Everything depended on her staying positive. This would pass, they'd find a new PEM and head straight to the nearest hospital. Darin would be fine. There was no way in stars she was going to watch him waste away. Not while she still drew breath.

Determined to fix their situation and get help, she checked her son's vitals before exiting the infirmary. As much as she wanted to stay longer and tell Darin they were doing everything they could to get him help, there were things that needed to be done.

She called out to the ship's computer on her way out of the room, "CACI, open up a commlink to Engineering."

A beep of acknowledgement preceded the click of a comm line opening and a slight background hum.

"Alton, I'm heading back to the flight deck now. Have you been able to make any repairs?"

No response.

It was unlike Alton to not be in his favorite broke-down chair in Engineering. If he wasn't in there, where would he be? The flight deck with Mina maybe?

A feeling of dread began to creep up her spine. Images of

Jamaal being jettisoned out into the cold dark vacuum of space flashed through her mind. Alton was a sensitive older man, but he was the furthest from suicidal she could think of. Stars, she was more likely to take the short step out the airlock than he was.

Despite the internal reassurance, she quickened her pace. The sense of dread rose within her.

Everything had gone to absolute shite lately. What should have been the haul of a lifetime in the Kyron Nebula, vaulting them to riches and freedom, had instead proven to be another corpse-littered battlefield. Just another place to bury loved ones.

Given that disturbing trend, it came as little surprise to Hailey when she opened the door to the flight deck and found Mina sprawled on the deck holding her head.

"Mina?" Hailey rushed over to her, concern softening the edge in her voice.

The doctor looked up at her, pupils dilated and pulsating somewhat. Had she hit her head somehow? A quick visual assessment of the room showed no signs of struggle or hidden attackers. No blood anywhere that Hailey could see, either.

How do you fight something you can't see? Stars! Just give me a target!

"I'm fine, I think." Mina reached up for assistance standing. She was so slight, Hailey practically launched her into the air. The doctor made a shocked *squeak* sound and cartwheeled her arms slightly to keep her balance. It was the first time Hailey had seen the woman lack her usual swan-like grace.

"Sorry about that, I'm used to heaving up Ja…" She almost said his name out loud. Picking his sorry drunk ass off the floor after a bender was something she'd never do again. Never have him playfully pull her down and laugh at her outrage.

Anger bubbled up through her grief. How *dare* he leave her! What right did he have to abandon her without so much as a word of explanation? How selfish! How incredibly self-centered was he? Maybe she hadn't known him as well as she had thought.

Mina was watching her, still clutching her forehead gingerly as if it throbbed under her palm. Her expression was a fluctuating mix of worry and agony.

No, it wasn't fair to judge Jamaal. There was obviously more to this story than just what he did. They were suffering some kind of attack. Maybe he did what he did in an effort to try to save them? She couldn't help but feel bitterness over being left out of the plan. There was no excuse for that. The rest, she would let go for now.

"Hailey, are you okay?" Mina whispered.

The question hung in the air for a long moment.

Sucking in a deep breath, Hailey set her jaw and said at last, "I'm fine."

Mina chuckled, then suddenly winced and massaged her temples. "They really should do away with the word 'fine' because it's so commonly misused."

A pained grimace twisted her lips. Admittedly, she was *anything* but okay at the moment. Her whole life had been upended in a matter of days—everything she had struggled to build, gone in moments. 'Fine' didn't even begin to cover it.

"I'll manage. What happened here?" Hailey let some of the old resolve back into her tone. She was done being weak. They had to get a new PEM and get out of there. One of those hundreds of derelict craft *must* have something that would work.

"I'm not exactly sure." Mina looked around the room, as if

looking for the source of her assault. "Sudden and severe headache, loss of vision, full-body pain. I could have been electrocuted, or maybe an aneurism?" She shook her head and shrugged.

"Well, I'm glad you're still with us." They shared a half-hearted smile. "Let's get that parts list from Alton, do this EVA, and get the fok out of here. What do you say?"

"Sounds amazing. I'll take two, please."

Hailey did manage a laugh then. Mina flushed with victory and mimicked 'scoring a point' on an invisible scoreboard between them.

Her lifted spirits were short-lived. With Jamaal gone, Hailey was the only qualified person to perform the EVA. That meant she'd need either Alton or Mina to oversee the operation on the flight deck.

While Alton was no slouch when it came to such things, he would be focused on prepping the *Andvari* for repairs so they could get turned around as quickly as possible. That made Mina the obvious choice. However, the recent revelation about the doctor and Jamaal threatened brain space that Hailey didn't have to spare at the moment.

A twinge of jealousy struck Hailey in spite of herself. The graceful doctor was everything that Hailey was not; sensual, extremely educated with brilliance to match, and soft curves that fit perfectly on her petite frame. Hailey, meanwhile, was all hard angles, lean muscle, and built for work. She felt like a barge by comparison. *Of course* Jamaal had been physically attracted to Mina; it would be ridiculous to deny it.

That wasn't really the question.

Why am I so upset about this? The thought was grim—angry, even. Now *that* was the real question.

Part of her had always loved Jamaal. He just had that way

about him—so bomaxed lovable. With his easy confidence and quick smiles, there wasn't a sexual creature in the system that wouldn't have romped with him if given the opportunity.

Not Hailey, of course. She'd held that line against fraternization as if her entire existence depended on it, despite there being no reason to do so as civilians. But she just couldn't see herself with Jamaal in that way, even though she found herself uncomfortable knowing he was with other people. Perhaps it was because they'd been friends while she was married, and that friendship was forever tied to Karej's memory. For it to turn to romance would somehow be a betrayal.

Hailey gave herself a little shake. *None of that matters now. Neither of us will have a future with him. We both lost a friend today.*

What was important now was saving her son and her remaining crew.

"Did Alton send you that list?" Hailey asked. "I figured he'd have been up here by now."

"I never got anything." The doctor looked around as if still trying to get her bearings.

Hailey strode over to the console and thumbed the comms for Engineering. "Alton?"

Again, nothing but the background hum of the machinery emanated from the open link.

The uneasy feeling Hailey had almost managed to banish suddenly surged back full-force. "I've been crewing with Alton for decades, and I can't think of another time in that history that he's missed two subsequent check-ins. That man *loves* his chair. The ship would practically have to be on fire for him to consider leaving it."

Mina's brows drew together. "Then we need to search for

him."

The two women exited the flight deck at a brisk jog.

As they ran through the metal corridors, Hailey couldn't keep her thoughts from turning to the worst possible scenario. There had been too much tragedy on her ship already. The fact that they were streaking toward the unknown one more time grated on her nerves. For someone who was usually the picture of control, she sure felt lost.

When the door to Engineering whisked open, the gentle hum of the ship's engines turned into a much louder rumble.

The room was empty. Alton's favorite chair stood solitary watch over the systems. Nothing looked out of place.

Well, at least there wasn't an unconscious body or pool of blood on the floor. That was a nice change.

"Hailey, aren't there supposed to be two thermalsuits in that locker?" Mina indicated an empty hook in the space where the suits usually hung, and the cabinet was devoid of all the accessories.

"Maybe he's in the ducts trying to prep the ship for a new PEM?" Hailey couldn't keep the anxious hope from her voice.

She eyed the remaining suit hanging in the locker, a plan forming in her mind. *I hate this day.*

CHAPTER 15

ALTON'S RIGHT SHOULDER ached. He grunted and tried to roll over but found he couldn't move.

Confused, he cracked open an eye and found total darkness.

Something wasn't right. His head was killing him, even more than usual. Where was he? The pain in his shoulder was near unbearable. When he tried to reach around to feel his back, his arm struck a metal wall. It was *right* on top of him!

Then he remembered where he was, and the panic flooded back.

Feeling around, he realized he was at the bottom of a shaft, cramped into a U-shape with his back pressing onto a hard object, likely his dropped flashlight—*again*, curse the blasted thing—and his head and feet pressed onto opposite walls. Stars, it hurt!

He had no recollection of how he'd gone from his wedged position to there. Presumably, on the verge of losing consciousness, he'd wiggled free and then fallen down one of the vertical junction shafts. The specific *how* didn't matter so much now, only that he needed to somehow get out.

Curling into the fetal position, he managed to awkwardly shift onto his knees. The now freed flashlight illuminated the cramped, metallic space. He must have been unconscious for a while, because the brilliant light hurt his eyes. Fumbling around half-blinded, he managed to grab the device and power the unit off.

Now all he could see was darkness and green-purple flashing splotches of after-images. His head still ached, as did his aged joints. They weren't used to this kind of intense physical use.

After several minutes of catching his breath and knuckling his aching hip, neck, shoulders, and… well, almost every part of him he could reach without kicking off a muscle spasm, he gingerly rose to a standing position and flicked on the flashlight.

Immediately, the reflective metal walls of the duct once again blinded him. This time, he squinted and gave himself time to adjust to the light before opening his eyes fully.

Once his vision adjusted, the first thing he noticed were the plumes of steam puffing out of his thermalsuit. Somehow, he must have torn it when he'd fallen. The suit itself had an active heating element built in to compensate for circumstances like this, but the energy cells weren't very big. He checked the readout built into the wrist of the suit: 'Temperature: 14.24 degrees C. Battery: 8.68%'

Perfect, woke up just in time to freeze to death! Couldn't I have just slept through it and passed gently? The thought made him chuckle despite his tenuous situation. What a way to go— freezing to death in the guts of his own ship. After surviving years in various wars and conflicts, harrowing engineering disasters, and that one trip to Sylvestra… Well, best not to remember *that* particular event.

Alton scanned the upper areas of the duct. He thought he could make out the area he had gotten stuck in quite a ways above, and there was definitely a broken and bent grate that he'd struck on his way down. Too bad it hadn't done its job and stopped his fall. Nothing irritated him more than poorly designed safety measures.

His teeth started to chatter. Not a great sign.

Thinking like an engineer, he scanned his immediate vicinity. Nothing of use. The walls were polished smooth, no handholds or ways to clamber back out—not that he relished the idea of that level of physical activity, but anything was better than death. Probably.

A flashlight, a thermalsuit, and his person. That was all that he had to work with; his pistol was nowhere in sight.

Again, the idiocy he had displayed in chasing after the intruder with so little information or support equipment just made him cringe. Why had he been so stupid? It didn't make any sense and was really unlike him. Retribution for Darin and Jamaal, he suspected, was his motivation for the reckless action.

Lamenting old age, he leaned his back against the wall and used the hand not holding the flashlight to cover the tear in his suit. It did little good; he could feel the warm air escape around his grip, as futile as trying to hold back blood pouring from a gut wound. Bringing a patch kit hadn't even occurred to him in his haste to pursue the stowaway.

Now, not only was he trapped down here in this cold, dark, metal box, but he was trapped with someone bent on killing off the crew one-by-one. If the cold didn't eventually get him, most likely this intruder would. Stars, maybe that was how he had wound up thrown down this shaft in the first place.

Something caught Alton's attention; the wall across from

him wasn't perfectly smooth like he had initially thought. There were tabs where it could be popped out—an access hatch. There was no labeling on it, which was mildly infuriating, but he might as well explore every presented option.

The thermalsuit was tight in the hands from the wrist down, which made it well adapted to detail work like popping the tabs out on the panel. It didn't take long before he had the cover free from the wall.

A long tone sounded inside the suit, and the wrist gauge flashed orange: 'Temperature warning, 12.00 degrees C.'

The damaged suit wasn't able to sustain the warmth he needed to survive. If he had the desire, he could likely do the math and figure out, to within a few seconds, just how long he had left to live. Would he rather know, or let it be his final surprise? It felt foolish to think that way, but he found himself circling the thought as he shone the light into the panel.

It was a power relay, consisting of various emergency fuse connections that served as a stopgap to prevent critical failures from cascading across the entire ship. The so-called 'Isolation Relays' were fairly standard, and unfortunately were not of much use to his present escape efforts.

With the cover panel pulled off and now in his way, he found it impossible to sit down; he opted instead to just lean against the far wall and brace his feet against the edges of the relay box.

The suit beeped at him again, the battery level flashing a warning to show it was critically low. With enough battery, he could have lengthened his survivability long enough to be discovered; with the minutes he had left, there wasn't a lot he could do.

He had probably been in the ducts an hour. How long

would it take for the scrambling crew of the *Andvari* to realize their unsociable hermit of an engineer was missing? Sometimes they went days without talking. Granted, a lot more was going on right now, but still...

I'm foked, aren't I?

It was a challenge to fight against the nagging voice in his head that started to tell him he had lived a good life and that he would be both remembered and missed. That didn't change the fact that he didn't really *want* to die.

As he crouched there questioning his life choices—as one was prone to do when faced with their untimely demise—he tried to focus on the relays.

A thought began to crystalize. If he were to damage a relay, it would immediately notify the ship's computer that there was a fault in the system and identify this exact panel. Hypothetically, it would alert Hailey that not only he was missing, but likely where to find him.

The drawback was, he had no way of knowing what system he was knocking out. For all he knew, he could be severing the power connection to their navigation systems, or worse, life support. The coding on the panel was of little help without a reference guide. It would all boil down to sheer luck—not his strong suit, much to his dismay.

Of course, there were really bad things that could happen, too, like disabling the anti-matter containment field on the pion drive. Catastrophic failure, indeed.

Unfortunately, his choices were either freeze to death or risk it. Sure, he was old, but he felt justified in his desire to survive. Hopefully, he didn't kill everyone, including himself, in his selfish effort to be rescued.

In doing a quick count, he found the panel had eighty relays. From his experience running the ship, he knew that there were approximately thirty critical system groups. Unfortunately, he didn't know where the branches of systems were located relative to this specific relay. He felt he was still relatively close to the main engineering hub, so these were still likely base systems.

That put his odds at disabling a critical system near fifty-fifty.

It either works, or you die. Great!

Alton squatted down with some creaking in his knees to scrutinized the panel. The panel was an evenly spaced grid of the unlabeled crystalline relays, which effectively acted as fuses. If he lived through this, he decided he was going to petition DGE, the ship's manufacturer, to pass some kind of color-coding standardization protocol to avoid situations like this.

There was really nothing left to do but…

He reached out to one of the central relays and yanked it.

It slid smoothly out of its socket.

For a second, nothing happened. Alton continued to hold his breath anyway. At least he hadn't pulled the fuse that included artificial gravity. Although, then he could've gotten out.

I can't win for losing!

That was when he heard the distant whine of alarms going off.

"Oops!" The exclamation was quiet, almost whispered, though it reverberated in the confined metal box he found himself in.

Now all he could do was sit back and wait for someone to come find him, hopefully before he turned into a grizzled old popsicle.

— — —

Mina had neglected to mention to Hailey that she was mildly claustrophobic. It was too late to complain now that she was shimmying through an access tube in a bulky thermalsuit.

"How's it going, Doc?" Hailey asked over the comm. The captain's voice had more static to it than Mina was used to; the tight metal space must be causing interference.

Mina tried not to think about the space being *that* tight.

"I think this kind of activity is over my pay-grade, Captain." She huffed out the answer as she continued to squirm down the metal tube.

If she were being honest with herself, she felt incredibly silly. Here she was wiggling like a worm into a freezing cold shaft. Sliding across her chest was making her breasts sore, and her hips were starting to cramp.

"If the good engineer isn't dead already, I'm likely to kill him and leave him down here."

No response came across the comm, but she hoped the comment had gotten another chuckle out of Hailey to break the tension.

Times had been tough, and Mina felt responsible for them being in the situation they found themselves now. It had been her suggestion, after all, that they proceed on course for the Kyron Nebula.

Trust me, it'll be the score of a lifetime! Her own words sounded hollow to her now.

They had all known there were risks to being this far out, but no one could have anticipated the level of difficulties they had encountered.

She felt significant guilt about Darin. That paled in comparison to the burning remorse that smoldered deep in her gut over Jamaal's suicide—a feeling like a vicious little animal was trying to claw its way out of her stomach. Thoughts of him made her eyes burn.

Never before had she met a man so full of life, so genuine, and... feisty? Was it okay to call a man that? Frankly, it had been a while since she had experienced any kind of interest in anyone, so she may be a little out of touch with the rules and protocols. She'd downplayed her interest, knowing the complicated relationship between Jamaal and Hailey. Truth be told, she'd hoped their physical relationship would grow into much more.

"What's the word?" Hailey sounded like she was barely containing a surge of anxiety. As a doctor, Mina was all too familiar with the cues, even by someone as normally calm and collected as the captain.

"I'm coming up on a junction now, but it's slow going in here. I'm struggling. I'd be forever impressed if Alton managed to get this far in on his own." Her hopes of finding the elderly engineer were rapidly dwindling proportional to the diameter of the access tunnel tightening around her.

As she shimmied her way deeper, she held up suddenly. *Was that a sound?* There was a rhythm to the acoustic environment of the ship, and the sudden discord of a stray *clank* echoing down an adjacent corridor stood out to Mina like ice dropped down the back of her shirt.

She held her breath and froze in place, straining to listen through the insulated helmet.

There it is again!

A noise *was* coming from somewhere off to her left, around the corner from the junction mere meters away. It sounded like someone navigating a tight metal tube, somewhat less gracefully than her own movements.

"I hear something up ahead, Hailey. I'm going to go check it out." Mina began to squirm forward again, with rekindled hope she'd find something other than a frozen corpse.

Her radio crackled, the depths of the ship interfering with the communications, "...be careful... don't do... okay?"

"Yep!" Mina replied enthusiastically, although she could only guess what had been said.

Get in, be careful, get him out, don't do anything stupid. Something like that, she imagined.

The junction was a six-way, unfortunately—branching left, right, up, down, and straight ahead. Although she was relatively certain the sounds had come from the left branch, acoustics down here could be unpredictable. It could just as easily have come from below and echoed up.

She had to trust her gut.

Navigating over the open expanse that plunged beneath her was somewhat discomfiting, but she managed it. In her youth, she had participated in a mountaineering expedition on Arisan Prime, a rocky crag-laden proto-planet, where she'd been pushed to her physical limits. Though not as acrobatically demanding, somehow being down in this confined space was worse.

The loud *clang* echoed again, from deeper this time.

Mina paused. *Was that the same sound?*

It was similar, but in this corridor, it seemed like it was coming from behind her. This time, it was less defined.

Another, much louder, *BANG* from directly ahead made her head whip back around.

Well, that was certainly closer than feels comfortable.

Another sound washed over her, gone before she could fully grasp it amid the cacophony of whirring and buzzing.

That almost sounded like a voice.

Mina felt around her chest for the switch to a small control unit built into the padded suit. "Alton?"

While not overly loud, the confined metal space made it seem like she had positively boomed the question into the world. It reverberated and echoed, even coming back around from behind her.

Great! So much for trusting her ears down here.

There was no response.

Up until this point, her biggest fears had been environmental in nature. Getting stuck, freezing, or running out of power in the suit. Now, a new fear caused her shoulder blades to itch. What if she wasn't alone down here? And she didn't mean the wayward engineer.

What if he hadn't become trapped or lodged in the narrow corridors but had been ambushed?

There *was* someone, or something, on board their ship attacking them, after all.

Another loud *BANG* sounded from up ahead. Was it closer, or were her fears playing tricks on her?

Mina released the button for the external speaker and heard the open line click off.

"Doc?"

The sudden loud voice inside Mina's ear made her jump.

"Still here, Hailey!" She took a steadying breath. *Although I maybe just lost ten years off my life with that scare!*

"Any luck? Time is getting short here. You're nearing the halfway point."

"I can hear something moving around down here with me. I called out with the externals, but no response." She paused, the commlink still open, then pressed on. "I don't mean to be alarmist or dramatic here, but do you think maybe our unwanted guest could be hiding down here?"

The pause stretched out longer than was necessary, and Mina's spine tingled again.

"Captain?" Still the line was silent after she ended her transmission.

After what felt like an hour, she heard the telltale click on the other side. "That's the halfway point, Mina. Get your ass turned around and get back here."

CHAPTER 16

"I SEE YOU, keep it coming." Hailey hung the comm unit up on a hook near the open hatch. The light bobbing down the corridor got brighter as Mina approached.

After a few moments, a puffy gloved hand reached out of the hole, and Hailey grasped it tightly to help her out. Mina looked awkward and somewhat comedic with the cream-colored engineering suit swimming on her small frame. Being slightly shorter than necessary to see out the helmet, she appeared like an obese two-legged bug.

Hailey sure was glad to see her.

Together, they released the seal on the suit and removed the helmet.

Mina gasped in some air and arched her back to stretch it. "Well, let's not do that again anytime soon, eh?"

Not really in the mood for levity, Hailey just grunted in response. They had a more pressing issue. "There's no real way to scan the interior access tubes of the ship for biological signatures, since those areas aren't connected to the normal environmental control systems," she explained.

The admission was painful. Hailey had never really

thought about it before, but she currently found that limitation to be incredibly frustrating. The lack of sensors in that maze of corridors made it an *excellent* place to stow away while also providing decent access to most of the ship.

As the doctor began stripping out of the six-sizes-too-large thermalsuit, she said, "Well, we can potentially reconfigure the sensors to penetrate some broader spectrums and somewhat fake a deep scan of the ship. I'm not an expert on that tech; it would be easier for Alton, but I can see what can be done."

The dainty woman stepped out of the heap of material and blew a stray strand of hair off her nose in the most unflattering way, eyes crossed and everything. Somehow, she made it cute. Not a word anyone would ever use to describe Hailey.

"Sounds good," Hailey replied. "Get it done. We need…" She trailed off as she noticed a flashing warning indicator light on the engineering console.

What now?

Following her gaze, Mina also noticed the light. "That can't be good."

Hailey jogged up to the console. There were several electrical alarms going off ship-wide; the power distribution system was suddenly reporting a main fault.

That was it. Hailey snapped.

She doubled-up both fists and slammed them on top of the panel, hard. It hurt her hands, but she hid her grimace by hanging her head. This was all just too much. Everything had been downright pleasant last week. How could *so* much go *so* wrong in such a short period of time? In just a matter of days, she had lost almost everything she had ever cared about.

A warm hand rested gently on the small of her back.

"We'll figure it out, Captain." Mina's voice was calm, clinical, sterile.

Hailey's breath was coming out in ragged gasps as she stared at the floor beneath the console. The faint red and amber flashing lights spilling in around the edges of her peripheral vision seemed to pulsate with the rapid beating of her heart. It had been a long time since she had felt this out of control.

Mina was talking over her shoulder, the soothing tone of a doctor giving bad news. *Can't she just join in the misery?* The bedside manner business could get really annoying. Hailey just tuned the doctor out and focused on her breathing.

There were really no good options at the moment, but she ran through the list anyway. Right now, their priority had to be finding out what was wrong with the ship's power systems. The last thing they needed was for the environmental controls to cut out. If one more thing went wrong with her ship, Hailey was likely to just scuttle it in the nebula and try her best to float home.

Next, they had to find Alton. No one knew the ship better than he did. They were at a significant disadvantage without him. If, between the two of them, Mina and Hailey were unable to repair the power fault, they'd need to reprioritize finding Alton. If he were dead... Well, one thing at a time.

From there, they had to get this intruder off her ship. Likely. whoever was on the ship was using the unmonitored access tunnels to avoid detection. That could also be what was wrong with the ship. Whoever was messing around in there was trying to force them to abandon the vessel.

A thought occurred to Hailey. If the intruder had purposefully caused a fault, it should show the location of the error within the ship's monitoring system.

Sucking in a quick breath, she stood upright and began tapping commands on the console.

Mina watched over her shoulder. Heat was still wafting off

her slender frame, carrying an aroma of sun-warmed sugar. A stab of jealousy struck Hailey. It wasn't fair that Mina smelled so nice after sweating for almost an hour in that thermalsuit.

For her part, the good doctor eyed the screen like a hawk, reading the information as it streamed through, completely oblivious to the restrained ire coursing through Hailey's mind. Most of this was likely projection, she realized. Knowing that didn't help in the slightest, though.

"There!" Mina suddenly said. "Go back."

Hailey admittedly had only been paying half attention to the screen while she nursed her tempestuous feelings. Rolling the traceroute back a screen or two, they found the fault. It was close, thank the stars! Just two junctions away from a nearest access hatch, several decks lower than where Mina had explored.

"That panel isn't far from where you just were, Mina. Could those noises you heard have been Alton?"

Hailey watched the woman consider briefly, then she shook her head. "There's just no way for me to tell. Noise carries strangely in those tunnels, not to mention the thermalsuit mutes everything."

Well, they had to start solving problems; too many were stacking up on them.

The panel was at least a solid location to start looking for either the intruder or Alton, and they needed to go see about repairing the power fault.

"I'm going to go down and check that relay." Hailey raised her hand when Mina started to interrupt, then continued, "I need you to start work on adjusting our sensors to do a deep interior scan—sensitive enough to pick up stealth tech, or thermal shielding, or however it is this intruder is hiding. I want whoever it is *off my ship*!" That last bit came out quite heated, and Mina retreated a step from her.

While Hailey wouldn't exactly call herself claustrophobic, she wasn't exactly built small and didn't relish the idea of being in the tight space. The access tunnels looked too much like the military coffins for her comfort.

"I'm going to set up a rapid winch system on this side and hook it onto the belt of the thermalsuit." The idea was slowly forming, Hailey's brain putting it together as she spoke. "When I've either dealt with whoever is down there or fixed the relay, I want you to hit the retract control and get me out of there without hesitation."

Pretending to not notice the doctor's slightly elevated eyebrows, Hailey scooped the thermalsuit off the floor at their feet and started climbing into it. At least she was more adept at donning it than Mina had been.

Years of training came back in a flash. It made her think of Jamaal. She half expected him to comment about her in that half-joking, half-flattering manner he had perfected over the years—some flippant comment about her perky breasts or tight butt that almost always accompanied her bending over to pull on any kind of gear. The absence of that now made her heart ache fiercely.

Losing him was going to stick with her forever.

A creak and groan announced that Mina had taken a seat in Alton's beat-up old chair, which was almost as cantankerous as he was. A small yelp from that direction announced that the chair had almost flipped her out onto the floor. Hailey couldn't help but smile; she had been there more than a few times herself. The only person that was able to navigate that dastardly piece of junk was its owner.

The rapid winch was back in the cargo bay, where it was normally used to either liberate loot from other derelict craft or to fetch stranded crew. Hailey wasn't sure there had ever been another occasion to deploy that particular piece of equipment *inside* a ship before.

Well, first time for everything I suppose!

As she jogged down the empty metal corridors toward the cargo bay, she felt incredibly groggy. Being a good leader in the Guard meant knowing when soldiers were being pushed too far. Hailey hadn't slept much lately, and what sleep she did get was fitful, at best. There wasn't much left in her reserves. If she had been her own CO, she would have demanded some rack time before this operation. Unfortunately, everyone was depending on her. There would be time to sleep when she was dead.

A grimace crossed her face as the door to the cargo bay opened. She *loathed* that old saying. Sleep was amazing! If she could, she'd curl up for an entire month; let someone else handle all this shite!

Just inside the door, she found the winch mounted to the wall opposite the hull doors along the bulkhead. Though it wasn't very large, it was boxy and *heavy*. Luckily, Jamaal had been doing some work in the cargo bay and had left a pneumatic impact driver nearby.

Bless that man for never once in his life putting away a tool!

The air-powered device sprang to life in her hand with a sputtering howl that made her ears ring, but it made short work of the heavy lug bolts affixing the winch to the ship. When the last lug was removed, the unit tumbled to the floor with a loud *CLANG*.

Hailey heaved on the unit and felt a twinge in her back—not quite a torn muscle but certainly more than a simple cramp. Frustrated, she glared down at the metal box with coiled cable wound tightly along a spool and a carabiner adorning the end. How in the stars was she supposed to get this back to the engineering bay by herself? Even straining her back, she had barely budged the thing.

"Shite!" she bellowed at the top of her lungs into the empty massive room.

Then, she grabbed the bomaxed thing and wrestled it onto her shoulder and stormed out of the room.

—   —   —

There was no way in the stars this was going to work. Not a chance.

Mina glanced over her shoulder at a loud bang and curse from Hailey. The captain was knuckling a spot about midway up her back, somewhere around the first lumbar or twelfth thoracic vertebra. If she had damaged that, she was in for a week of soreness.

It appeared as though the captain had maneuvered some other equipment over to help hold the winch up near the hatch so she could drive some heavy-duty bolts into the ship's structure. While it definitely wasn't going to win any awards for aesthetics, hopefully it would help in a pinch. Mina was glad that Hailey had thought of it, and maybe a bit annoyed she hadn't insisted on mounting it for *her* exploratory mission into the ducts.

She turned back to the mess she had made of the ship's sensor arrays. After almost an hour of trying to reconfigure the system into a broad-spectrum pulse that was directed inward, instead of the usual outward, she was becoming increasingly frustrated.

Nothing was working the way she *thought* it should. Granted, she was far from a technical engineer. Her expertise was in pattern recognition and diagnostics, not root system programming. Still, with a little luck, she thought she could pull off what she was trying to do. It wouldn't be pretty, and Alton would no doubt give her a tongue lashing once they found him alive and well.

Holding onto the hope of locating him was becoming increasingly difficult. Every minute that passed, the odds of finding the old man alive dwindled.

"Okay, I'm going in," Hailey said.

While Mina herself had felt like she was literally swimming in the chunky fabric, Hailey looked like a statuesque ancient warrior ready for battle. She filled that bulky suit in an extremely flattering way, somehow enhancing her already intimidatingly sturdy frame. She was a formidable woman in all respects. It made Mina feel like a helpless child just to be near her.

After a nod of acknowledgement, Mina watched as Hailey swung fluidly into the shaft. With that initial momentum, she was halfway to the first junction without expending so much as an additional breath of effort. It made Mina sniff in annoyance; she had been mostly out of breath just from clumsily clambering through the hatch. The whole thing had impacted her ego in several silly ways.

Click.

"Okay, Doc, I'm making a beeline for the panel, but I sure would feel better if we had a scan of the immediate area. I'd hate to stumble into an ambush."

"Working on it, Captain." Fingers flying across the console, Mina tried to keep the creeping self-doubt out of her tone as much as was possible.

There simply wasn't a good way to cover the *entire* ship with the external sensors. Frankly, what she was attempting to do was mildly dangerous. Bombarding the ship with sufficient levels of electromagnetic radiation to get past the ship's shielding was not a recipe for longevity.

How could she circumvent the safety measures in such a way that allowed for achieving what she was looking for *without* harming all those on board? That was the question.

With one finger rubbing at her lips and the other tapping impatiently on the backlit console, a thought suddenly occurred to her. The issue wasn't that it couldn't be done; it couldn't be done *all at the once.* However, sensor sweeps could be conducted in the various spectrums, from multiple arrays, and have the information composited and analyzed together. However, that approach would be slow—perhaps pointless for their present efforts. However, seeing as it was her best option at the moment, she programmed the arrays and pushed the settings beyond their theoretical limits, then initiated the sweep.

Immediately, data began streaming across the viewscreen above the main control console. A progress bar just said 'CALCULATING', and after a few moments, had not updated. Not a great sign.

"Okay, Captain, I've begun a sweep of the area. Unfortunately, I'm unable to target specific regions of the ship and achieve a broad-spectrum scan. No estimate on completion." This time, the glum tone definitely carried.

"Copy that, Doc. Keep me updated. I'm approaching the second junction now. If I'm right, the panel should be just ahead and below." Still there were no sounds of exertion, just calm and focused determination.

Mina was no soldier, but if she ever had to go into battle, she'd want to follow someone like Captain Suro. Her confidence and poise was infectious.

Suddenly, with nothing immediately pressing to attend to, Mina found herself pacing back and forth across the small platform that served as the control deck, intently staring at the unhelpful progress bar. Why even have an indicator if it didn't at least give an approximation of completion status? It seemed ridiculous!

On a whim, she pulled out her handheld and used it to radio Hailey. "I'm going to go check on Darin, but call out of you need anything."

"Good idea," came the immediate reply.

Mina glanced once more at the infuriating 'progress' bar—more like '*lack* of progress' bar—and hurried out.

CHAPTER 17

THE JUNCTION WAS just a meter away, finally, but crawling through the tunnel in the heavy thermalsuit was beginning to tax Hailey. On top of that, it was hot; the sealed garment trapped her heat, turning it into a sauna despite the frigid temperatures outside. She fully expected to find Alton dead of heart failure from the effort of getting this far.

Hailey reached down to her belt and drew her sidearm. She released the safety and did a quick check to make sure it was in firing condition. As much as she was able, she wanted to get battle-ready, just in case the intruder was hunkered down waiting for her.

She rested her head on the smooth metal wall and took a few calming breaths while listening to the area around her. There was something, she couldn't quite make it out, but there was definitely *another* sound in her direct vicinity.

Sadly, there was no quiet way to approach. Lumbering in the bulky suit through a metal echo chamber made stealth out of the question.

Well, let's do this thing. Another of Jamaal's favorite sayings.

Stars, she missed him. There was a certain comfort in knowing there was someone trustworthy always watching her back. Figuratively and literally. She'd appreciate both in equal measure right about now.

With a sudden surge, she pushed off hard with her legs to propel herself halfway out over the open junction. It was a precarious position, with her upper half completely exposed, but what she lacked in defense she intended to make up in offense. She scanned the area with her pistol.

Her heart leaped. The crumpled form of a body in the missing thermalsuit lay at the bottom of the shaft.

Her flashlight beam painted the garish scene with harsh shadows that warped her perspective. The figure certainly looked like it could be Alton.

A quick assessment of the area showed a bent and snapped grate. If Alton had fallen down this shaft, he could have died from the impact. It was easily ten meters.

No sounds registered to Hailey's hearing, though that wasn't saying much with the deluge of ambient noise from the ship humming around her. It was like being in a cave immediately adjacent to a gargantuan waterfall. Still, she had to get down to check the body. Any hope she had of finding Alton alive was mostly gone now. This had quickly gone from search and rescue to a search and recover mission.

Hailey grasped the opposite side of the vertical hatch with her hands and then eased her legs over one at a time. She struggled to get balanced as she braced her feet against the sides of the shaft. Cursing the ship's designers for their lack of accessibility planning when it came to the innards of her ship, she began to ease her way down the shaft. The added weight of the suit made it an excruciatingly slow process.

After an agonizing descent, she finally dropped heavily

next to the limp form. The body was positioned in a seated position, legs folded halfway up the opposite wall, with the heavy helmet pinning the person's face to their chest.

With measured, deliberate movements, Hailey aimed her pistol at the top of the helmet and reached with her other hand to pull the head back so she could peer inside the clear visor.

Alton!

His eyes were closed, but a faint fog pulsed on the inside of the visor. He was still breathing.

"I found him, Doc! He's in bad shape, but I don't know the extent of his injuries. I think he fell. I'm going to hook him up to the winch." All sneakiness or caution were gone from her voice, it was time to act. There was a soldier down, and she *would* save someone!

As she gave her report, Hailey unhooked herself from the carabiner and gingerly reached behind Alton to clasp it onto the belt of his suit.

A discordant noise snapped her to attention. The metallic pinging coming from above was somehow out of time with the rest of the ambiance.

She raised her pistol toward the overhead junction while attempting to use the panel as some semblance of cover. Except, no fire and death rained down from above.

The sound was also gone. Had she imagined it?

No, there was something moving up there. She could *feel* that she was being watched—a slight twitch and tingle on the back of her neck that made her fine hair stand on end.

I need to get us out of here. Doesn't matter what is or isn't lurking in these tubes.

She returned her attention to the task at hand. As she went to move Alton, she noticed that he was grasping a crystalline power relay. Upon closer inspection, she noticed the blank spot in the open access panel where he'd yanked it out.

Well, that explains the system errors!

Alton had obviously used it as a way to signal them that he was trapped and needed help. That was one mystery solved. If only he had pulled the plug on something *less* significant to their survival. On the flip side, if it had been anything less critical, she may have ignored it while tending to more pressing issues. Then he'd be dead.

His cleverness constantly surprised her.

In two smooth movements, she grabbed the relay and plugged it back into the system.

One problem solved. Now for the rest.

"Hyko, cover the…" Her heart lurched.

It hurt *so much*! Life was never going to be the same without Jamaal's companionship. A significant portion of her adult years had been spent with him close at hand. More than a friend, as intimate as a lover. They had been *partners*. That was all gone now, quick as flipping a switch.

Nothing will ever fill this hole.

Mourning him wouldn't get her or Alton out from the tunnel. She tried to focus.

Their escape would be tricky. There was no safe way to cover herself and control the ascent of the unconscious lump of a man. They would be completely unprotected, but she didn't see a way around it.

"Doc, I'm going to make my way up first without the harness." Hailey began to shimmy up the metal shaft by bracing her feet and back against opposite walls. It was noisy, precarious, and if she slipped there would be no stopping her tumble down.

"Copy that, Captain," Mina acknowledged on the comm. "I just checked on Darin; all good there. Running back to the winch now. Just let me know."

As she neared the junction, her shoulders began to burn with the exertion of keeping herself wedged in the shaft. There was no good way to do the next part.

With a heroic shove, she launched herself up to the side of the junction opposite where she had heard the noise and grasped the ledge with her left hand. She smacked the wall hard, her shoulder and left side protesting the impact. Once stable, she quickly drew her pistol from her belt again and aimed it down the opposing tunnel. Nothing moved in the dimly lit metal tube. A quick scan of the other passageways showed little else of note.

The strain on her shoulder was becoming too much. She wasn't quite in the same shape she had been when she was a soldier, plus the thermalsuit added a considerable amount of weight. Bracing with her legs, she holstered her weapon and began pulling herself up into the shaft. As much as she was able, she listened to the area around her, hoping to avoid an ambush.

Finally, after what felt like an eternity exposed to easy assault, she rolled onto her back in the corridor, gasping in great puffs.

"Doc, I'm up. Ease Alton up slowly, please. That winch—"

The steel cable line screeched across the corner of the metal shaft as the winch activated, letting out an excruciating high-pitched whine. The line stopped suddenly, and Alton slammed into the side of the wall with a hollow *thud*.

"Easy, Doc!" Hailey bellowed into the comms. "That thing is meant to reel in *foking spacecraft*! Alton would be pissed if he found out you were calling him fat."

"Sorry! Shite, I'm so, so, so very sorry!"

Never had Hailey heard the doctor sound panicked, but

there it was. She wasn't sure she had ever heard her curse, either. *Not as unflappable as you appear, eh, Doc?*

The situation was so absurd, it actually made Hailey chuckle a little bit. As incongruent as a feeling as mirth could be, while all their lives hung by a thread—Alton's in particular. Yet, here she was laughing. Luckily, she wasn't transmitting over the comms. The doctor would likely demand some kind of psychological evaluation if she'd heard it.

Failing that assessment was a very real possibility, Hailey realized glumly.

Her amusement faded.

Tentatively, the cable began to draw Alton upward in lurching fits and starts, which was arguably worse than the initial jolt.

"Slowly. Light but *constant* pressure," Hailey urged.

In response to her coaxing, the cable began to grind at a uniform tone across the edge of the metal, and Alton rose toward her.

"There it is. Great job, Doc."

"Let me focus, Hailey!" There was genuine stress in Mina's voice. Like she was gritting her teeth while talking.

A sudden impulse drew Hailey's attention toward the adjacent shaft. She jerked her head to the side in time to see a shadow darting around a distant corner.

She drew her pistol again, as slowly as she dared, while she whispered into the comms, "I'm not alone down here, Mina. I'm going to clear Alton from the vertical shaft and then leave it to you."

How the rotund body was going to navigate the two corners was an issue she would have to ignore for now.

Sorry in advance for the beating, buddy!

Alton finally got within arms' reach, and Hailey braced

against the sides of the shaft as best she could, while keeping an eye bent toward the corner the mysterious figure had disappeared behind. Once she had a fistful of thermalsuit, she heaved with everything she was worth. Her muscles screamed at the awkward angle. Offering what little guidance she could, she left the bulk of the work to the winch to pull him over the edge. If he caught on the lip, there was a very significant risk of harming the old man.

Hailey hated how prone they both were to attack. Had she been the one waiting for an opportunity to strike, this was it. An easy two-for-one deal.

The last heave cleared Alton from the vertical shaft, with the exception of his right knee. There was a sickening series of wet snapping sounds as the limb caught, like breaking the ends off ripe celery stalks.

Hailey's stomach lurched. She rolled over with Alton, and their visors smashed into each other.

He was awake, his face stretched in rictus of an agonizing scream that was muffled by the sealed suit. His bloodshot eyes cast about wildly, obviously blinded by the pain. Hailey tried to restrain him, gripping him tightly as he thrashed, fighting unseen foes.

There wasn't time for this, they could be attacked at any moment.

Hailey then noticed that the lights inside his helmet had gone out. The suit had no power, which meant he was rapidly cooling. Cursing her carelessness, she tried to do the math on how quickly he would freeze to death in the supercooled conduits. There were too many variables, but she knew it wasn't long.

With as much strength as she could muster, she gripped his helmet and put their visors together. She exaggerated mouthing the words, "Get out now!"

The wild look faded somewhat, but tears streamed down Alton's cheeks, and she noticed trails of frost forming behind them.

"Doc, he needs out, quick!"

No response, except Alton was ripped from her like a leaf on the wind. She heard the thud of him hitting the junction and felt the reverberations of it under her body. That was going to leave a mark.

With little more time left than to snatch a quick breath, she leaped across the vertical shaft opening and propelled herself as quickly as she was able toward the corner where she had seen the figure.

Now that the initial crisis was over, she was furious. Lucky for her, she had someone to take it out on.

I'm coming for you!

CHAPTER 18

A LOUD *CWATHUMP* echoed through the access tunnel as Alton unceremoniously flew out of the shaft and tumbled to the floor. Mina shut off the winch, her relief turning to renewed concern when she saw his right leg sticking out at an unnatural angle.

Fingers of steam curled up from the evaporating ice particles that sparkled over his suit as Alton thrashed on the floor, trying desperately to get out of the garment.

Mina kneeled next to him and all but tore his helmet off. The hiss of the seal coming apart was punctuated by the loud, unrelenting, stream of curses issuing from the man like a torrid flood bursting through a dam.

She recoiled from the onslaught, her eyebrows shooting up her forehead to the point where it actually strained the skin. This was a master class in the use of obscenities.

Alton finally sucked in a breath, and bellowed one final, "FOK!" before passing out cold, his head, drooping softly to the floor.

He certainly swore like a soldier, though Mina hadn't heard from the man directly that he had served. "Well," Mina chided quietly, "I hope that made you feel better."

The thermalsuit was turning red around Alton's twisted knee.

Mina took a calming breath. *This is going to be messy.*

Her medical training kicked in, and she began cutting off the suit around the injured limb. The many layers and internal heating coils of the suit spread aside to reveal a ghastly injury. His kneecap had been peeled back, almost to the point of being completely removed. There was extensive bruising and a very apparent patellar tendon avulsion protruding from the wound. This would require facilities beyond her capabilities to repair, even with the aid of the autodoc.

Sounds of gunfire erupted from the access hatch. The shots came in rapid bursts of three, a total of twelve.

No screams or cries of pain.

"Captain?" Mina heard the quake in her voice, but she didn't care. She was no fighter. If something had happened to Hailey, there wouldn't be much that she could do by herself. The sudden gravity of their precarious situation fell fully on her shoulders.

There was no response.

Mina glanced around the room, looking for... what exactly? A weapon? She would have to stretch her memory to recall the last time she held anything in violence. Still, having *some* method to defend herself was the most prudent course of action, right?

"I'm headed back out, Doc." The somewhat garbled transmission from Hailey was a balm on Mina's rattled nerves. The captain's voice sounded tired; not injured or in distress, just exhausted. "I think... I don't know, Mina. I think I may need to talk to you. Professionally, if you know what I mean."

That was probably the most terrifying admission that Mina

had ever heard. The feeling of dread that had been tickling her neck was a sudden frigid deluge dumped down her spine.

"Okay, Hailey. Whatever you need." Thank everything that her mentors had drilled the importance of clinical separation into her tone. Every part of her insides were writhing with trepidation, but at least she had regained mastery of her own voice.

"Fokin' short n'curlies!" Alton suddenly exploded, a geyser of vulgarity mixed and spittle rising out of his red face.

The comment raised a lot of questions, but this wasn't the time to ask.

"How are you feeling, Mr. Kress?" Something about the nature of Mina's work always caused her to default to more formal address of her patients.

"Bomax, how do you think I'm feeling? I feel like twice-turned-over SHITE!" He sat up anyway, his usual calm demeanor suddenly replaced with that of a cantankerous old man. "What the bloody ass trails took you both so long? I had to rewire the suit to squeeze more time out of the thermal shielding!"

"I don't know what *any* of that means, and frankly, sir, I don't care to have it explained at the moment. What I can tell you is that we did our utmost to solve the *plethora of problems* we have been handed in short order." She hesitated as he began to inhale a great breath, but she headed off his forthcoming outburst with one of her own, "You've gone and right properly destroyed your leg, and possibly your brain from the cold. So, if you'd like to keep pissing straight for the last few years of your miserable life, I'd suggest you shut that mewling quim of a mouth you've got there and listen to me!"

Feeling quite proud of herself, she relished the absolutely stunned stupid look on his face. There were several words in there that she had *no* clue what they meant, having just been recently introduced to them by Alton, but she thought she used them right, based on the previous context.

"Yes," Alton coughed out. "Yes, ma'am." His tone was properly subdued now.

Hailey swung agilely out of the hatch, and she landed in what struck Mina as a heroic pose, with one knee down, fists pressed into the floorboards. Like the seasoned veteran she was, Hailey unsealed the helmet and stripped it off as she stood.

The look on her face was one that Mina had seen several times. It made her stomach drop.

Those were the eyes of the haunted. Of the survivors. Of the guilty.

Hailey was definitely not in a good place.

"Captain Suro, let me get Alton patched up enough to be comfortable. Then, we can talk."

—

Mina wouldn't characterize her chat with Hailey as particularly forthcoming, but the woman opening up emotionally to *any* degree was a big step. In the course of Mina's evaluation, she discovered that Hailey had torn a muscle in her shoulder and hyper-extended two of her fingers on her left hand during her excursion into the ducts. As expected, the injuries were shrugged off without so much as a request for a painkiller. She had finally gone off to bed for a quick rest.

Alton had settled into his disaster of a chair and was snoring peacefully, despite her recommendations for him to recuperate in his bunk. He swore up and down that he had never once fallen from the chair, sleeping or not. Mina didn't know how that was possible; the thing was a menace.

With every fire out, or banked for the time being, Mina found her way back to the infirmary. Darin's condition was unchanged.

Who would have thought that someone being in a coma still would be the bright side to a day?

That was not a great thought to have, as the ship's medical officer. It made her feel like she wasn't doing her job properly. She certainly *felt* like she was doing everything right, but so much had gone wrong. Was this her fault?

No, it was whoever was initiating these attacks. The notion that they were under constant threat from within was disconcerting at best, and downright debilitating at worst. Unfortunately, it was also quite easy to *forget*, as well.

With little to do for Darin, except check fluids—both in and out—which seemed within normal measures, Mina went up to the flight deck. Now that Alton had reclaimed his seat of power in Engineering, she'd be able to continue her work in an area that was a touch more familiar to her.

Half expecting to find Hailey lurking in the captain's seat despite her intention to get rack time, Mina cautiously opened the door. Thankfully, the room was empty.

The fact that she was, presumably, the only conscious person on the ship—which was host to a violent intruder—was not lost on her. As soon as she had checked the small room for any hidden foes, and finding none, she sealed the door from the inside. Hailey would have a fit if she came to the flight deck to find Mina locked inside; it was a significant breach of protocol. A reprimand from the captain was a risk she was willing to take.

There was a very real fear of being alone that Mina wasn't used to experiencing. Their ship suddenly felt very small, and very dangerous.

With just a few clicks, she transferred the altered sensor program to the pilot's station. No elegant scanning solution was jumping out at her. The previous sensor sweep she had initiated *still* had not calculated an approximate time to completion. Certainly not great news. At this rate, the calculation would run for months.

The primary issue was, in fact, relatively straightforward. The ship had internal sensor arrays to monitor life-support systems and the crew, but it was only applicable in the *habitable* portions of the ship. These monitoring systems were quite limited in size and scope, only scanning for a narrow band of data within a portion of the ship. The more sophisticated sensor arrays were on the exterior of the vessel, directed outward into space. Even if she could finish the sweep in a timely manner, it wouldn't provide a clear picture of their own ship.

If only there was a way to look at their ship from a remote vantage…

That's it!

There *was* a way! The *Andvari* had a handful of small probes, which the captain normally reserved for delicate or dangerous wreck exploration—containment leaks or other kinds of hazards that made a boots-on-hull approach too risky. Mina had never actually *used* one before and didn't know the first thing about it.

It was her best shot.

Backing out of the ship sensor array menus, she tracked down the probe command tree. It was completely foreign to her. If she had any other options at her disposal, she'd abandon the effort in favor of a tried-and-true approach. As it stood, though, it was the probes or bust.

After experimenting with a few exploratory commands, and accidentally initiating a firmware reset on one of the probes—oops—she thought she had a basic enough understanding on how to deploy them. Now it was just a matter of setting the target and the range for the scanners to process. Which, why hold back at this point? Desperate times called for *all* the sensors.

The process turned out to be somewhat simple, and everything appeared to be properly set. Of the four probes, one was dormant during its reboot, and three would go out and do independent broad-spectrum scans of the *Andvari* in two passes. They would upload their data, and the ship's computer would process it into a multilayered spectral image. Seemed reasonable enough.

As she committed the flightpaths and programmed the three probes, a flashing button lit up in the bottom right corner: 'Deploy'.

Something about that giant, bold, bright-red flashing button made her anxious. Had she done this correctly? How much of this should she have asked permission to use?

Hesitation was the patient-killer.

She smashed the button with her teeth clenched tightly. *Here goes nothing!*

Indicators appeared on the augmented HUD, showing the crisscrossing arc flightpaths of the probes that she had programmed. As the sensors started streaming data, her filters began to piece together the various bits of spectral information that was collected. It was a considerable amount of data, but this is what probes were designed to do. Regardless, it was a much quicker process than her ship sensor sweep idea would have been.

The progress bar was screaming toward completion by the

time the probes had finished their first full circuit around the *Andvari*. No actual images were visible yet, as the data was crunched in the background, so she just sat and watched the data stream across the console while wringing her hands in worry.

Well, there wasn't much to do at this point other than wait. Might as well do said waiting with a hot cup of tea.

That decision made, she turned from the screen and unsealed the door, which immediately snapped open.

Mina screamed.

Clenched fist raised, ready to bludgeon her, and a savage snarl twisting his face, Alton stood mere inches from her.

"Stars, girl!" The bellow had a slight accent she couldn't place, an uncharacteristic slip from the old curmudgeon. "I about bashed your face in. Why was this door locked?"

The room wobbled from the sudden increase in her blood pressure; she felt a touch faint. From the rabbit-like thundering in her chest, her heart must be near to bursting.

"You could've *knocked*, Alton!" The words came out a breathy rasp as she tried to regain some of her composure.

The confused expression on his face made it pinch in and resembled a hairy prune.

"Why would I do *that?*" A simple question, but so very much *him.*

"Never mind, what are you doing here? You should be resting!" She jumped back into doctor-mode when she realized he was leaning heavily on a bent-up piece of metal conduit to keep the pressure off his damaged leg.

"Rest," he harumphed loudly through his frazzled beard, "no one's got time for that!"

Then he noticed the data streaming across the console and the conspicuous probe targets still circling around the screen with flashing targeting reticles highlighting them.

"I deployed the probes," she admitted boldly. May as well attack it head on.

Alton had been drawing in a large breath, probably to launch into a tirade. With her forthright admission his teeth clicked back together, and he grunted instead.

"I see that." Was all he said, in a rolling grumble that reminded Mina of a distant thunderstorm.

Something about his tone irked her. While he was taking a nap and trying to freeze to death down in the engineering section, *she* was the one that was trying to save all of their asses! How dare he? How DARE he! Their Captain was fast asleep, their security officer had airlocked himself after having some kind of nervous breakdown, the ships engineer was trying to kill himself playing hero, and Darin had been attacked by some kind of hostile trespasser.

In a flash she, was ready to break her icy exterior and yell Alton down, wounded or not! He wouldn't even think to…

"Smart."

Wait, what?

With all the grace of a rolling square boulder he hobbled over to the console and poked a few commands. Then nodded to himself. "Well done. I should've thought of this before. Hailey's always so bomaxed frugal with these probes, I sometimes forget we even carry them." His face dropped. "Oh, you bomaxed fool!"

What happened to the praise?! Mina's face flushed. "Sorry, Alton, I—"

"No, not you. Me. The relay I pulled… shite!" He began tapping commands rapidly on the console.

Mina looked over his shoulder to trying to see what was the matter, but nothing jumped out to her untrained eyes.

"What's wrong, Alton?" she asked softly after almost a minute of him working without offering any kind of explanation.

"The power fault caused a micro-failure in the antimatter containment hold. With the PEM offline, the system defaults to bleeding off antimatter to prevent a single massive breech."

"What does that mean for us?"

"I don't know yet." He didn't look up from his work, but he blew a puff of hot breath through his beard.

A ship's mechanical systems were as much a mystery to Mina as neurosurgery would be to most people. It sounded like there was good news mixed in with the bad—that the ship's safety measures were functioning properly. Nonetheless, leaking antimatter didn't sound great.

After two more minutes of furious typing and numerous swears, Alton let out a long sigh of relief. "Stars, that was close."

"What happened?"

"That venting safety feature was meant for instances when a ship is traveling under thrust. We'd matched drift with this infernal starship buffet, so we're barely moving, cosmically speaking. An antimatter cloud had built up around us, and we're incredibly lucky there wasn't a spontaneous annihilation reaction. Certainly, if we'd initiated a full burn of the drive while in the cloud, we wouldn't be here to have this conversation right now."

Mina gulped. "Ah." She paused. "Uh, but we haven't moved. So...?"

"I've temporarily disabled the drive and have stopped the venting. We will be clear from the dangerous area by the time the lockout is up."

She nodded. "Crisis averted, then."

The scan data was compiling on the screen. Alton looked it over, and a spark suddenly ignited in his eyes. "Of all the bomaxed craziness."

Mina's heart skipped a beat. "Oh no. What now?"

Alton shook his head incredulously. "The antimatter cloud coupled with the other environmental factors seems to have created a slight spatial distortion around the ship. This scan data is coming in more like a transdimensional data capture."

"That's… interesting." She didn't really know what that meant in practice, but she was just happy to hear that the ship wasn't about to explode and that no equipment had been damaged in the antimatter cloud.

The old engineer stroked his chin. "The flight pattern for the probes is well done. Should punch out the results much quicker than if you had just used a single."

Isn't that the point of having multiple probes? She didn't say it out loud, but it definitely made her feel a little snarky.

"I hope I'm not around when Hailey realizes you've blown all her probes though." He blew a chuckle through his beard, but it sounded half-hearted. Like, almost as if he were doing it for her benefit.

"What do you mean?"

He looked at her incredulously.

"The probes are single use and crazy-expensive. They burn through all their power scanning and sending data. Once that's done, they usually drift off once they lose power and their navigation systems malfunction." He eyed her skeptically. "You didn't know that, did you?"

She gulped reflexively.

Then he did laugh, uproariously. Such was the extent of his mirth that he doubled over and almost fell flat on his face, the makeshift crutch tangling in his shoulders and legs and causing him to wince in pain between chortles.

The sight was simultaneously infuriating, and infectious.

Mina soon found herself chuckling lightly alongside him. It felt good to laugh again. The last few days had been nothing but nail-bitingly tense, soul-wrenchingly painful, and an overshadowing sense of hopelessness had washed over them all. This little bit of levity seemed to reinvigorate her somehow. Maybe there was hope for them? Quite possibly they could survive this and save Darin at least. Maybe even collect enough salvage to pay off the ship and make Jamaal's tragedy not in vain. Not worth it—never that. But at least not worth *nothing*.

Then they both noticed the image fuzzing into existence on the screen.

"Holy mother of…"

Mina left Alton standing at the console gaping and she ran faster than she'd ever moved in her entire life. The corridor blitzed by in a blur of steel.

"Hailey!" Her scream echoed around her as she sprinted. The terror in her voice gave her goosebumps. Distantly, she realized she had never been so scared of anything before in her life.

That's when *it* attacked the ship.

CHAPTER 19

HAILEY JOLTED AWAKE. The pain instantly made her feel woozy, causing the room to spin even while flat on her back in bed. Residue of whatever dream she had been having made it seem like she had heard someone scream.

Blood thumped painfully along the sides of her head. Even the dim light in the room was excruciating, hazy rings surrounding each fixture. She squinted, trying to clear her vision.

A sudden jolt to the ship tossed her several centimeters into the air and spilled her to the floor. She groaned from where she landed; that bump to the head certainly wasn't going to help things.

Another impact rumbled along the length of the ship.

What in the...?

The thought was unfinished as a massive shudder tossed her against the far wall of her quarters. Alarms sounded and warning lights flared to life.

"Hailey!" Even through the sealed door, the chorus of sirens, and the metal grinding on metal protestations of the *Andvari*, she heard the scream. It sent a sudden chill down her back, and a flush of heat to her chest.

With a hiss and an onslaught of sound, the door opened to reveal Mina.

A sudden discomfort clenched at Hailey's heart, like a fist tightening around it. She had seen this look before—normally on the faces of soldiers, bathed in firelight, blood, and death. Hailey flashed to a hundred moments just like this one. The wild animalistic portion of her mind wrestled with the vain attempt to hold on for just one more minute, a few more seconds. She had heard stories of soldiers drowning and attacking their rescuers in their hysteria.

Mina had that look in her eyes at this very moment.

"Doctor Hurn, I need you to calm down," Hailey said, in her broker-no-shite CO tone. She stood to face the frantic woman.

"But Hailey, you haven't seen... You don't... It's *out there!*" As she spoke, her voice rose in both octave and speed.

There was a protocol in the military to how to handle these moments, and Hailey had always deployed it with great efficiency.

With a full backswing and open palm, she *slapped* Mina across the face. The impact caused her head to whip to the side, just in time to catch the full-bodied backswing across the other cheek.

As expected, the woman went slightly limp standing there, her knees giving way. Hailey caught her under the arms and stepped her over to the edge of the bed. There, she let her fall onto her rump.

As she kneeled, Hailey shook out her hand. Stars, slapping the woman's face had been like whacking a boulder. All hard angles and bone.

"Would it kill you to eat an extra ration every now and

then?" Hailey said, kneeling in front of the stunned woman as she attempted to focus.

"Wha… what…" A dribble of blood had begun to form on a broken edge of Mina's lip, and both cheeks were beginning to blossom with a wonderful ruddy brown-red. Somehow, it made the woman's already enviably luminous skin look even more fetching.

The ship rumbled distantly. While the initial sirens had been silenced, likely by Alton somewhere else on the ship, the flashing lights continued their persistent pulsing.

"Focus," Hailey said sternly.

"You… you *hit* me?" It was posed as a question, but the incredulity it was laced with made it half accusation.

"Yes, I did. Old Tararian Guard trick to cure FOF Syndrome."

"FOF…?" Mina brought her hand up to wipe away trickle of blood as it left her lip and began to slide down her chin.

"Fight or Flight, battle-panic. Whatever you want to call it." Hailey stood and offered her hand to the seated doctor. "You ready to face this?"

All the rosy color she had just worked so hard to get back into the woman fled.

"Hailey, there's something you need to see," she breathed.

Back straight, shoulders back, Hailey said forcibly, "Whatever it is, I will face it and fight it to my last breath. The question I have is, am I doing it alone, or are you coming with me?" She glanced meaningfully at her proffered hand.

Mina considered for a moment, gave a worried shake to her head, then she closed her eyes and grasped Hailey's hand in a firm grip.

Hailey smoothly pulled Mina to her feet, and the two women stalked out into the hall together.

"Tell me everything you know." Hailey picked up the pace to a light jog.

Mina fell in beside her, huffing out her answers as they ran. "I used your probes... er."

Hailey looked at her, brows drawn down in disapproval.

With a guilty smile, Mina continued, "Sorry about that. Yeah, used all but one, and was going to try to get a scan of the intruder..."

There was a long dramatic pause. It drew on until Hailey began to get irritated.

Then she continued, "I found it, Hailey."

It?

Something about the way she said it sounded ominous.

That clenching feeling came back, and a frigid tightness crawled up the left side of her neck and into her jaw.

"What is 'it'?" That seemed like the obvious question.

"I... don't know, but it's bad." After a moment, she added, "It's *very bad*."

The door to the flight deck was open, revealing Alton half-standing, half-hugging the back of the pilot's chair. His hair and beard were a tangled mess, like he had been sleeping face first in a pillow, and his brows were drawn together so hard they were touching.

"We have two escape pods. I think we need to move Darin in and..." Alton began without preamble.

"We are not abandoning ship until I've seen what..."

Then she saw it.

On the console was an overlaid spectral imaging data composite of the *Andvari* and the surrounding space.

Clutching the outside of their ship was the... *something...* that had everyone so worked up.

Invisible to the naked eye but clearly represented on the

broad-spectrum scan, an enormous creature had entwined itself around their craft, its mass of ethereal tentacles dwarfing the *Andvari* like a grain of rice in a giant's hand. It seethed with power—a magnitude reminiscent of mythical monsters she had read about as a child. Ancient. Magnificent. Deadly.

The scale of it was almost beyond comprehension. Larger than the biggest craft she had ever seen, by a factor of ten. Maybe hundreds!

No physical data had been collected, but the broad-spectrum scan had picked up several readings that extended beyond the observable reality of spacetime. The area around the ship was one massive spatial anomaly, registering like a ship about to execute a jump. Except, this *monster* was coming through it. It was coming for *them*.

The *Andvari* rocked and shuddered in the thrashing, twisting grip.

A shower of sparks and a loud thunderclap sounded from the console, and reflexively they all dropped to the deck. Except for Alton, who more or less just let gravity do the work.

Pain suddenly gripped Hailey. Blinding, searing agony bored in behind her eyes. Someone was screaming, and it took Hailey a moment to realize it was her own voice. Next to her, Alton's eyes were rolled back in his head and he was writhing on the deck in a seizure. Mina moaned nearby with her hands gripping the sides of her head.

As sudden as it had started, the pain diminished, then retreated. All three of them were left in various levels of anguish on the floor.

Through the open door, Hailey could hear something else. A distant sound, echoing down the metal corridor from the aft of the ship. A scream.

Darin!

Desperately, she struggled to her feet, battle energy surging through her.

Pain she could handle; she had been trained by her instructors to endure the worst. Cemented in the core of her very being.

But her maternal instincts were also in play. Nothing— *nothing*—would stand between her and her suffering child.

Her vision swam, echoes of the pain causing her body to quake with the aftereffects of the intense distress. She felt drunk, stumbling and staggering down the hallway as it shuddered under the leviathan's grasp.

There was no way for her to really tell whether or not the entity was still actually twisting them about, or if her disorientation was her own warped senses from the pain she had just endured. Something was telling her it was all in her head. But even if it *had* stopped, how long would their reprieve last?

The doorway to the infirmary loomed ahead, and she staggered up to it.

When it opened, she was immediately stunned by the level of damage done to this section of the ship. Pressure lines had ruptured, spewing environmental gas mixtures into the small room. An entire cabinet had been torn from its mounting to the bulkhead. Thankfully, the falling case had missed her prone son, but from the looks of things, just barely so.

Darin's back arched taut against the restraints holding him to the exam bed. His face was purple from prolonged screaming. Blood dribbled down his arms where the thick belting was cutting into his skin.

Hailey's couldn't readily see anything attacking him or that might be causing him pain. Maybe he had suffered the same mental attack they had. Could this be related to his coma? How would someone in a coma handle being telepathically assaulted? From what Hailey understood, you had to be conscious to have any kind of innate defense against such things. The pain in his howling voice broke her heart into a million pieces.

Hailey ran to his side. Any attempts to touch or provide comfort seemed to make the screaming intensify. There was nothing she could do. Nothing she had been able to do for Jamaal, either.

For the first time in her life, she felt truly helpless. She wasn't able to help *anyone*! Some ship's captain she made. Maybe she deserved all this. To lose everything, so close to the riches she and her son had always dreamed of finding.

"I'm sorry, Darin," she blurted out through choked-out tears. "I did the best I could!"

She rested her head on the table next to her son as he screamed, only ceasing to raggedly inhale another breath. At some point, he had screamed so hard he had torn the flesh in his throat, and subtle gurgle sounds mixed with his agonizing wails.

Then, it stopped suddenly. His teeth clicked shut and he fell limp to the table.

A crunching feeling hit her hard in the chest, like a delicate vase shattering. She tentatively reached out and checked for a pulse.

Thank the stars!

His heart was beating strong as ever, thumping wildly from the outbursts and pain. Maybe he had just passed out from lack of oxygen from the yelling, or from shock. Or, maybe whatever attack had pressed into his mind had finally subsided. Whatever the reason, she was thankful it was over.

For now.

"Hailey," a gruff voice said behind her.

Turning, she found Alton leaning heavily on the doorway, with a strip of metal gripped white-knuckled in his hand to keep himself supported on his injured knee. Blood stained his mustache and beard a blackish red, where it had dribbled out his nose and down his chin.

"Alton, what's happening?"

There was such sturdiness to him, it was something she had come to depend on over the years way more than she had ever realized. Even now, despite being attacked by something the size of a *foking planet*, he drew himself up as straight as his injury would allow.

"I don't know, Hailey, and frankly I don't care." He harumphed loudly through his beard, cleared his throat, and spat a disturbingly large glob of bloody phlegm onto the glass-littered floor.

"Is that... *thing* what's been messing with us on the ship?"

Alton grunted a noncommittal response. "It's not entirely *here*. From the looks of the image, it's reaching down from a higher dimension. No telling what a being like that could do to electrical systems or people's minds."

"Our ghost."

The ship shuddered again.

"I don't understand why it didn't physically interact with us before," Alton said. "Maybe the scan made it angry."

Hailey's heart pounded in her ears. "Did it make all those replicas of our ship?"

"If I had to guess, yes."

"But *why*?"

Nothing about the situation made sense. Assuming the creature was behind all the strange goings on, it had exhibited a varied and bizarre set of behaviors. From messing with their perception to small-scale destruction, it was strange that it hadn't exerted more power.

"Why hasn't it destroyed us already?" Hailey asked. "We may as well be an ant compared to it. Yet it's mostly just been in our minds, messing with us."

"Your guess is as good as mine. It's almost like it was…"

Realization dawned on her. "Studying us," she completed for him, barely above a whisper. "What is this thing? Why would it care about *us*?"

"Doesn't matter. What I do know for sure is we need to get off this ship. Like, yesterday."

She couldn't agree more.

"How?" Hailey asked, trying to quiet the other questions swirling in her mind. "Our escape pods don't have the range we'd need to get back into permitted space. Not before we all asphyxiate, at least."

Alton chewed at his lip in thought, his brows drawn down. He had that look he always got when he knew she wasn't going to like the answer to the question.

"Spit it out, Alton. You'll find I'm not in the mood to argue on this one."

"I have some ideas, but you're not going to like them very much." The words tumbled out slowly, reluctantly.

"Only one way to find out."

Alton nodded slowly, watching her closely through bushy brows. "You'll have to suit up and go get us a working PEM."

He was correct; she already hated this idea.

"Out *there*? Are you insane?"

Not only was it a bad idea, but it was also likely pointless, anyway. They hadn't even *located* a functional PEM yet. Stars, she wasn't even sure if they *could* now. Hailey had figured they'd do an EVA and search a few of the derelict craft at a time. That was absolutely out of the question now.

"We can do this, Hailey. You're just going to have to trust me." Abruptly, his shoulders sagged and his gaze dropped to the floor; even his wild beard seemed to deflate. "Have I ever steered you wrong?"

No, he was steadfast and reliable as the stars.

Still…

There was nothing she could do except nod, which he returned brusquely.

"I'll be down in Engineering. I don't know why this thing stopped it's attack, but we need to move quick before it does so again."

Time was not on their side, Hailey knew this, but she watched the older man hobble down the hallway and out of sight before she could pull herself into action. While she didn't exactly know what his plan was, she could tell just from the way he was acting that it wasn't at all something she was going to like; he had been correct in that regard. He was *usually* right, though, as bomaxed annoying as it was. As uncharacteristic as it was for her, she was going to take a backseat on this one.

She stretched her back out. It snapped, ground, and clicked as it usually did—too many injuries sustained over one lifetime and not enough money for the good repair shops.

As she left the infirmary, Hailey thumbed the comms console next to the door. "Mina, find us a PEM on one of those starships. I'm headed to the port-side airlock to suit up for an EVA to retrieve it. I'll need you to chair for me."

Hailey didn't even wait for a response. She was suddenly so tired.

At this point it didn't even matter if she *had* a second chair for the op. There was something that needed doing, and it fell to her. That was fine; she had broad shoulders for exactly this reason.

The ship was in as rough shape as she was. Lights flashed, pressure releases fired all along the corridor, which created a carnival house-of-horrors type effect. Once the pride of all her hard-earned credits, the hope for a legacy to pass on to her son, now it was just a battered ruin. Much like she was.

The walk to the airlock prep room was slower than she felt like she should be moving. Her motions had a weight to them, like it just wasn't worth the effort. Not that she was reluctant; far from it. Much like her ship, it was almost like the energy had been sucked from her.

In the airlock prep room, she was met with a solitary EVA suit hanging on the wall, since Darin's had been cut apart after his accident. She stared at the name patch affixed to the suit's chest: 'HYKO'.

An immense sense of loss welled in her chest again. He'd been there to look after her in life, so it was fitting that she'd wear his suit now in an effort to save what remained of the life they'd built together. She thought he'd like that, wherever he was.

"This one is for you, Jamaal. Help us out if you can." Half prayer, half plea, she stepped into the suit and began the process of sealing it up.

CHAPTER 20

THE TWINKLING SPECK of light Mina was tracking on the viewscreen drifted slowly toward the boundary of her visual range. She flipped a switch on the control console, and a reticle appeared on top of a magnified image of Hailey racing toward their potential salvation.

Alton was relatively certain that the PEM Mina had identified through a weak power signature would be compatible with their ship's systems. Getting the main power up and running again meant they would have jump drive capabilities again, once they could get close enough to a nav beacon for a lock. It was their best hope of escaping from this place of nightmares.

Unfortunately for them all, the recent attack on the *Andvari* had severely damaged their sub-light pion drive, so the ship was currently free-floating. That made the EVA particularly dangerous, since there was no way to adjust trajectory. Hauling the PEM and loading it at speed, and with no navigation systems to negotiate the exchange… Well, it was going to be dicey at best.

In any other circumstance, Mina would be nervous about

overseeing her first EVA. With everything the way it currently was, there was no other choice; nerves were out of the question. It was like doing her first amputation in the field. A doctor never *wanted* to take a person's limb, but once the bone saw was out, it was a foregone conclusion. Walking Hailey through her EVA was much the same; she was in the command chair now whether she liked it or not.

The reticle provided relative and actual velocity, distance from target, and the angle of Hailey's approach. The captain was a pro; all of her adjustments were minimal and only when absolutely necessary.

"Looking good out there, Captain."

All things considered, it had been relatively quiet since the enormous entity had been unmasked. The tremors throughout the ship had subsided, and no one had reported seeing any more shadowy figures or strange sounds.

The results of the scan hadn't yielded *all* bad news, she supposed. They had ruled out an actual intruder on board the *Andvari*; the only living, physical beings visible in the scan had been the crewmembers. So, at least there wasn't a stowaway... not that the fact some nightmarish *thing* had them in its clutches wasn't a big enough problem.

Mina couldn't help wondering if this was all for nothing. How could they run from something so *immense*? It was like a guppy trying to flee from a shark. Pointless. Inevitable. But they had to try, right? That was the deal with survival; the instinct to keep life going, even for a moment longer, was hardwired in. The mind wanted to survive, whether or not the heart thought it was possible. That was something she had experienced a lot in her profession—the death of spirit before an expiration of a body.

"Approaching the target."

The sound of Hailey's voice over the comms shook Mina from her wandering thoughts. Something about the abstract nature of a physician always caused her to be a bit pensive when lives were on the line.

"Sounds good," she said after a brief pause. "Grab it and get back."

"How's my relative vector?" Hailey prompted.

After a quick scan of the data, Mina replied, "You're plus two point six k-m-s and delta eleven degrees."

"Not too shabby. It's all going to be lost once I get in the vessel. My readings here are showing it's matched velocity to the *Andvari*. Can you confirm?"

Not having the same level of experience as everyone else who staffed the flight deck, it took Mina a minute to locate the proper menus. After keying in the required commands, a new tracking reticle blossomed to life on the screen and illuminated a non-visible target off in the distance.

The relative velocity of the spacecraft showed as zero. That couldn't be. Their own speed had been all over the place in the attack from the giant 'space leviathan', for lack of better term.

It gave her a chill of trepidation.

Verify and cross-check.

The comm clicked on, private line for Engineering designated by three rapid clicks, "Alton, you there?"

"Mostly. How can I help you, Doc?" At least he was back to his usual grumpy and distracted self.

"Have you adjusted our velocity in any way since the... uh... attack?"

There was a drawn-out pause. Mina was just beginning to wonder if she should repeat herself when Alton's voice came across again. "Hold on."

Wasn't that a simple 'yes or no' question? Nothing like

being trapped in the jaws of a monster to make one a bit snippy when it came time for patience.

While she waited, Mina checked on Hailey. The reticle was still visible, but the speck no longer was. The two targeting reticles were barely a finger's width apart now on the display, and closing quickly. Hailey would be boarding the wreckage very soon.

"Doc, are you seeing what I'm seeing down here?" Alton's voice had a curiously terrified quality to it. "The grid of ships is locked to us. Perfectly."

"That's what we're trying to confirm up here. Our vector has changed since our initial approach to them... and they've matched to *us*." Being relatively certain of something and confirming it with an expert were two totally different things.

"That's correct."

Bomax!

She flipped back to Hailey, "Captain, I confirmed, and so did Alton. You're correct. We are V-locked to the target."

"Acknowledged," was all that came back.

If it wasn't for everything else that she had experienced, Mina would have said that the uninhabited target ship perfectly matching their velocity was impossible. Not only was it *that* ship, but the *entire grid* of ships that had adjusted to match their flight path so as to appear motionless. There was no doubt left in her mind that the space monster was behind it, though she had no idea what it meant.

The two reticles flashed orange; a proximity warning. Then they went red and merged into a single target—the duplicate *Andvari*.

"This is unreal," Hailey said over the comms. "It's almost an exact replica. Even the door codes are the same."

"I don't like this at all, Hailey. Maybe we should come up

with another plan." Nothing about this was feeling right. Nothing *at all*! There was a practice in medicine: if too many coincidences lined up in your favor, you're overlooking something. They were missing something major, of that she had no doubt.

"Too late, Mina. I'm here, and going to grab this thing and get back. I won't sightsee, I promise."

The flippancy of the comment made Mina chuckle. Here she was out in space with some kind of never-before-seen space monster, and the captain was cracking jokes. Hailey was brave, or absolutely insane. Maybe a little of both?

"Okay, I'm nearing the engineering bay," Hailey said. "I can tell that this was built to *look* like the *Andvari*, but it isn't. There are some really old components in here. But it's a close approximation, for sure."

"I thought you said no sightseeing?" Mina wish she didn't sound so scared.

Hailey chuckled over the open line. "Just keeping my eyes open and communicating, Doc. Keep your pants on."

That had been something Mina had noticed as she spent more time with her new crew. The more stressful, terrifying, and calamitous the situation, the more *military* they all seemed to get. This had been true for every single one of them, even Darin, but in no one was it so apparent as with Hailey herself. Even her humor changed, became more barracks-level-banter. Casual disregard for fear, like she couldn't be bothered with it, and it was silly that others allowed it.

Not that Mina was some fainting ninny. She had seen some serious shite in her day and knew she had a tougher stomach than most. Even so, comedy was the furthest from her mind as she could push it.

Nevertheless, as much as Mina hated to admit it to herself,

the casualness with which the captain approached their situation was somehow immensely comforting. If Captain Suro was unperturbed by what was happening, and joking, well… it couldn't be *that* bad. Right?

Unless it's all a front. That was a very real possibility.

Mina *loathed* being managed.

Moreover, she absolutely detested that it was working.

— — —

The eerily similar engineering bay door snapped open in response to Hailey's input command. While not an exact replica, the craft was close enough to make it easy for Hailey to identify what she needed and how to approach it.

Silently thanking whatever madman had put this together out of scrap—perhaps the work of the transdimensional leviathan?—she navigated over to the PEM. The unit was still registering energy activity, according to her handheld scanner.

"Alton, I've found the PEM, and it's functional."

"That's great news, Hailey. You need to extract the core. Remove the pins and withdraw the unit. No need to be too terribly gentle with it—it's suspended in a vacuum and far from delicate. Rip it out and get back."

Hailey got to work. Using an impact hammer she had carried on her belt from the tool locker, she began ripping the restraining pins off the cage housing. With Alton's assurances that she didn't have to be surgical, she opted for haste over care.

"Hailey," the comms crackled to life with a terrified whisper from Mina. "I don't mean to alarm you, but I think something is happening over here."

That was ominous-sounding coming from the usually poised doctor.

"I'm half done, Doc, hang in there."

No response.

With renewed urgency, Hailey gritted her teeth and managed to unseat the crystalline voydite structure from the cage. It was difficult in zero-G. Every subtle push or twist caused her body to react poorly. It wound up being a constant dance of to-and-fro that could drive a person crazy. The discarded bolts pinballed around her within the engineering bay silently.

The thickly insulated gloves were designed with fine-motor needs in mind, but still there was enough dexterity loss that it made her feel clumsy, especially when time was of the essence. As bolt after bolt was removed, the power core began to jiggle in its housing.

Just a few more!

The PEM finally drifted free of its moorings. The voydite crystal nanostructures that composed its casing were an interesting blend of purple and black structures blended together to form a simultaneously swirling and crisscrossed pattern. It was a fascinating hunk of technology, but the only thing she cared about right now was that it could power her ship and get them out of this horrific nebula.

Using the padded case she had strapped to her back for the purpose of carrying the unit back safely, she secured it to herself and shoved off the now empty housing cage with her feet to glide toward the exit.

The good thing about zero-G was that it was easy to build up significant velocity with very little exertion. The corridors streaked by in a blur. This had been Darin's favorite thing in all the universe; that was something she had gotten from his father. It tugged at Hailey's emotions a bit to think about.

The open airlock door whizzed by her and she was met

with open space. The nebula cast the area in its garish myriad of colored lights, but the high contrast of it also blocked out all of the neighboring stars. The effect was somewhat disconcerting, as it appeared brighter and darker simultaneously. Fortunately, her helmet had a built-in ship tracking system, which outlined the *Andvari* lurking a few thousand meters away.

"HAILEY!" The voice peeled like thunder inside her helmet, so loud and high-pitched it made her wince.

A rippling of space around the ship, almost like a heat shimmer, began to form. The waves stretched from just above the ship and undulated far out into distant space. An energy, like jade-colored static, billowed and rolled following the odd shimmer.

It reminded Hailey of the Rift.

Her blood ran immediately cold.

The leviathan tore through the dimensional veil, sliding into the prime-material plane with a bulbous eruption of energy made physical.

Fear gripped Hailey like a vise. All she could do was stare. What engulfed her ship was equal parts magnificent and petrifying. With its dozens of tentacles writhing around a central core of iridescent energy-laced abdomen, it vaguely resembled some form of deep sea creature. There were no visible eyes, mouth, or features. Just the arms and the main body.

Several of the tentacles began to tear and bash around the *Andvari*. The reticle in her helmet's HUD began to flash as damage reports listed along the sides.

A subtle hiss sounded in her head momentarily before utter quiet. Communications were down between her and the ship.

As she slammed the throttle wide-open for the small thrusters on her suit, she hoped there'd be something to get back to. The thought of being adrift in space didn't sit well with her. Especially since Jamaal…

All she could do was navigate closer to the assault.

Small explosions from damage to the ship illuminated the underside of the beast. It seemed to *draw in* the burning gas and somehow absorb it.

"What the fok *is this thing*?" Nobody could hear her, she knew. The magnitude of the statement echoed through the silence of her helmet.

They were dead.

There was no way to fight this thing.

It could devour a planet if it wanted.

All she could do was try to get back to the ship and *run*!

CHAPTER 21

FIRE BURST FROM the nearby panel in a shower of heat, pressure, and hot twisted bits of metal. Mina was sure there was sound that accompanied it, but all she could hear was a painful ringing in her ears. Decompression warning indicators were flashing all over the flight deck. It was time to seal this room off before she died.

She scrambled on all fours like a wild animal, unable to hear and her vision swimming between the violent concussions. Smoke was rapidly filling the central corridor in great black billows issuing forth from the flight deck.

Molten bile rose into the back of her throat, and she felt like she was going to vomit. She reached up from the floor, looking for the emergency seal lever on the door. It was too high; she'd have to go up into the smoke layer to pull it.

She did vomit then—a dainty little sick-up that would've probably been considered cute by most standards. It burned her throat, nose, and eyes. Holding her breath and grasping wildly at the doorway, she was finally able to find the lever and half-pulled, half-fell with it in her hands back to the metal floor.

The bulkhead doors slammed shut with a thunderous boom of finality.

Oh good, sounds are coming back!

Everything had that distorted 'underwater' kind of sound to it, but she could faintly make out the tones of metal grinding against metal. The ship groaning in protest as it was mauled by their unseen assailant.

Desperate, suffering shock, and in a near state of panic, Mina gripped her handheld to her face and screamed into the comm, "We have to abandon ship!"

The indicator lit up, showing that she was receiving communications, but it was no use. She couldn't hear well enough yet to make out the voice of whoever had replied to her message.

"Alton, I'm going to ready the escape pods for evac!"

Again, the indicator flashed chaotically.

Another massive shudder rocked the craft like a leaf on a stiff breeze. It flung her against the far wall of the corridor. The impact was mostly to her shoulder, thankfully avoiding her head. Still, there was a cracking sound inside her skull, and an intense fiery pain shot through her shoulder into her arm and hand.

The surgeon in her immediately considered the damage. Probably fractured at a minimum, with additional tearing, bruising, and who knew what else? None of that mattered if they couldn't escape, though.

Mina ran, in a zigzagging and flailing path toward midship where the escape pods were. Thankfully, they were right next to the prep area for the airlock, so Hailey wouldn't have to travel far once she arrived.

With her hearing returning, Mina was beginning to be overwhelmed with the sheer *volume* of the sounds around her.

Alarms chimed, CACI calmly issued damage reports, the comms were blaring.

"Mina!" Hailey was roaring, "Do *not* activate the escape pods until we are all on the ship! Do you hear me?"

What *nonsense*! They were out of time!

This is what I always do, isn't it? Run away when things are at their worst.

The irony wasn't lost on her that she was running, yet again. Just like that fateful incident when her colleagues and patients were counting on her, but she'd bolted from the pressure. It cost her everything—her career, her social status, her future. Hunting space scrap was her penance.

Here she was again, running from another disaster. Leaving people to die, abandoning her patients so she had a better chance of living.

She didn't care. She was a survivor.

Hailey could take her chances on the *Andvari*, but Mina was getting out *now*!

The escape pod door opened with a hiss. The inside was a complicated mess of straps, emergency supplies, and high-powered beacon equipment.

Regrettably, Mina realized she knew next to nothing about escape pod protocols. She was aware that they couldn't jump to subspace and relied on mostly sub-light engines. So, the idea of programming a jump to immediate safety was impossible. They'd have to navigate away from the danger.

For a moment, she hesitated. Maybe Hailey was right and attempting to flee was a bad idea. These pods were mere lifeboats. Even a small bit of debris in their way could rip them to shreds, let alone this behemoth that was currently using their entire *ship* as a plaything.

Foolishness! They were so tiny compared to the *Andvari*

itself, the pods would be able to sneak away while the beast was distracted.

It doesn't need to just be me. She'd left patients behind before, and that decision had haunted her ever sense. But those were strangers, not the people she'd grown close to over the past year. She knew she had to run, but she didn't need to go alone.

Focus. You can get everyone out.

Reading over the posted protocols, which were obviously written by an engineer, Mina began the power-up sequence of Pod 1. As it initiated and did whatever it was that it had to do, she began to power up Pod 2 in the same way.

Then, she raced down the hall, illuminated by flashing amber and red warning lights.

The infirmary would never be the same. Just too much had been broken or damaged. The floor was completely littered with glittering shards of glass polymer, spilled pills, salves, and injectables—all the materials she'd managed to salvage from the previous onslaught in the infirmary. Now, there was nothing left to save.

Navigating the floor was a tricky feat. A pang of regret stung her chest. What she had done here, she had been immensely proud of. When she had first come on to the team, their infirmary had been little more than a rickety old table and some painkillers—a *lot* of painkillers.

Now, it was all ruined.

As quickly as she was able, she unfastened the restraints on Darin's arms, chest, and legs. A particularly bad lurch of the ship sent her sprawling across him. Pressed up against him as she was, she felt helpless. He was almost twice her body weight; how did she expect to get him to the escape pod?

With a heroic effort, she managed to get the boy into a

seated position and draped his arm over her shoulder. Another heave and she grunted as he slid off onto the floor, almost taking her with him. The kid was *solid*!

Mina began to half-carry, half-drag the limp figure of Darin across the floor. It wasn't long until his bare knees were leaving a crimson trail of blood behind him. Thankfully, the infirmary was a small room—little more than a closet really— and they were soon out into the hallway. Here, she propped him up against the bulkhead and picked the larger glass bits out of the spots where he had been dragged.

"Mina? MINA! I'm almost back. Don't do anything until I do. Stay focused! We *can* survive this if we work together!"

Hailey's voice penetrated Mina's panic for a brief instant. The woman was insane. They would be dead if they stayed here a minute longer than they absolutely had to.

Memories flooded back to her in a rush. Of fire, and blood, and bodies strewn about a triage center. Of a transport vessel crashing into a city center. Limbs, and bits of body flung about and draped over twisted metal like some macabre and bizarre work of art. It was the day she had lost everything...

Well. It didn't matter.

She wasn't going to suffer the same fate twice.

If Hailey and Alton wanted to stay, fine. They could stay. She was getting off this death trap, and likely never venturing out into space ever again.

CACI chimed in over the symphony of destruction, "Escape Pod 1 has calculated the nearest potential active sector and is prepared to launch." Followed by an identical message for Pod 2.

Perfect, time to go! Mina hauled Darin up as best she could. This time, without the height imparted from the table, she had to mostly drag him across the floor by his arm, face first, his hair hanging down to cover his features.

She had only gone a few meters before she had to stop and push sweaty hair out of her eyes, breath puffing out in great bursts of fog.

She glanced around the corridor. Ice crystals were beginning to form on the walls of the ship. Their environmental systems had been damaged, or the ship's hull had been breached deep enough to begin freezing the systems internally. Either way, it was a death sentence, both for the ship and anyone still on board.

Any doubt she had about fleeing vanished.

If it was the last thing she ever did, she would be getting off this ship!

She heard her comm activate again, as well as the ship-wide channel, "Alton, I think Mina is going to take one or both of the escape pods and try to flee. I need you to stop her!"

Again, the ship-wide channel clicked on, "Alton!"

There was no response.

The intersection that turned off into the prep room, airlock, and escape pods wasn't far away now. She could see it just ahead. Her arms burned from the effort of dragging Darin's dead weight down the corridor. Streaks of blood marked their trail back toward the infirmary.

CACI chimed in again, "Deck pressure critical."

As she rounded the corner, a dark figure detached itself from the wall and swung something at her. Her vision exploded in flickering silvery splinters of light. She heard more than felt her body hit the floor. The barely regulated nausea came roiling back and she gagged on bile deep in her throat, coughing and spluttering.

Several sets of feet swam in her blurred vision right in front of her face.

"Easy there, Doc. I don't want to have to put you down." Alton's voice had an eerie tone to it as it echoed inside her thudding head. "Just stay put and we'll leave it at the warning shot, okay?"

The hunk of conduit he had used as a crutch thumped on the metal floor as he made his way to the first escape pod. Not that she could *see* what he was doing—but she knew. He was powering it down, the fool!

Even the thought of trying to stand caused her to groan in agony. The dancing lights in her vision had diminished enough she could see, albeit just barely.

Darin groaned nearby where she had let him fall face-first onto the floor.

Blurrily, she attempted to focus on Alton, who was standing in the first pod, presumably going through the power-down sequence. Tears stung her eyes, both from frustration and pain. What was he *doing*? Why weren't they trying to escape? What was wrong with them?

Trying to think clearly was a challenge. She likely had a concussion.

There would only be one shot at this.

Hesitantly, she looked over at Darin. A pang of guilt stabbed through her. Abandoning patients seemed to be what she did in times of crisis. Some doctor she made. There was nothing for it; his mother was the one making the decisions here. Mina just refused to go along with it. She wasn't ready to die. Least of all like this.

Out of the corner of her eye, she noticed Alton glancing her direction. She stilled, faking unconsciousness. After a moment's assessment, he returned to his work. Vaguely, she could hear him mumbling to himself.

If she was going to make a move, this was the moment.

Summoning all the energy she could bring forth, Mina surged into a crouching position. Simultaneous with Alton's warning shout, she leapt toward the second escape pod's door. She hit the deck hard, face-first, the metal flooring abrading her cheekbone. With much more dexterity than she'd realized she possessed, she curled her legs up and let her momentum roll her fully into the pod.

"Mina, no!" Alton shouted.

Reaching up, she hit the switch to initiate launch.

The door sealed instantly, with a roaring hiss and thump.

Alton's distraught face appeared in the window, and she could faintly hear him pounding on the door. Thankfully, his shouts were completely muted by the thick doors.

A sob escaped her raw throat. Whether from relief or disgusted guilt, she couldn't be sure. But the levy broke.

The countdown sequence was already underway, and it was only fifteen seconds.

With the last scraps of her flagging energy, she pulled herself into one of the seats. The weight of her decision was falling heavily on her, sapping her will.

Still crying, she strapped herself in, the final restraint clicking closed a moment before the pod shuddered loose of the *Andvari.*

Just like that, she was free.

— — —

"*Fok!* Mina initiated Pod 2!" Alton bellowed through the comms.

Hailey was twenty meters from the airlock, but she noticed the spinning amber warning lights that indicated an imminent pod launch. Unfortunately, that was the side and area she was approaching at a rapid speed. She wasn't entirely sure she had enough fuel remaining in her pack to avoid a collision with the pod *and* slow her approach enough to prevent splattering across the hull of her own ship. Not a great situation to be in.

"I'm going to be coming in fast Alton," she said through gritted teeth. "Ready a rescue tether."

The pod launched directly at her with the sudden iridescent glare of the sub-light engines.

Hailey slammed the lateral thrusters on her pack in an attempt to dodge the incoming vessel.

It was going to be tight.

The escape pod ripped by her at a safe distance, but the uncontrolled firing of her suit's thrusters had sent her into a pinwheel headed toward the *Andvari*. The gravitational force strained her ability to keep conscious.

She grunted with the effort, panting to try to keep her blood oxygen rich enough to not pass out. In an effort to stabilize her tumble, she fired her suit's thrusters frantically. It didn't help.

The *Andvari* closed in.

With a sudden shrill *CRACK*, she smacked the hull right above the airlock door that she had been aiming for, one of the few open areas not covered by a translucent tentacle. A sickening bone-crunch echoed mutely through her body on impact. More alarming than the potential of broken bones, moisture began to form on her visor and be sucked toward a spiderwebbing crack across it.

The moisture, she realized, must have been her sweat being drawn off her face toward the tiny fractures in the polymer. Thankfully, the cracks were small enough that the moisture seemed to be doing a decent job of sealing them. On the flip side, there was no way to know how damaged the integrity of the visor was—nor how long the fluid would protect her from decompression, or asphyxiation.

Hailey realized with a start that she was borderline conscious. Gasping rapidly, she closed her eyes to ignore the rapidly diminishing image of her ship. She had struck the hull and bounced off. The impact had dazed her enough that she had neglected to attempt to grab onto something, and instead had ricocheted out into space.

A bright light abruptly flashed around her, the color of coral and sunrises. The explosion left a cascade of cyan and cerulean after-image blobs in her vision.

Something struck her chest, *hard.*

Warnings flashed in her visor. Pressure levels were rapidly dropping.

Whatever had punched her in the chest had pierced the seal of her suit.

That was a death sentence, sure as being naked in space.

Despite the nausea it caused, she kept her eyes closed.

Hailey let her arms go slack, allowing her momentum to carry her off to her eternal sleep in the depths of space. Something had always whispered in the back of her mind that this was the death that awaited her.

Dreams flashed in her mind; of dying a twisted old crone, warm and comfortable under a sea of heavy blankets, surrounded by generations of her children with eyes full of love, fear, and loss.

Memories tumbled through her mind. Of her husband and their first meeting. Their first touch. First kiss. Of giving birth to Darin, the pain mixed with a thrilling sense of *what might be.* Of Jamaal, and all the times he had held her as she wrestled with the losses in her life.

Those thoughts were unceremoniously yanked from her as

her momentum stopped with a painful snap of her arms. Whiplashed, partially blinded, and rapidly venting oxygen, she felt her momentum shift, swinging like the end of a weighted pendulum.

Another yank and she was rapidly moving in the opposite direction.

Amber warnings indicated she had minutes, if not seconds, of pressure left. She'd begin to freeze or suffocate soon.

A turbulent wave slammed into her from the direction of the explosion. The *RATA-TAT-TAT-PLINK-BANG-TAT-TAT* of bits of flying debris peppered her suit and helmet. There was a painful tearing feeling across her arm and stomach. Trails of tiny crimson spheres begin to gather in her visor. Something had cut her, and she was bleeding quite badly inside her suit.

The explosion nearby began to fade.

So did her vision, clouding and collapsing in on itself.

Everything went black.

CHAPTER 22

ALTON FELT ANOTHER rib crack. His hand kept slipping in the blood pooling on Hailey's chest.

"C'mon, you mean ol' hag!" Alton panted out between huffs.

The blue, lifeless face just stared back at him slack-jawed.

This wasn't going to work. He fell back onto his ankles, barely able to breathe. He was too old for this shite! Already he was completely winded, and he had only been applying chest compressions for a few minutes. Sweat dripped freely down his forehead and ran off his nose to the floor.

"I'm not going to let you die like this, Hailey!" Alton roared, surging back to his knees and placing his hands in the proper place on her chest.

The laceration across her stomach was deep, but not deep enough to have pierced the gut. She had most likely asphyxiated from a lack of oxygen in the suit once it had been cut. The offending grapple that he had fired at her as she had cartwheeled through the air lay nearby, covered in blood and fabric strands.

Alton grabbed up another nanoinjector and slammed it

into her heart. It automatically injected whatever lifesaving wizardry was trapped inside. He had no idea what he was doing, having only gone through basic field triage five decades ago in basic training. Cursing with every movement, he flung the empty injector aside and resumed chest compressions.

The skin of Hailey's bare chest was blue and waxy. From the moment he had ripped open the pressure suit with his teeth and pocketknife, her skin had been icily cold. Definitely not a good sign, but he'd be buggered if he let that stop him from trying.

The auto-ambu bag attached to her nose and mouth pulsed rhythmically and beeped to the beat he was supposed to be applying the compressions. The sickening protrusion of broken ribs did little to resist his weight as he bore down.

Usually, he'd have pulled her to the infirmary and hooked her up to the autodoc. Unfortunately, the whole infirmary looked as if someone had set a bomb off in it. Almost to the vial and bottle, everything had been spilled and smashed onto the floor. Bloody streaks traced back to the table where Mina had dragged Darin through the debris-strewn room. The autodoc itself was a shattered ruin of what it had once been. So, this was the best he could do—deploying field medicine in a blood-soaked hallway just inside the airlock.

Tears started to leak from his eyes, mixing with the sweat and blood smeared across his face.

"Hailey," he sobbed out, "I can't keep going like this, girl. I need you to work with me!"

Her face bounced slackly, mouth agape with the clear facemask-like device over it. For all he knew she was shaking her head 'no' at him.

His vision was growing cloudy, and a definitive pain was starting to become unbearable in his sides. If he kept this up, he'd be joining her in the grave.

At least the attack on the ship had stopped as abruptly as it had begun. There would be time to dwell on what had happened there later, he supposed.

If it was even worth it.

Frustration began to mount in him, and he kept going with the compressions while glancing around him at the spilled contents of an emergency kit. Technology hadn't changed overly much since his bygone days in the Guard, but it had been just long enough that he didn't immediately recognize everything.

"Stars, girl, WAKE UP!" The shout echoed down the halls.

His compressions had lightened up, and his hands slipped in the blood from the wound. He fell heavily across her torso. The smell of her blood was a strong, sweet metallic that contrasted sharply to the acidic vomit he had found in her helmet. It all gnarled together in his nose with the antiseptic smell of the sterile ship atmosphere. This was a smell he associated with loss. The stench of trauma centers in hospitals, of field surgery centers from the Guard.

"I'm so sorry, Hailey!" he cried but couldn't bring himself to lift himself off her. Not being a small man, he felt like he was crushing her. *She can't feel it anymore...*

The thought broke him. He wept like a child. He could feel her broken ribs under him as he raggedly hacked alternating sobs and curses.

"Get off me..." The words were spoken so softly, he almost couldn't hear them.

Like he had been struck by lightning, he practically *launched* himself off her body.

Hailey was removing the straps from the ambu bag attached to her face, which was still pulsing and pushing air.

"Oh, stars," Alton cried. "Stars! Hailey, I thought I had lost you!"

Color was returning to her face, but she still looked like death warmed over.

"Help me sit up," she spoke in a breathy whisper.

Alton complied, although he thought it was the worst idea ever.

As she sat up, she noticed the laceration across her stomach and the three deep punctures where the ends of the grapple had punched into her torso. She traced the jagged laceration and poked at the holes.

"Did you…" she gasped quietly. The words were near inaudible to his old ears, so he leaned down toward her. "*Shoot me?*"

That brought a half laugh, half sob, from him.

"You're bomaxed right I did, girl, and I'm likely to do it a second time if you ever scare me like this again."

Hailey smiled this time, just a slight twisting up of the side of her mouth.

"Help me stand. I need to get to the flight deck." Hailey reached out to him.

There was no reason to fight her. They had to escape, and with only the two of them conscious, well… there weren't a whole lot of good options at the moment. He levered her up to a wobbly standing position.

"Is *it*," she motioned around the hallway, "still here?"

No reason for *her* to explain the 'what' she was referencing. The 'Leviathan' that had killed them one by one.

"As far as I know."

"We need to forget about the plan to replace the PEM. The ship is already lost."

He couldn't disagree, so he only nodded solemnly in

response.

"Well, let's get to it." Hailey took an unsteady step.

"Easy there," he chided. "You've lost a lot of blood and had a close call. Pretty sure we lost you totally for a number of minutes."

"You really think you'd get rid of me that easily, Grandpa Al?"

He stopped and stared at her mutely. Despite a heroic effort to resist it, his bottom lip quivered.

Hailey just patted him on the back and moved toward the corridor wall, in an almost stumbling fall. Then she looked back at him with that same half-smile. He had always been fond of that one.

"I never thought I'd hear you call me that again." Tears stung his eyes.

"Yeah, well," she breathed softly, "that was all a long time ago."

She had a point.

After a few more shaky steps toward the flight deck, she said over her shoulder, "I know we're both hobbling around here, but I need you to get Darin loaded up into that escape pod, Alton. We're going to abandon ship as soon as I can find a safe way to do it."

That would be a trick, now, wouldn't it?

It was a grim thought, with images of Mina's escape pod being ripped to shreds like an old can of rations. The sub-light drives had been damaged so quickly they had left a small glowing haze in the section of space where she had been. The Leviathan didn't want them to escape. That much was certain.

The protests died on his lips. The best thing he could do would be to see to Darin's safety and then help her figure out a way to get out of the beast's clutches.

The boy lay where he had been spilled onto the floor beside the escape pod door.

His great-grandson.

Alton suspected that Darin knew, but the two had never spoken on the topic. The boy had just been too close to Jamaal, who had known from the beginning. There was no way that Jamaal had managed to keep that secret, was there?

With his waning strength, Alton heaved Darin up into the pod seat and strapped him in. Then, on a whim, he scooped up the medical equipment and gave him a quick once-over. Nothing had changed—aside from the fresh abrasions—despite all the excitement.

Not knowing whether to be relieved or upset over that, he set the medical equipment in the pod and began a power-up sequence. He only grumbled a little bit about having *just* powered the thing down.

—   —   —

Hailey hurt. Badly.

Unfortunately, she thought her body was still mostly in shock from the near-death experience. Everything was moving slowly, like through syrup. Lights were too bright, sounds too loud. Her motor functions were stiff and awkward simultaneously. Her brain knew what to do, but the connection between her mind and actions was somehow sluggish.

The doorway to the flight deck stood closed and sealed tight.

Warning indicators told her everything she needed to know.

The flight deck was completely depressurized.

Time to go.

Spinning, she decided she'd go do what she needed to do in her quarters.

The walk was a short one. Once insider her small room, she eased herself gingerly down to the desk, which had a glass-topped console on it. After authenticating herself, she began a final captain's log.

Hailey had always hoped she'd never have to do one of these. The final report to be laid to rest with the ship as it hurtled out into space, adrift forever. At least until some scrapper like her showed up to pick its bones.

Like everything else in her life, her report was brief, succinct, and without frills.

A thought occurred to her, and she loaded up data on Mina's failed escape attempt. If things had turned out any differently, she would've had a difficult time watching one of her crew members die. However, in this case, Mina had abandoned them all out of blind panic. Much like Jamaal had done, actually. There were other forces at work there, though. Such could be the case with Mina, but she didn't think so. She had just gotten scared and ran.

Did she feel remorse? Absolutely. Mina had been a member of her crew, as such she had a responsibility, a duty to protect them all. Failing that duty stung. Still, the doctor had the potential to have been a close friend, part of the family-she-chose. The loss of that potential friendship hurt her heart.

That was no excuse for succumbing to panic. That put them all at risk. It was inexcusable, and had Hailey been on board during the attempt, she likely would have taken Mina's life herself.

Shaking herself and feeling a stab of pain from the myriad of wounds across her chest, she turned her mind back to figuring out exactly what had transpired while she was drifting back to the ship. She watched a replay of the sensor data.

The escape pod had launched into space. Before it could get too far, however, the Leviathan had reached out and torn it to bits.

Hailey leaned back in her chair and sighed. *Well, that's going to be a challenge to avoid.*

A monster as big as a planet that was able to materialize, reach out, and pop a ship like an overripe pimple on a teenager's ass. Great. Wonderful. Fantastic!

Hailey ground her teeth in irritation.

The action hurt her face way more than it should have. Then she remembered her delicate situation. The whole surviving the *still very recent* ordeal.

Probably should take it a little easy on myself for a bit. For whatever reason, the thought didn't sit well with her.

As she rolled the footage back to play it again, she watched for something, *anything*, that she might be able to use to assist them in an escape.

Launch, seconds pass, destruction and death.

She watched it again.

And again.

There was nothing. They were going to die here.

The *Andvari* really was going to be the 'last ship she ever had'.

All they could do was make a run for it.

Hailey filed the footage with the logs, began a backup, which she set to upload to the escape pod's memory banks. She then started a hibernation sequence for the ship; it would trigger when the power level went critical and would send it into a long-term low-power storage state. The data could last for a thousand years without further damage to the ship. Hopefully, someone would find the information useful.

With all of her captain's duties managed, she gathered up what personal items mattered most to her. Which, as it turned out, wasn't that much. She left the room, without so much as a glance over her shoulder.

CHAPTER 23

ALTON PLAYED THROUGH the report past the destruction of the escape pod and the bursting of its sub-light drive. The explosion was immediate and destructive. Mina had never stood a chance.

"Alton, I've got the ship set up to hibernate." Hailey had a defeated tone, not one that he was used to hearing from her.

"We're all set up for a pod launch, and Darin is secure on board." He bit his lip, grasping for something positive to add to help lighten her burden. "I also packed the pod with enough emergency supplies for a month. And, what little amount of salvage we had so at least we won't be broke when we get picked up."

Upon review, it didn't really sound as upbeat as it had in his head.

"Great," was the only morose response.

The comms clicked off without any kind of sign-off.

Alton sighed heavily, stirring his facial hair and setting off an itch under his beard.

Feeling pretty glum, he accessed the hull recorder data again. This time, he noticed the file had been accessed by

Hailey from the captain's quarters. Of course, that made perfect sense; the files would be included in an after-action report for the final log—especially considering there was a loss-of-life that would need to be documented.

He wanted to watch the footage and analyze the data for different reasons. There *had* to be a way to escape. What had happened with Mina didn't give him much hope. As the footage played out, and the data streamed by, it was apparent to him that the beast could kill them with minimal effort whenever it chose. For some reason it was toying with them, and likely had been from the very beginning.

That begged the question: *why?*

What was its motivation for doing this? If the thing had wanted to kill them, and had the unlimited potential to do so on a whim, why drag this out? Why mess with their minds? Was it just sadistic? That seemed unlikely for something so powerful.

Although, he considered, there were beasts found in nature that found great enjoyment in playing with their food before they consumed it.

He shivered uncomfortably.

"I don't want to be eaten," he grumbled.

The lack of information they had on this thing was frustrating. If only they had complementary data to the limited set they had from the ship's systems.

But they did!

Doctor Hurn had deployed the probes. Maybe they had still been operational when the escape pod had been destroyed. That would give him *all* the data!

Excited about the prospect for further intel, he furiously keyed in the commands on the engineering console to access the probes. Thankfully, it appeared all but one was still operational. Likely that one had been struck by debris or destroyed in the explosion.

Two is better than none!

The data began to stream in, and he reconciled it against the data the *Andvari*'s logs, putting everything in sync. He then streamed it from launch to destruction.

Over and over again, he watched the hull monitor feeds and scrutinized the streaming data. Frame-by-frame, high-speed playback, then a loop of it playing forward and winding back on repeat. Nothing!

Leaning back as he watched, he let his mind wander.

Launch, travel, boom.

Boom, travel, launch.

Launch; was completely unremarkable. Save for almost slamming into the tiny spec that was Hailey, racing back toward the craft to save them all with the new PEM core. Well, that and the massive multitude of ethereal tendrils whipping around the *Andvari* and escape pod.

Travel; again, unremarkable save for the aforementioned abnormalities. The readings from the escape pod were nominal; without intervention from the Leviathan, it would have fired its sub-light engines and been headed for the nearest heavy-traffic area and deployed emergency beacons. All standard protocols. Normal operational standards.

Boom; the end.

There was nothing…

The footage began to play in reverse, rolling back toward the launch.

Alton sat bolt upright.

Clumsily, he rolled the footage back.

The diaphanous tendrils of the Leviathan whipped out and tore through the escape pod like paper. The engine exploded…

All the tendrils recoiled instantly! Like a child's hand touching a hot pan.

He thought back to the conditions during the transdimensional scan and the attack that followed. The creature had been mostly just messing with their minds up to that point, but as soon as Mina had deployed the probes, the creature had made its first large-scale assault on the ship. Something about the antimatter cloud compiled with the broad-spectrum scans bothered it; it hadn't directly, physically interacted with them until then.

We must have hurt it.

That was only one instance, though; not enough to establish causation. But he did have a more recent piece of evidence.

When the creature had whipped the escape pod with one of its tendrils, the pod had lost containment of the onboard antimatter used in the vessel's pion drive. The probes were still functional at that time, resulting in similar conditions to the first incident. Again, the Leviathan had recoiled from the site of the explosion.

Excitement bubbling up for the first time in what felt like a year, Alton referenced the probe data to verify the observations. *Yes!*

He could only hazard a guess at why the seemingly powerful creature would react so negatively to those conditions. Perhaps existing in this dimension and holding a restricted physical form was challenging. The spatial distortion created from the antimatter explosion and numerous frequencies from all the scans might make it difficult to maintain its reach across the dimensional veil.

No matter the reason, there was hope!

Alton choked back a sob. *Maybe we can actually survive*

this.

—

"Have you lost your mind?" Hailey asked as soon as Alton finished sharing his plan with her.

He scoffed in reply and crossed his arms across his burly chest defensively.

Hailey stared at him wide-eyed.

The two squared off in the airlock prep area. They had done what they could to prepare the remaining escape pod for an undetermined amount of travel time.

Odds of a swift rescue generally weren't great; space was a big place, and they were particularly far outside the beaten path. Having additional resources might prove significant. The pod was packed to the brim with medical equipment for Darin, food, water, additional pressure suits, helmets, tools, and anything else he thought might be necessary for long-term survival in the small space.

"You can't be serious," she pressed when he didn't respond.

"I am," he barked. "Deathly so, in fact."

While Hailey didn't look well, at least her color was improving. Before he had dropped this bomb on her, he had sat with her and shared a quick meal of bland rations. The mush always caused him some significant digestive discomfort, but it had been more for her than it had been for him. Often, he'd rather go hungry than force the disgusting gruel down his throat.

The meal had done little to curb Hailey's ire, however.

"You want to blow up the ship while we shoot the escape pod," she pointed toward the outer hull of the ship, "out there with *that thing*?"

Well, when she put it like that it *did* sound a little crazy. That was neither here nor there.

"Pretty much sums it up," he said instead.

They just stood there looking at each other, she aghast, him stoic and unflinching.

"You're space-sick," she finally said.

He almost smiled. At least she was getting a bit of her fire back. Although, if she had been in peak condition, she'd likely bodily thrown him out into space. "It hasn't beaten us yet," he said.

"This thing could have killed a hundred times over by now. Attack, withdraw. It doesn't make any sense!"

Alton caught her gaze. "It was messing with us, Hailey. Pushing us to our limits. Seeing what we would do, where we would crack."

"But *why*?" Her eyes were wide with desperation, all the loss and abuse piled up and becoming too much to bear.

"I don't know, Hailey. I wish I had answers, but this one is above my paygrade. If we can stun this thing, though, then we can escape." They had been over this already, but he needed the plan to sink in.

"We're too far out from rescue. With all the supplies and medical equipment for Darin, the three of us won't fit…" She caught the twitch of his face. Her eyes went even wider, if that were possible. "You're not coming with us."

It wasn't a question. She had ferreted out his intentions.

While he had hoped to keep this part of it under guise for a little while longer, there was just no way to maintain the secret forever. The simple fact was that a mass release of the *Andvari*'s antimatter reserves would require manual overrides, which meant a person needed to be present. Add to that the fact that the escape pods were designed to only fit two people comfortably, three only in the direst of circumstances, and he was already out of a ride.

May as well go out doing something useful. He drew in a long breath in preparation for substantiating his case.

Hailey wasn't having it, "No."

His objections died on his lips.

There was no arguing with her when she was like this. As bullheaded and pissy as her mother. Stars, but he missed his daughter something fierce!

He brought out his secret weapon—his grandfatherly tone, all warm honey and dripping affection, "Hailey…"

"I said no, and last I checked I was the captain of this ship."

He raised a bushy eyebrow at her.

Now it was her turn to cross her arms defensively, jaw set so hard it caused her cheeks to twitch with the effort.

You get more with honey than you do vinegar. That had been his mother's favorite saying. The strategy was not his strength, not nearly as much as it had been hers, but he deployed it so rarely that hopefully it gained him an advantage.

Again, he spoke softly, reached out toward her, "The choice is between my life and your son's. My great-grandson's *life*, Hailey. I'm old—too old to be fighting transdimensional space monsters. Let me do this. I *need* to do this."

He sucked his lips in over his teeth and puffed his cheeks out.

Tears brimmed in her eyes.

The fight was won.

It was time to get on with the plan.

He wrapped her up in a hug as tightly as their battered bodies allowed.

"I'm sorry." She whispered into his shoulder. "We wasted

so much time being angry with each other."

"Nonsense, girl." He pushed her back so he could look her squarely in the face. "After what happened with your mother, well... I guess I turned into a grumpy old shite. What can I say? It's genetic."

She smiled half-heartedly at that. The family had been full of a bunch of grumpy assholes for sure!

Alton reached out and roughly wiped the tears from her cheeks, his own beard was feeling a bit more moisture than was probably proper. Those tears he ignored; best not to draw attention to them. "I'd not trade our time crewing these old wrecks for anything in the whole universe. You can bet your too-skinny ass on that."

He gently maneuvered her toward the pod.

"Get strapped in. We only get one shot of this, and no do-overs. Clear?"

She nodded firmly, a slight tremble to her lip. "Crystal."

"Get to it then." He bent over to scoop up his fallen cane.

As he paddled off, he heard her climbing over the mountain of gear in the pod to take her seat.

Everything was pre-programmed; they'd just have to be spot-on with their launch. Too early and they'd be killed by the monster. Too late, and well—they'd die in the blast. The timing wasn't impossible, but it certainly could've been a whole lot easier.

The good news was, the thing that surrounded them was so vast, it likely functioned on a scale where noticing something the size of the pod would take a bit of effort. Alton had a plan to extend that with a little distraction of his own—a little something he had learned with his time in the Tararian Guard.

Before approaching Hailey with the plan, he had seen to

preparing it all, knowing it was the only way. Even had she flatly refused, he would've gone through with it. Far better to be able to say goodbye on the terms he wanted.

Stars, but he loved that girl mightily. She was so much like her mother, it hurt his heart to think about. He recognized the parts of her that were her father, the tenderness lurking just below the cold exterior. The need to be acknowledged. His daughter had always been completely self-motivated. No need for the 'atta-girls' and shoulder-pats. Give her a duty, and a cause, and she would strangle it to death with her sheer force of will, then stand back and let others claim the credit for her efforts.

Alton could leave this existence knowing he had done the best he could with the hand he was dealt. Sure, he had made a disproportionate share of mistakes, but those had been some of the best learning moments of his life. He didn't really believe in an afterlife, but he hoped he would be pleasantly surprised to find Beth waiting for him in some form or another. He'd sure like to hug her one more time.

The same went for his other loved ones. Wouldn't that be a nice surprise?

Hobbling into the engineering bay, he sat in his favorite chair and began a string of commands to initiate his plan. All in all, the idea was relatively straightforward.

He would first send out a flurry of small bits and equipment that he had loaded into the two cargo bays, and scatter sand—so to speak. Then he'd do a soft-undock of the escape pod, so it didn't fire the sub-light engines. It would drift out with the other debris, and hopefully escape notice until it had enough distance that Alton could override the *Andvari*'s antimatter containment safeguards and then blow up the entire ship in spectacular fashion. During the explosion, the pod would fire the sub-lights and make its opportunistic escape. Textbook strategy.

He set the comms to an open two-way line so they could talk freely without the need to transmit. "Okay, I'm going to do a bit of razzle-dazzle to kick this show off. Hopefully, if this thing is lurking around, it'll take the bait and you can sneak out the back door. I'd like to give you as much distance as possible before I hit the big-red-button."

"Give 'em both barrels, Pop."

Something happened then that Alton hadn't expected, he smiled wide enough to show teeth. He couldn't remember the last time he had done that. The expression was one his daughter had wielded with reckless abandon.

Alton began inputting commands for the next stage of his plan. Frustratingly, self-destruct protocols were often a long sequence of events that would trigger slowly enough to allow personnel to abandon ship and achieve a minimum safe distance away. He needed to force a rapid critical failure. With a little careful maneuvering—

He froze, an instinctual chill running down his spine.

Slowly, Alton turned around in his chair.

Standing behind him was a figure, formless and dark as the deepest space. A featureless void, like a cutout of reality in a bipedal shape.

"*Your plan will not work, Taran.*" It wasn't so much a voice, as an *impression* of a voice. Alton couldn't tell if it was actually speaking inside his head, or the *feeling* was being pushed into his consciousness. "*You should give up your plans for war now. You cannot hurt us. We are eternal.*"

"Hailey, starting this off a bit early, hope you're ready!" Spinning, he slammed down the control for the cargo bay door release.

Obviously, he had disabled every alarm and warning ship-wide, so there was no announcement, no countdowns, no whirling lights. Just a notification that the order had been executed.

The figure still stood behind him, he could *feel* the presence now. A deep-rooted echo of some primal fear, long absent but never forgotten. He noticed his hands shaking, and he risked a glance over his shoulder toward the figure.

It stood looking off to the side, it's lack of substance making it a disconcerting caricature of a person.

The only active sensor was the monitor on the escape-pod side of the ship. He would wait until Hailey had disembarked before triggering the antimatter release. If he could do it while this thing was *in the room* with him, maybe he could do a bit more damage to it?

"*You were warned,*" the thing said. "*You have not changed. You will pay.*"

Alton didn't like the sound of that at all, but he tried to ignore it.

Pain ripped into his head, like feedback from a speaker magnified a half a million times on top of each other. The sudden unrelenting agony dropped him where he stood.

Such was the level of torment that all he could do was writhe in muscle-locked agony. His fingers formed claws, his eyes so wide they tore at the corners of the sockets. His mouth stretched, tearing his dehydrated lips. His old back arched off the floor until the crown of his head pressed into the deck.

The pain slowly intensified. Some far-off part of Alton wondered how that was even possible.

It was only then that he became aware that he was screaming. A wholly unnatural keening that he would've thought was beyond his vocal range. Somehow, he was able to sustain it without being able to draw breath. Time had become completely irrelevant, or nonexistent. The only thing that subsisted him was his total anguish.

Thought became all but impossible.

"*Now, betrayer,*" a voice said amidst the turbulent storm of torture, "*you die.*"

CHAPTER 24

"ALTON!" HAILEY SCREAMED the words at the speaker panel. Her voice broke with the effort to penetrate the blood-curdling screams spilling into the pod through the comms.

Then it abruptly stopped. Like a feed had been switched off.

Complete silence.

The trap had been sprung; Alton had initiated the distraction. And something was horribly wrong.

Hailey was intimately familiar with the sounds of death, how a person died when under intense pain. Despite her railing against the idea, she knew that Alton was gone.

That presented a significant issue with their plan.

Someone needed to trigger the chain reaction that would stun the Leviathan enough to allow the pod to flee. If it were even possible, this was their best chance.

The responsibility fell onto her shoulders. For whatever reason she wasn't disappointed; there was a feeling almost like relief. A captain wasn't supposed to leave a doomed ship with a subordinate. Sure, there was no *actual* rule against it. Arguably, it was a stupid rule. A captain normally had critical mission data that subordinates didn't, so having all that knowledge get lost with the ship was rather poor command.

Still, it hadn't sat right with her that she was relying on Alton's sacrifice to rescue her son. Her grandfather had already forfeited much in his life, this had been too much.

He died anyway.

That stung.

Unfastening the restraints, she leaned over and planted a lengthy kiss on her son's forehead. Then she held his face, memorizing everything she could about it, affixing it prominently in her mind.

"Do good, son." The whisper hung in the air as she initiated the launch sequence with a five hundred-second delay. She synchronized the countdown to her watch. *One final mission clock.*

Hailey exited the pod and sealed the hatch behind her. With one last caress of its hull and prayer to the stars for her son's safety, she ran toward Engineering as fast as her brutalized body would carry her.

She saw Alton the moment the door opened. The sight of him stole her breath and punched at her heart. The old man was twisted and coiled in unnatural angles for a person his age. His face was stretched and smeared with blood streaming from his nose, eyes, and mouth. His beard had crusted over with red-black blood.

Worse, his hands still twitched, and his lifeless face still moved in vacant spasms. He almost looked like a doll. The light was gone in his too-wide eyes, but the body refused to be still, with his head rolled over and his arms moving languidly. The *life* gone from them; it was horrible. This was a twisted and debauched mimicry of life.

As she entered, she did everything possible to avoid

looking at the eerily slow writhing form of her once grandfather.

Focus on the mission, she told herself.

Almost half of her time had elapsed. The disconnect of the escape pod would happen with one hundred seconds to go, and the firing of the engines at the zero count. They had agreed that timing was everything for this to work. The worst part about it was, she would have no idea if she had succeeded or if she had inadvertently murdered her own son in the attempt.

Not exactly the 'rest in peace' she had hoped for.

Thoughts and fears of that sort were poison; she had to focus on the here and now. The plan *would* work, and her son *would* escape! That was all there was to it.

A quick check of the debris field showed that it was scattering further than she had hoped.

Bomax!

The cover of debris would be too far gone to provide any kind of smokescreen for the escape pod. Their timing was already irreparably off.

She needed to come up with a secondary diversion, and she had less than ninety seconds to figure it out.

Wildly, she scanned through system's menus, desperate for inspiration to strike. They had already jettisoned everything they could. Plus, she didn't have enough time to haul anything to the cargo bays. The debris distraction idea just wouldn't work now.

Running out of time, she turned and looked at the engineering bay, scanning for anything that might trigger a half-cocked plan.

The ship was in ruins. It was barely held together with hopes and dreams at this point.

A thought occurred to her.

The monster had to know how much damage it had done to the ship. It was *riding* them through space; it had to feel that the vessel was coming apart at the seams.

If Hailey could nudge it a little in that direction, maybe the thing would be distracted by the ship coming apart and miss the pod making its run.

There were mere seconds to decide.

It was risky. Compromise structural integrity too fast, or too much, and she'd be ejected into space before she could initiate the destruct sequence. Do it too slow, and it was for nothing anyway.

Fok it!

Hailey sat down in Alton's chair, which thankfully didn't try to spill her out onto the floor like it always did. She rotated the aft starboard maneuvering thrusters one hundred eighty degrees and fired it full, sending them into a harsh lateral spin. Then, she fired the top thrusters at full. The vertical shift did what she was hoping, sending them into an untamable tailspin.

The forces on the damaged craft were too much; physical strain caused every bulkhead to bulge and bend. The warnings had been disabled, but she knew the ship was screaming in pain much like its engineer had just minutes before. This delta spin was a death sentence for the healthiest of craft, and one on its last legs would only last seconds.

It was becoming increasingly challenging to stay rooted to the chair. Blood dribbled out of her nose. Her head swam from the rotational force exerted on her.

Something appeared behind her, like a hole in the room in the shape of a person.

"Nothing you do now matters, Taran." A *feeling* bellowed inside her. *"You will not escape punishment."*

She checked her watch. Four hundred seconds had

elapsed.

Darin would be drifting away from the ship now.

"Punishment for what?" she screamed at the apparition, bits of the engineering room beginning to tear loose in showers of sparks, gasses, and flashes of metal.

Keep talking, you piece of shite!

There was an overly long pause in the response. Hopefully, it was having to focus too much of its attention on keeping the disintegrating ship together.

Then it spoke again.

"*The accord you have broken!*" The feeling inside her head said, dripping venom. It was like ice being pressed to her midback, it grated against her very existence. Was it just her imagination or did it sound distracted? There was less focused malice to the thoughts inside her head.

It's working!

Standing from her chair, she turned and faced the thing.

Thirty seconds!

Darin would be halfway to minimum safe distance by now.

"What accord? We've never even heard of something like you! What are you talking about?"

Again, there was a delay, and the void-like substance-less shadow-person seemed to vibrate in place, the edges fuzzing out.

Hailey reached behind her and placed her hand on the initiation button.

FIFTEEN SECONDS!

"*You think you can deceive me, betrayer? I KNOW YOUR MIND!*" The thought-voice roared inside her head with accompanied pain the likes of which she had never thought possible. It was as if molten metal had suddenly been poured into her skull.

Somehow, she held on for ten more seconds.

With every shred of her being, she bellowed through gritted teeth at the figure, "*GO FOK YOURSELF!*"

She smashed the button.

EPILOGUE

GINA DITURI DIRECTED the *Oberon* out of subspace, welcoming the sight of stars against the velvety black backdrop of deep space. While subspace was pretty to look at, it never sat right with her to think about being outside the realm of normal physical reality.

"Easy does it," the First Officer ordered from the raised command mezzanine of the flight deck.

"Always, sir," Gina said with a slight smile. It'd been a long day, and she was looking forward to some much-needed rack time.

With the jump complete, Gina's work was finished for the shift; she began shutting down her station to hand over to the next Navigator on duty. The key tasks for the next several hours would fall to the analysts to log reports and come up with and action plan, so there wouldn't be a lot to do by way of course-plotting.

The *Oberon* was a massive Class V merchant freighter, used mostly for hauling colonization packages to new worlds. 'The Bear of the Black' is what the captain affectionately called his ship. Gina almost never cringed anymore when she heard the nickname. Well, mostly.

It was Gina's third rotation on board the ship, and only her second as resident crew. Though civilian in classification, the vessel operated with military precision and formality. A good number of the crew were ex-Guard, so it made sense. As a colonization ship, they ventured into places beyond normal civilian transit zones, preparing for the inevitable expansion of the Taran Empire.

Their current assignment took them near the Rift—the former warzone where many planets had been destroyed during the centuries of conflict. Now that the enemy threat had been eliminated, a number of former colony worlds were prime candidates for re-population. The *Oberon* had been hauling supplies to a staging post on Aleda in advance of new residents traveling to the nearby worlds.

The nature of their work meant extended shifts, so getting to bed as soon as possible was a necessity. Consequently, she tensed when the specialist at the Tactical station called out an unexpected report.

"Sir, we're picking up a large energy reading coming from the Kyron Nebula, bearing three-one-two-mark-five."

The First Officer looked down his hawkish nose and stood stiff-backed. "Navigation, bring us around so we can use the long-range directional scanners."

"Aye," Gina acknowledged. *So much for getting to bed right away.* She entered the coordinates into the ship's navigational computer.

Excited chatter erupted from the Sensor station.

Bakal, at least Gina thought that was the man's name, looked up to the First Officer sharply. "Sir, we have long-range imagery on an explosion."

"On screen, Bakal," the First Officer instructed.

The center viewscreen illuminated the dark interior with a busy HUD, displaying a teal-ish-white ribbon of light billowing outward. Then, the flashing light winked out.

"What was that?" the First Officer.

"Inconclusive. Some kind of spatial distortion…" Abruptly, Bakal leapt to his feet, "Sir!"

A reticle had begun flashing a bright pulsating red on the viewscreen. An emergency signal had come into range.

It was the duty of every spacefaring vessel to respond immediately to any detected distress call. That was standard protocol.

"Set a course," the First Officer instructed.

Fingers flashing across her console, Gina calculated the distance to the signal's origin based on the readings, adjusted for flight time, and programmed a short subspace jump to intercept the beacon's source. Normally, only military vessels would have access to the nav beacons this close to the Rift, but they'd already been issued access codes as part of their expeditionary mission.

The subspace jump was almost instantaneous. When the cloud of the spatial distortion cleared, the viewscreen updated with an image of their target.

"Sir, it's an escape pod registered with the salvager *Andvari*," Bakal said while he scrutinized the information readouts displayed on his console.

An unusual energy wave, followed shortly by an escape pod. That didn't bode well.

"Any survivors?" the First Officer asked.

"One, sir."

Gina watched as information was passed back and forth between the various systems. She was ordered to match speed as close as she was able to get to the pod. As it turned out, less than ten meters separated the *Oberon* from the target by the time she had synchronized their velocity.

Then, the magic happened.

Orders were barked, readings were called out, and Gina got to watch on a series of helmet cameras as the Strategic Operations team was deployed in the rescue mission. They would go out, secure tethers, and then be reeled back in.

As they landed on the pod, one operator moved to peer inside the small portal, broadcasting the imagery to the *Oberon*'s main viewscreen.

Inside was the strangest scene that Gina had ever seen. A man, not much younger than herself, was strapped to a chair with what appeared to be bits of medical equipment snaking around him. The remainder of the pod was an odd assortment of what appeared to be food, water, and engineering equipment.

What in the stars happened on the Andvari? Gina thought suspiciously.

"Let's get that man on board and head to the nearest port-of-call with a major hospital. Dituri, find me something close and with expert facilities. Bakal, I want a deepscan sweep of the entire area. Make sure there are no other survivors floating around out there."

Gina kept half an eye on the rescue mission playing out on the viewscreen as she got to work. A search revealed the nearest hospital was Icarus Station, nicknamed the 'Port of New Hope'.

"Well, if that isn't a fitting hospital to take a deep space survivor, I don't know what is," Gina mumbled to herself as she transferred the coordinates to the Command relay and the ship's navigation console.

"What was that, Dituri?" asked the First Officer above her from his catwalk.

"Nothing, sir!" Stars, the man had good hearing.

Not that Gina would ever know what really happened, but she let herself daydream about the survivor's story. Had it been pirates lurking deep in the Kyron Nebula? Had a new Rift ripped open while no one was looking? Or had it been an inside job? Sabotage and betrayal? It was fun to think about.

Once the escape pod had been successfully captured and stowed, Gina swung the *Oberon* around and initiated a subspace jump for Port of New Hope.

Then, she stretched in her chair and stifled a yawn with the back of her hand. She really needed some rack time.

Up in the mezzanine, the First Officer took a call on the command line. Gina strained a bit, trying to pick up the conversation.

"…Had better contact the Guard," said the faint voice over the comms. "We found a data log. You won't believe this."

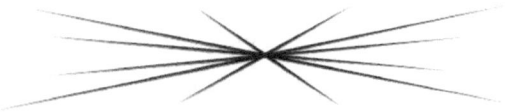

The attack on the Andvari was just the beginning. A new transdimensional menace threatens to send the Taran Empire into civil war.

THE STORY CONTINUES *EMPIRE REBORN...*

Break the treaty, be destroyed.
We forgot.
Now we pay the price.

Jason Sietinen's investigation into a mysterious starship attack uncovers a chilling truth: the Taran Empire has inadvertently broken an ancient treaty with transdimensional aliens.

Now on the cusp of galactic war, Jason must find a way to unite the Taran worlds, including the lost colony of Earth, against the mounting alien threat.

Except, how do you fight an enemy you can't see or touch?

ADDITIONAL READING

Cadicle Space Opera Series by A.K. DuBoff
Book 1: Rumors of War (Vol. 1-3)
Book 2: Web of Truth (Vol. 4)
Book 3: Crossroads of Fate (Vol. 5)
Book 4: Path of Justice (Vol. 6)
Book 5: Scions of Change (Vol. 7)

Mindspace Series by A.K. DuBoff
Book 1: Infiltration
Book 2: Conspiracy
Book 3: Offensive
Book 4: Endgame

Verity Chronicles by T.S. Valmond & A.K. DuBoff
Book 1: Exile
Book 2: Divided Loyalties
Book 3: On the Run

Shadowed Space Series by Lucinda Pebre & A.K. DuBoff
Book 1: Shadow Behind the Stars
Book 2: Shadow Rising
Book 3: Shadow Beyond the Reach

AUTHORS' NOTES

From James Fox:

Let me start, as I normally do, with expressing my sincere gratitude for you reading this book. Without your interest and dedication, none of this would be possible.

This book in particular, was quite a lot of fun for me. Not only was it my second novel, but it was a quick break from the intensity of The Sol Saga and the sprinting to the finish line I had just completed on Book 1 of that series. I hadn't even realized that I needed the mental break, but I am extremely glad I did.

World-building is exciting. I'll be the first to admit it. There's just something special about getting to try to think about the *whole* of something. Solving problems, creating, *digging deep*! That complex troubleshooting is exactly what I yearn for in storytelling. How can I convey this incredibly intricate social dilemma in a way that simultaneously makes sense *and* is entertaining? Yeah, none of that happened with *In Darkness Dwells*, because it wasn't my world to begin with!

"Well, shoot! This'll be easy, I'll be done in a month."

Not quite.

I think I wound up writing, scrapping the *entire* thing, reworking, deleting, and writing again—no less than four times. The total-words-in on this book has to be over 200k. Seriously. I had a solid outline, that Amy and I had worked on together. I knew what I *wanted* to do with the characters. I did all my pre-production on developing their backstory, interpersonal relationships, etc. I just could *not* capture the right tone for the writing.

Let me back up a minute, if you'd indulge me. See, I'm a fan of A.K. DuBoff. I freaking *love* the Cadicle Universe. There's a lot about that Universe that reminds me of my own family—not that we're gifted psionicists… not that… certainly not! Just the way they relate to each other, some of the things they say and do, it just really bumps that nostalgia button for me.

So I was probably about 75% complete with the first draft of the manuscript, almost to the point where I was going to share what I had, when I did a read myself. See, I don't read as I go. I purge. I watch the movie in my head and write along. This time though, I wanted to make sure it was my best work. And, I like to improve on things. So, with Sol Saga Book 1, the editors identified several things I consistently did that were incorrect. That bothered me. I wanted to make sure I wasn't doing any of those things.

As I sat down to read it, I realized very quickly that it sounded absolutely *nothing* like a Cadicle novel. It sounded confused. The story was decent. Characters were compelling. The pacing was passable. The *voice* was off. It meandered. I tend to be long-winded, and digress with regularity. (As I'm sure you're well aware.) The writing and style in the Cadicle Universe is clean, quick, witty, and intelligent. Not ponderous and pontificating.

After I finished the whole thing I realized two things. First, I had a mildly interesting plot. There was tension aplenty, and I really was digging the whole suspense-thriller-scifi mashup that was going on. I also realized that I had neglected to write any Gifted characters into the story at all, which was something altogether alien to the Cadicle Universe as a whole. I had a couple decisions to make.

Ultimately, I enjoyed that these were just normal people dealing with something VERY NOT NORMAL. It upped the tension for me. There aren't a lot of points of view of "normies" in the Cadicle Universe. So, this was a little unique in that regard—and possibly would be of interest to the readers. That got to stay.

The plot was solid but needed some tightening up. I was pacing a 150k word count novel, not the target I was given. This was also one of the bothersome things making the book sound out-of-character with the rest of the expanded Universe.

I stepped away from the project for a little while. During this time away, I had many more conversations with Amy, not just about the Universe, but about life, and general things. When she'd ask how IDD was coming along, I'd wince and say, "It's about half done." Which was quite possibly true at the time—I wasn't exactly sure anymore!

After that break, I got back to work. I got to the 50% mark on my word count goal, just in time to take a month-long vacation, camping across the United States. I packed up my portable solar equipment, and loaded the manuscript on my laptop. Nothing like writing from the river's edge!

I finished the official manuscript of IDD in the hills of Northern Georgia, eating some of the best BBQ I've ever had, enjoying the company of some amazing people. Which contrasted terribly with how ruthless I am to my characters by the end—I'm a monster, I admit it.

All this to say, it was a fun journey. Not at all what I expected it to be in the beginning. I'm immensely grateful to Amy and all the incredibly talented authors in the expanded Cadicle Universe for allowing me to be numbered in their ranks. I hope I did the world justice, and you, the fans, enjoyed it!

Perhaps I'll have the opportunity to write more? Maybe there are some plans percolating about what Darin does next? I guess, for now, that is up to you, the readers.

Be safe out there, and read on!

An additional note from A.K. DuBoff:

Thank you so much for reading this book! I hope you enjoyed it :-).

This was a fascinating project to work on in a number of ways, and it's been a lot of fun to work on!

First, it's the only co-authored novel to-date that was brainstormed face-to-face. I had the opportunity to sit down with James and talk about the new transdimensional baddies in the Cadicle Universe and what those beings might be able to do. We came up with a lot of interesting stuff, and that has shaped many the events in the larger story with this next era of the Taran Empire.

What it came down to is we needed something that would scare Wil Sietinen. Not an easy feat. But, I think we've done it.

As James has admitted, he'd pretty brutal to his characters. This was a perfect fit, because I knew from the start that I wanted there to only be a lone survivor of a ship attack where the aliens had been studying the crew. If you've already read *Empire Reborn*, you know where the story leads. This was, obviously, a much darker tone than typically found in Cadicle novels, but I wanted to do something different. This threat is real. It's serious. Not everyone is going to be able to solve this problem and walk away unscathed.

I love that this book is a tale about regular people thrown

into an extraordinary situation. So many of the other novels in the universe have featured people with unique roles or abilities. This is a raw book about people trying to do their best with what they're given.

The other thing that made this such a great collaborative experience is James' deep familiarity and fandom of the Cadicle Universe. His work on the pilot script for the TV adaptation didn't require him just to *read* the books, but to *internalize* them. The script ended up deconstructing the characters and story and putting them back together again in a way that captured the essence without being a verbatim copy. I don't know how a person could go through that exercise and *not* come away with a deep understanding.

That background informed a lot of what we did in this book. What had been done before? What would be something different to add to the universe? What would we set up that would be a ramp up from the threat of the Bakzen and the Priesthood?

We had a unique opportunity to tell two stories in one. There is the tale of *Andvari* and its tragic fate, but there is also the larger story of the Taran Empire facing an enormous threat they don't fully understand. The two tales are interwoven, but they can be read in either order.

Whether you read *Empire Reborn* first or if this is your first introduction to the Cadicle Universe, I hope you have enjoyed the ride. There is much more to come!

Thank you, as always, to my amazing beta readers John Ashmore, Jim Dean, Kurt Schulenburg, Steve DeBacker, Gil Forbes, David Frydrych, Doug Burnham, Manie Killian, Eric Haneberg, and Leo Roars. We've been working together for quite some time now, and I trust them immensely. The book you have just read is better for their involvement, and it means so much to have that amazing support team.

Many thanks also to my amazing proofers who help add the final polish. You are incredible!

Much love and gratitude to my husband Nick, my parents, and to James' family for their encouragement and support. As I have said before, writing is far from a solitary endeavor. I feel so fortunate to be surrounded by amazing people.

More in the Cadicle Universe is coming soon. Until next time, happy reading!

ABOUT THE AUTHORS

JAMES FOX

Native American and Californian, James Fox is a natural storyteller. After graduating from the Academy of Art in San Francisco, with a BFA in Directing, he founded Dawnrunner Inc. in 2006 and has championed the company through numerous award-winning projects. As a writer, James devotes his energies to the careful crafting of compelling characters and diverse worlds. In addition to writing books, James is a multiple award-winning screenwriter and director.

www.thejamesfox.com

A.K. DUBOFF

A.K. (Amy) DuBoff has always loved science fiction in all its forms—books, movies, shows, and games. If it involves outer space, even better! She is a Nebula Award finalist and *USA Today* bestselling author most known for her Cadicle Universe, but she's also written a variety of space fantasy and comedic sci-fi. Now a full-time author, Amy can frequently be found traveling the world. When she's not writing, she enjoys wine tasting, binge-watching TV series, and playing epic strategy board games.

www.amyduboff.com

www.ingramcontent.com/pod-product-compliance
Lightning Source LLC
Chambersburg PA
CBHW020053180626
46812CB00006B/2316